Calamity Rayne Back Again

CALAMITY RAYNE
BOOK TWO

LYDIA MICHAELS

Calamity Rayne Back Again
Calamity Rayne 2

Print ISBN: 978-1-957573-29-8

Romantic Comedy

Disclaimer

Calamity Rayne Back Again is the second book in the Calamity Rayne saga. ***Calamity Rayne: Gets a Life*** is book one. Starting the series here is like finishing the second half of someone else's ice cream—you know some good chunks are missing.

*For Gayle.
Love,
MumblesMcMichaels*

How did I get here?

1

Sometimes a fleeting moment can be the most monumental, fundamental, and defining part of a person's life. It seemed exciting things always happened fast—waterslides, parties, orgasms... But some defining moments ended in heartbreak.

I'm the asshole who wishes she could be a mermaid and not have to adult. Unrealistic. I know. But I still think it at least once a day.

Now would be a great time to swim away and forget my worries faster than Dory forgot Nemo. But that wasn't an option. Shit just got real and I had to pull up my big girl panties and walk into an adult rated nightmare. I'd never been more terrified in my life.

Turning the corner into my best friend's

hospital room, I took an emotional sledge-hammer to the heart. Her beautiful face was pale, her head half shaved, and a jagged line of black thread tracked down her skull. My beautiful Elle was broken.

So pale and still, so battered and lifeless, the sight of her stole the breath from my lungs. Despite knowing my best friend by heart, I hardly recognized her lying comatose before me.

The utilitarian white sheet disguised her body and made her appear small and meek. Elle was anything but meek. She had enough backbone for the both of us. This was not my Elle.

Toothy knots stitched across her temple further disturbed her ravaged face. The fluorescent lights bleached her skin, throwing dark bruises into sharp relief. Every trace of familiar comfort found in her presence vanished as stark fear impaled my heart.

Knees buckling, I gripped the doorjamb, fighting back a sob as everything inside of me wanted to run. There would be no running. I had to face this because Elle would do anything for me and I wanted to do just as much for her. I had to shove my fear aside and get in there, talk to her, tell her everything would be all right. That's what best friends did.

The soles of my sandals weighed me down.

My heart stuttered and plummeted into my feet as I braced for the unimaginable and tried not to flinch in horror. I needed to be brave, for her, for me, for anyone who doubted she'd come out of this. She *would* recover.

Her unconsciousness seeped into me, a hollow pain too vast and encompassing to fully describe. No matter how I tried, I couldn't cross the threshold.

"You can come in."

Inside the room, a woman in scrubs inspected some sort of tube hooked between Elle and a bag of clear fluid. I willed my legs to move, to carry me those last few steps to my best friend's side, but a shiver stole over me, paralyzing me as half my world was decimated.

The happiness I owned only hours ago drifted like a whisper through the silence, too low for anyone else to hear. My peaceful little world of guarantees had crumbled to dust, little granules of heartache settling into my bones and leaving me stiff with uncertainty.

Gone. Broken. Divided in two. And I selfishly mourned the life I'd just found, forcing myself to let it go so I could be where I was needed most, present, in this nightmare with Elle. There would be no returning to Hale as long as Elle was hurt. I knew that, but my heart struggled to accept it, pulled so tightly between two worlds I feared it might rip in half.

My toes twitched as my foot slid over the sanitized linoleum, too immobilized by trepidation to bend my knee and actually lift into a full step. Elle was the unbreakable one. She was the achiever, the confident beacon I looked to when questioning the trajectory of my life. And there was absolutely no sign of life coming from her now, just the slow, chirping pulse of the monitor wired to her body.

My other foot edged forward, and then the next until I slowly shuffled across the room. The nurse continued to fiddle with intimidating medical devices as I approached the bed, never letting her out of my peripheral.

I had questions, lots and lots of questions. A tear teased at my jawline, clinging for a chilling second before falling away. How could this have happened? When would she wake up? What was the last thing she said?

All of those questions seemed irrelevant and juvenile, despite the gnawing ache to have them answered. My fingers stretched to the bedding, pressing lightly into the shape of Elle's arm and dragging lightly to her hand.

"Hey," I rasped. The word sent a surge of chills up my spine and I shivered, trembling with anxiety.

Something signaled me that the nurse was about to exit. "Is she... Is this ... a ... coma?"

Never in my life had words felt so awkward in my mouth. I knew nothing about medical stuff aside from what I learned from soap operas. My ignorance slid another layer of distress onto what was already an unbearable burden.

"Right now, she's on a lot of medication to make her comfortable. Rest is good after a trauma."

What the fuck kind of answer was that? I felt unbearably stupid, too ignorant to even gauge the severity of Elle's true situation. "So she'll wake up when the drugs wear off?"

"Eventually."

"When?"

"You'll have to speak to the doctor. Are you family?"

Breath labored past my clenched teeth. I was a little rabbit about to be chased away by a big hawk. "She doesn't have family. I'm it." Well, there was Tyler—and Chris, but I'd explain all that later.

"Visiting hours are over at eight. You're welcome to stay until then." She gave a polite smile and left the room.

My feet, no longer as heavy as they were when I first entered, rounded the bed toward the chair. Was someone else here? The seat faced Elle as if someone had already positioned it.

My weight fell onto the cushion just as my knees collapsed. I drew back the sheet and found Elle's discolored hand fastened with some sort of monitoring clip and an IV punched through her vein. The skin had already begun to bruise beneath the medical tape.

My attempt at gentleness caused my hands to shake. I scooped her fingers into mine and pressed our palms together, relieved to feel the heat of her skin.

"Hey," I greeted again, watching her eyelids for any flicker of acknowledgment. There was nothing. "I'm here."

The machine chirped and my shoulders lowered, my forehead pressing into the crisp linen of her bed. Brow resting on the mattress while the weight of her fingers filled my hand, I stared at the floor. Bed wheels, wires, outlets, devices... This place wasn't home. Tears blurred my vision as I stared at the white tile.

Drawing in a deep breath and gently withdrawing my fingers from Elle's, I lifted my head and reached for my phone. "If they think I'm leaving you in this scary place alone they're out of their fucking minds."

8:01. Yeah. I wasn't going anywhere.

I opened my last text to Hale, the one where I let him know I was in the cab leaving the airport. He'd written back, but as I read the word *Good* my phone shut down.

"Shit."

I looked around the room for Elle's belongings, hoping she might have a charger, but there was nothing.

"Where's your purse?" Maybe it was with her car.

Stuffing my phone back in my bag, I glanced at my luggage by the door. I should move it out of the way. But what if some nurse named Ratched showed up and told me I had to leave since visiting hours were over? Maybe I could hide.

"God, grow up, Rayne," I mumbled.

Huffing out a breath, I slouched back into the chair and stared at Elle. "You know I won't leave you. You wouldn't leave me."

Elle was always there to tell me how to do things like an adult. Thank God, because a lot of times I fell back on philosophies that didn't work, like, shut your eyes and you're instantly invisible. I rarely made the right choice as a first decision. That's why Elle was so essential. She could predict my immaturity and tell me how to handle life's curveballs before I got pegged in the head with a fast one. That and the fact that

I loved her and she was one of the few people who actually loved me back.

So this... This was like being hit with cannon fire.

"How do I get them to let me stay?"

I stared at her face, noting her pretty, blonde eyelashes and the natural, plump curve of her lips. A sad smile twisted my mouth as something inside of me eased and a bit of my tension unraveled. She wasn't going to wake up right now, but she was alive. Eventually, she'd heal. Baby steps.

"Okay." My shoulders lifted as I drew in a galvanizing breath and straightened my spine. "I'm going to tell them I'm staying. I'll be right back."

I covered her arm with the sheet and gave her a reassuring smile she couldn't see. What was the worst that could happen? They'd say no? A vision filled my mind of me freaking out, legs flailing, arms dragging IV towers down the hall as an orderly hauled me out of the hospital. Not really an option. I'd simply have to be an adult and get permission.

Tucking my suitcase inside Elle's room, I scanned the hall for the nurse's station, wondering which nurse had the nicest disposition. The one with cats and yarn balls on her scrubs was probably a pretty good mark.

Pulling back my shoulders, I centered myself, hiding away all signs of Calamity and honing my Davenport skills. Davenports had a knack for conveying entitlement and getting exactly what they wanted. I'd just pretend I was one of them.

Go time.

I reached the desk in only a few surefooted strides and smiled at Kittens. "Hi."

The nurse looked up from her phone and grinned. "Can I help you?"

No mention that it was past visiting hours. Good. I decided to offer something before I asked for something. Remington, the patriarch of the Davenports had taught me that negotiating trick.

"Do you need anything signed for Elle Tuttle? I'd be the person to help with that." That sounded good. I was making myself essential.

"I don't think so. I believe the responders pulled all her information from the scene of the accident."

"Oh." *Don't panic. You're still relevant.* "Do you know when the doctor will be back? I'd like to speak with him or her. I'm Elle's next of kin."

Okay, that last little fib just sort of fell out. But really, who else would be here? She'd be fine with that white lie and she was all that mattered right now.

"You're family?"

Elle's parents passed away within a year of each other, so as far as family went, her brother, Chris, was it. He'd only make things worse. "We're sisters."

Oh crap, the fibs were getting fatter. I was a terrible liar. Time to expand. Make it believable.

"Our last names are different because I was married. Divorced now." I waved my bare fingers, which had never felt the weight of a diamond ring. "Such a messy thing—divorce. Todd was a real piece of work." *Todd?* "By the time all was said and done I was too exhausted with the paperwork to follow through with reverting to my maiden name, so Meyers it stayed."

For the first time in my life, I was grateful I was thirty. All of that shit could have actually happened. Not that any of it had. I was only a few weeks deep into my first real relationship.

Feeling pretty confident in my lie, I smiled at Kittens and realized by the speechless look in her eyes that I might have gone too far. *Okay, reel it in. That was definitely TMI.*

"Sorry. My mind's a mess. I just flew in from Florida. I didn't get much sleep last night, and I haven't been thinking clearly since I got the call about Elle—my sister."

Kittens nodded with what appeared to be sympathy. "I know it's hard to think positive right now, but I've seen a lot of patients recover from much worse."

There was no need to fake the comforting effects of her reassuring words. "Thank you." Collecting myself, because I needed to secure my place in Elle's room, I cleared my throat. "Would it be possible for me to get an extra blanket and a pillow? I think I'd like to stay by her side tonight."

"Of course. Coming from Florida on such an unexpected trip, you probably don't have anything arranged. Let me see about getting some things brought to her room. You can wait with your sister. It shouldn't be long."

Relieved and impressed that I earned the permission I needed, I sighed. "Thank you so much. I honestly couldn't handle leaving her right now."

"Completely understandable."

The walk back to the room was victorious. But, as I entered, my anxiousness to tell Elle what I'd just accomplished shattered. Elle was unconscious. A sense of loneliness stole through me, piercing the bubble of achievement and leaving me deflated and once again scared.

No little distraction would overshadow the truth that she was in bad shape. So I settled into my chair and took her hand. It would be a long time before I'd feel comfortable letting go. "I'm back."

Floating Through Time

2

For the first time in my life, I was in love. Not crushing on a boy, but grown-up, sexy-time love with an actual man. An incredible man. It didn't seem fair that at that same moment my heart was breaking.

"You should eat, Rayne."

My gaze lifted from the hospital bed I'd been staring at for the last several hours and shifted to Tyler. "I have no appetite."

"Have you eaten anything since you left Florida?" Sliding his bulky body into the corner chair, his assessing stare burned through me.

His concern was a whole other presence in the room. He didn't seem capable of looking at Elle, which was understandable, but I wished he'd stop looking at me.

My withered appearance wore the stench of communal travel. Wrinkled clothes and greasy hair exploited every missed hour of sleep. The skin beneath my eyes literally burned from dashing away tears, but the last thing I cared about was vanity—I simply never had, and there was no point in starting now.

My heart cracked when Remington Davenport, my eccentric, billionaire boss told me the news about Elle. Another chunk chipped away when Hale, my boyfriend and boss's son, hugged me goodbye like he might never touch me again. It was a combination of those moments and actually seeing Elle in this condition that shattered my heart so severely I had a hard time recalling the girl I was twenty-four hours ago.

So, yeah, food wasn't really on my priority list at the moment. "I'm not hungry."

Tyler sighed and shut his eyes, pressing the back of his head into the recliner seat until the stiff leather creaked. He stuck to the corner like a shadow, his words intruding as a gentle reminder of his presence every so often.

"Is this going to affect your job, being here?"

My job? I had a love/hate thing going on with my job. I loved it because it brought me to Hale, but he wasn't all I loved. I loved my boss, too, the grumpy, old bastard. However, loving a man like Remington Davenport meant hating him fifty percent of the time, too. He was an enormous, wealthy pain in my poor ass.

I didn't know how this time away would affect my job, but I knew I wasn't finished with the Davenports. Not by a long shot. I was pretty certain my job was secure, at least that's what they all said when I left.

"It shouldn't."

"You don't sound too sure." Tyler's realist personality didn't always inspire confidence. Elle usually acted as the balance between us, me the pessimist, her the optimist, Tyler the realist.

Tyler liked to shoot out random doubt bullets, little ballistic, heat-seeking reality checks that knocked me on my ass from time to time. I hated when I started questioning things. I was not what one would call a heavy thinker. But when I hit thirty I went on a soul-searching adventure to shake up my life. Lots of heavy conundrums since then.

Working for Remington Davenport was my version of Jack Kerouac-ing across the country on someone else's dollar. Okay, maybe Jack Kerouac-ing wasn't the right term. The Davenport lifestyle was galaxies away from roughing it in the woods. But there had been some soul-searching and it turned out, I'm actually pretty complicated.

Not that I'd invested my time in anything as extreme as ending world hunger or solving global warming. We're talking strictly about girl problems. I've been inflicted by all of them —the butterflies, the strange twitterpated sensations one gets when near a certain someone, the gawky misfortunes that happen regardless of how hard I tried to imitate class and grace. Simply put, I was a fucking disaster, a steaming, hot mess. A calamity—thus the nickname. It'd been a rough haul...

I typically got a kick out of four-letter words, but *love* was a new one in my vocabulary. Sometimes kids said *shit, fuck, dick, twat,* or *piss* without knowing what the words actually meant. Grown-ups had a habit of tossing out the word *love* without ever really knowing the actual definition first hand.

Me, I was one of those grown-ups—until recently.

Hale loved me. All of me. And I loved him. We were L-O-V-E sitting in a tree and I wanted the world to know that I'd finally found someone. Aside from Elle, there weren't many who could tolerate my weird quirks. Hale, Elle, Tyler, and my mom did not scare easily. They were my people for that very reason.

Remington should probably be lumped into that tolerant clump. I mean, there had to be some reason he hired me. I was easily the worst personal assistant on the planet, no business acumen, zero typing skills, the attention span of a gnat, and the grace of a goat... But those Davenports loved me. And I loved them.

My hand closed around Elle's, drawing comfort from the warmth of her fingertips. I wanted to shake her, demand she wake up and look at me. I wanted someone to tell me this would all be okay, but those guarantees weren't coming and I was stuck in this silent room trying my best not to break.

It had never been so hard to put on a brave face, but I forced the words out, needing to hear some sort of reassurance. "It'll be fine."

"Did you get to talk to the doctor?" Tyler asked.

"Yeah." Anxiety made my chest tight so I breathed through my mouth. "He came in around seven this morning. The nurse said until Elle shows signs of waking, he'll be checking in every few hours."

"The nurses seem nice. They let you sleep here?"

I nodded. "If anyone asks, I'm her sister."

"Are you okay?"

Drawing in a deep breath, I gave Tyler a wan smile. "Yeah. Just thinking."

"About work?"

He seemed to be fishing for a distraction. "Sort of."

"I haven't talked to you since you started. How's it going?"

I left Oregon only a month ago, but so much had changed "I love it. It's exciting and fast-paced. I meet a lot of interesting people and live in an incredible mansion in Key West." The first half of the month had been spent on *The Lady Parr*, Remington's yacht—*one* of them.

"What's your boss like?"

My smile turned genuine. "We're polar opposites. He's a conservative egomaniac with the virility of a Fidel Castro." Little known fact, Castro slept with thirty-five thousand women, one during every lunch and dinner of his reign. My boss was sort of like that, but *not* with me.

He managed to sleep with many young, pretty things, despite his four marriages. Yeah, Remington didn't really respect the word *fidelity* unless it was in reference to a bank. I wasn't praising these attributes. I personally disdained them. But the facts were the facts. Remington was a pig.

Tyler scowled at me. "Do you have a thing going with him?"

"Ew! Gross! No." I tried not to gag. "He's a total chauvinist. And he's *old*."

"Good. I don't think I could handle the image of that."

I scrunched my nose. "Why would you imagine it in the first place?"

"If you said you were having an affair with him my mind would've gone there."

"Well, stop it."

I sheltered my boobs with my arms. Staring at Tyler, I concentrated on the crotch of his jeans until his hand dropped protectively over his lap. "What are you doing?"

"Picturing your penis."

"*Why?*"

I shrugged. "Fair is fair."

He sighed and rolled his eyes—so very Ty. At least we distracted ourselves for a few minutes.

Not that I'd tell Tyler that I recently discovered how much I liked having sex, but it was definitely notable news I wished I could share with *someone*. Not only did I like it, I looked hot having it—at least with Hale. He had this mirror at his house in Georgia and one time we...

Stop.

My brain—and my body—couldn't handle sex recollections at the moment. I'd gone almost a complete lifetime without a carnal appetite, but Hale opened my eyes to a literal smorgasbord.

Figured, now that I started enjoying sex, I'd have to go without. Maybe I should think of it as fasting rather than some sort of starvation.

"Will you go back to waitressing?"

"I like my job with the Davenports." My words tumbled out on a wave of panic. Going back to serving fries and beer filled me with a terrible sense of meaninglessness. Nothing against waitresses. I was one for the majority of my life. But now I wanted something more ... impactful.

"I was just saying, you have options if you want to stay around for Elle."

Waitressing might actually be my *only* option. I *needed* to be here until Elle recovered and there was no telling how long from now that would be. My gaze lifted to her battered face.

"Her hair will grow back." Tyler's words whispered through the silence. The least of my fears, but one of the few guarantees we had to offer each other.

I nodded, appreciating his attempt to console me.

God, it was suffocating in this room, stuffy, yet there was a steady chill to the air. I shut my eyes and tried to picture Hale sitting beside me. A tower of unshakable strength and calm control. Devastatingly handsome, tall, broad shoulders, athletic build, dirty blond hair, and those signature gray, Davenport eyes.

He could be intense and tender, balancing the two with utter perfection. We were so different, yet so perfectly suited for each other. Hale smelled like authority. I smelled like catastrophe. He showed me that sex could be phenomenal and I, well... I let him.

He was selfless and noble and so much a man to admire if you could actually see beneath the stuffy, reserved façade he wore for the rest of the world. Hale had deep feelings and honorable secrets. For instance, he adopted a little girl who needed a dad. That was the clincher that tied my heart to his.

Even now the truth made me sigh. He was the best man I'd ever met, and through some freak turn of events, we found each other.

A nightshift nurse entered the room. "Pardon me, hon. I just want to check her IV."

I watched as she inspected the many tubes connected to my best friend. My stomach hurt as I wondered if Elle felt any pain. A shiver climbed my spine as my vision blurred, her shimmering image appearing far too delicate for such a strong woman.

When the nurse left, I looked at Tyler. "Has anyone called Chris?" Elle's brother wasn't my favorite person, but someone should have notified him by now.

"I left him a message. Don't know if he'll get it."

Chris had once been a fun, normal guy until he got involved with drugs. When Elle stopped supporting him he robbed her blind. Not only did he steal her debit card and clean out her accounts, he stole her oven. Who steals an oven? He took other things too, her jewelry, some furniture, and her laptop. But the oven really got to me.

"I hope he doesn't come here," I muttered, knowing his presence never brought anything but stress to Elle's life.

"I was sort of hoping the same, but I had to call him. He's her brother."

I stayed at the hospital until seven that evening, knowing I needed to get home, find a phone charger, and sleep in a real bed. I ate some sort of pastry from a vending machine on my way out of the hospital but was pretty sure it expired in the nineties.

I took a cab because my car had been in my mom's garage since I started working for the

Davenports. When I climbed out of the taxi and stared at my childhood home, a crushing ache formed in the pit of my stomach. Back again.

Everything inside of me demanded I shouldn't be there. I was supposed to be taking care of Remington, in Florida, with Hale. Moving forward. This felt like a humongous step backward. Reminding myself of the circumstances that brought me back to this place only intensified that ache, heaping a good amount of guilt into the stew. I was here for my friend and, as much as I'd expected to be somewhere else, I accepted that this was where I wanted to be—with Elle. I was just tired, and juggling so many conflicting emotions wasn't helping matters.

I lugged my suitcase to the porch and the door opened before I even slid my key into the lock.

"Hi, honey," my mom greeted softly, eyes heavy with worry.

I'd been so good about keeping my tears locked inside after the first shock of seeing my friend, but my mom's concern and Elle's continuous stillness, on top of my lack of sleep and abundant hunger, was a weight I could no longer bear.

My face pinched, as a high-pitched wheeze

scraped past the lump in my throat and my shoulders drooped forward on a sob. My mom pulled me into her arms, hugging me tightly.

"I know, sweetie. She'll get through this. Elle's strong, honey."

I wept inconsolably, as my mother ushered me into our little kitchen and sat me at the table. She continued to offer words of hope, but nothing would erase the memory of Elle's battered face from my mind.

"They had to shave part of her head," I cried.

"Hair grows back, Rayne."

But Elle was a hairdresser and her hair was lovely, nothing like my plain, brown, poker straight mop. It was her source of pride and they'd cut it away. Her face had been so battered, it hurt to see her wounds.

A plate of cookies slid in front of me as my mother patiently waited for me to sniffle through the last of my tears. "Thank you."

"You need to eat. I figured cookies would do the trick."

I peeled back the plastic wrap and broke off a crumble, but even homemade cookies tasted like sawdust on my tongue. I'd *never* been too sad to eat.

Sliding the plate aside, I stole a napkin from the basket on the table and blotted my eyes. "Do you have a charger?" Hale was probably going nuts trying to reach me.

"It's in my bedroom."

Too tired to talk, I lurched to her room. The familiar, dated décor welcomed me and distressed me at the same time, every glimpse of my surroundings a strange reminder that I was far away from my other home.

Sliding the plug into my phone, I sat on the edge of my mother's bed and waited for any signs of life—a reoccurring theme for the day. When the screen lit, several messages and texts appeared, but I ignored them and dialed Hale.

"Rayne?" he answered midway through the first ring.

I curled onto my side and held the phone to my ear, shutting my eyes so my tears wouldn't make the screen slick. "Hi."

"Oh, babe." Two words, but I knew he understood. Never in my life had I wanted to touch a person as much as I did in that moment.

"I'm sorry I didn't call sooner. My phone died and I left my charger at your place."

"Have you been at the hospital all this time?"

"Yes. She's..." My voice seized. "I'm so scared, Hale."

"Shh... We don't have to talk about it if you

don't want to. Just shut your eyes and pretend I'm there with you, holding you tight."

My arms closed over my hollow belly as my eyes squeezed tighter. I could almost feel his strength banding around me.

"Everything will be okay, Rayne. I'm here."

For the first time since returning to Oregon, I felt an acute sense of balance return. "I love you."

I knew he wasn't there. I knew they were my arms hugging me. But if I could just believe for a minute that they were his, maybe the pain and fear would stay at bay.

"I love you, Rayne. Don't worry. I'm not letting go."

The Things We Shouldn't Think

3

I went to the hospital every day for three solid weeks and there was no improvement. Seeing Elle hooked up to a feeding tube truly terrified me, that I might never hear her voice again. Hale called every morning, texted throughout the day, and was the last voice I heard at night before I went to sleep. But even he couldn't cheer me up.

Realizing Elle wasn't getting better meant making some tough decisions. I needed to stay in Oregon for my friend, but staying without an income would be impossible. There was no choice but to return to work and that meant going back to the bar where I'd waitressed since college.

"Are you sure that's what you want to do?

If you need money—" Hale protested and I cut him off.

"Hale, I can't live off your money. I can't leave until I know she's okay and I have no idea how long it will take before she's back to her normal self." If that was even a realistic goal.

His objection came in the form of silence. Although he understood my circumstances, I knew he'd rather send me money than see me get tied up in commitments that might hold me here longer.

Taking his money was out of the question. Remington had given me a credit card when I left, but I couldn't use his money either. Nor could I expect my mother to revert to supporting her thirty-year-old daughter.

"I don't want to be a burden on anyone."

"You're not. Rayne, let me help you. Please."

"You are. In other ways."

As much as I appreciated his offer, I'd always managed to support myself. Even when I decided to give up a well-paying teaching career, I'd made things work. My independence was my only testament to adulthood, and reverting to a time when others supported me broke some sort of cardinal rule in my head.

"It'll just be temporary," I repeated for myself as well as him. "I promise."

Thankfully, he accepted my decision without further argument and my previous employer welcomed me back with open arms.

Placing the bar tab on a table occupied by a young couple, I forced a smile. It was tough keeping a pleasant expression while waitressing and serving drinks, but most of the patrons at the bar were my old regulars and knew through the grapevine about Elle. So my lack of congeniality was mostly excused.

"I'll take that whenever you're ready." It was a familiar script with the same lines day in and day out, but I knew it by heart and not having to think too hard about how to do my job helped me focus on other issues in my life.

Shuffling back to the kitchen to check on my next order, I blew out a slow breath. My anxiety had tightened to such a strangling knot in my chest I sometimes had to concentrate on simply breathing.

It wasn't just Elle's health. It was everything.

While Elle remained unchanged, Elara, Hale's daughter, was growing like a weed. Hale sent me pictures often, and every time I saw her little peanut face with those silver Davenport eyes my ovaries grew more depressed.

Elara wasn't mine and I didn't pretend to have any claim to her, but she'd shown me babies weren't so scary. I mean, having a child of my own would be disastrous, like riding a bike with a flaming seat and no brakes as it raced down a steep hill through a Civil War-like rendition of Bull Run where bullets were binkies and cannons fired diapers full of baby shit. But, again, not my kid. Hale managed to ride that bike just fine.

I couldn't keep a plant watered. But that didn't mean I couldn't appreciate everything Hale was doing. Elara was his responsibility. I was only a bystander—a bystander who really missed seeing her boyfriend's daughter up close and personal.

So much was happening and I was missing it. Never in a million years did I expect Elara to garner so much of my affection. But with each passing day, I missed her almost as much as I missed Hale. And with every ticking minute, came the certainty that they were surviving just fine without me. All of them—including Hale.

Not a good place for my mind to go. If Elle were awake, she'd tell me to knock it off and assure me that the distance between Hale and me wouldn't change our love. But if she were awake and could tell me that, there really wouldn't be a need for me to be here. And without her generous guidance, my mind seemed to spiral into the darkest depths of my own doubts.

God, I was completely dysfunctional without my best friend. She was my Jiminy Cricket. Without her, I was just...wooden.

As I finished up my shift, I approached Tyler at the bar. He often came there to read, which was rude, but that was just who he was. "How was she today?"

He closed his book, using a cocktail napkin as a placeholder. "The same."

It was wearing on all of us. Chris, Elle's brother, had never shown up. He called Tyler back and said he would, which filled us with dread, but in true Chris form, he broke his word. It was probably for the best.

"I think I'm going to head over to the hospital once I cash out my tips."

My phone pinged and I lifted it from my apron pocket. Hale. His text, a simple *I miss you,* should have made me smile but it only added to my stress. Three weeks of good morning chats followed by a slew of redundant texts throughout the day and one solid goodnight conversation did not equal the level of intimacy we had in Florida.

Every time I got another *I miss you* it subliminally hit me as a *you're still gone and time is moving on without you...* I shouldn't complain.

At least he was thinking of me. If the *I miss yous* ever stopped I'd be devastated. But I wanted more. I didn't want to miss him at all. I wanted us to be together.

Tyler looked at me and sighed. "Sleep at home, Rayne. She's not going to wake up."

Everything inside of me went rigid as his words stabbed into the endless worry I tried to hide. "Shut up, Tyler."

His face paled as he realized what he'd said. "I didn't mean it like that. I meant tonight." True regret showed on his face, as all color leached from his cheeks. "I didn't mean that."

I touched his hand. We were all short on sleep and high on ugly emotions. "I know."

He shook his head and mumbled, "I just meant tonight."

I nodded because it hurt to say he might be right, but chances were she wouldn't wake up tonight, or tomorrow, or the day after that. It had been three weeks and nothing had changed.

It was as if we were all in a coma, holding our breath until the moment Elle opened her eyes and we could all start living again. What if she never woke up?

Don't think that shit. Take it back. Take it back now!

I take it back. She'll wake up. It's Elle. She has to wake up.

Right?

There was no reassurance. Only cold silence.

Disregarding Tyler's advice, I drove to the hospital. When I entered Elle's room I froze. A bed, made and empty, filled the hollow space.

"What the fuck?"

Pivoting, I bolted into the hall. Kittens, otherwise known as Nurse Ally, looked up from the desk with a start as I crashed into the counter. "Where's my friend?"

A doctor glanced at me while reviewing a file with the family members of another patient. Ally shook her head, a look of confusion flashing in her startled eyes. "Your sister?"

"Elle Tuttle, where is she?"

"Let me check." She typed something into a computer. "Jenn, do you know if they moved any patients today?"

The other nurse stepped to Ally's side. "The Tuttle woman? They moved her around noon. I have her paperwork somewhere. Let me check."

"Was something wrong? Why did they move her? Did she wake up? They were supposed to call me if she woke up."

"I don't believe there's been any change."

Ally sent me an apologetic look. She understood. This other nurse was too distant to get it. I'd only seen her a handful of times on this floor.

"Check faster. How do you lose a patient?"

The other nurse pursed her lips. "She's been moved to the fifth floor, but visiting hours are over—"

I ran to the elevators and repetitively jammed my finger in the button until the doors opened. Breaking into a sweat, I tried to calm my nerves, but my stomach was cramping painfully.

They would have called if anything changed. They had my number and specific instructions to call either Tyler or me.

I walked briskly to the nurse's station on the fifth floor and managed my words carefully. "I'm looking for Elle Tuttle. She was moved here from the second floor and I don't know why."

The nurse checked a chart. "She's in room five-ten."

I glanced at the room numbers. "Why was she moved? What ward is this? Did something happen? I should have been contacted if there was any sign of change."

"This is long-term care." She wheeled her chair back to a desk and grabbed a file, flipping it open. "I don't see any notes regarding her status today... Hmm... That's strange. I'm not sure why she was moved from two. There's been no change."

No one had any answers. Nodding, I turned and went in search of five-ten. When I saw the placard, my stomach twisted. I slowly pushed open the door and my jaw unhinged.

Elle lay peacefully on a freshly made bed, looking much like she did the last time I saw her. But the room was *huge*. A mauve loveseat was against one wall and a large arrangement of flowers sat on a dresser. Angling my neck, I peeked through the door into the room next door. That room looked normal. Small, with two beds separated by a curtain. This room was like a hotel, but with wires and scary machines.

I shuffled to the bed and brushed my hand over Elle's fingers. She needed a manicure. "Hey."

Silence.

Dropping my purse on the loveseat, I inspected the flowers. It was a stunning arrangement of lilies and exotic tropical blooms that overpowered the scent of disinfectant in the air. Digging through the petals, I found a card and smiled.

Get well soon.
~The Davenports

THAT'S WHEN IT CLICKED. THIS WASN'T the doctor's decision. It was theirs. They'd had Elle moved, probably demanding the room include suitable seating for visitors, knowing Tyler and I were frequently here.

I removed my phone and dialed. I'd speak to Hale in a bit, but first I had to call the person who unapologetically threw his weight around to get his way.

"How's the room?" Remington answered and I grinned at the familiar, gruff sound of his voice.

"Thank you."

He grumbled. "Does it have a sleeper sofa? I told them to make sure it had somewhere for visitors to rest."

Wiping the tear from my lashes, I nodded. "It does. Thank you, Remington."

I couldn't express how much his gesture meant, so I repeated my gratitude over and over again. Once I pulled myself together, I asked, "How are things there?"

"The cast comes off tomorrow."

Sad I'd miss the big reveal after taking care of him for so long, I tsked. "You must be thrilled."

When Remington suffered a heart attack at the beginning of summer he'd also taken a nasty spill and broken his foot. That's where I came in. I was hired to compensate for his lack of mobility. Some assistants were right hands. I was a left foot.

"It'll be nice to finally get around. There's a chance I might have to wear a boot, but we'll see about that."

I rolled my eyes. "If the doctors tell you to wear a boot, wear the boot, Remington."

Again, he grumbled. "How's your friend?"

I had no news regarding Elle, but the room change was a great distraction. As I spoke to Remington I wandered around the space, scoping out the bathroom and cabinets and babbling about nothing in particular, but he acted like everything I said was interesting.

"We miss you, Meyers."

My heart pinched. Remington didn't talk about his feelings easily. "I miss you, too."

"Fall courses start up soon. Have you looked at the roster?"

He'd been trying to talk me into going back to school for business, but I had no interest in returning to college, especially now. I already had one degree I didn't use. It seemed cumbersome to have two.

"I'm a little busy working at the bar and being here."

"Sign up for a class, Meyers. It'll do you good. You could study while you keep watch over your friend."

"We'll see."

I wouldn't. Despite his offer to pay, I was all the way in Oregon and life seemed too unpredictable at the moment to make big commitments. Sure, I could take something online, but since Elle's accident, my brain had gone on vacation. Sometimes it took me five tries to type an order into the register at work. I was in no state of mind to learn.

"Thanks again for the room, Remington." I sensed him getting tired and considered the time difference between here and Florida.

"It's nothing. You take care of yourself, Meyers. Hurry up and come home."

The line went dead and I shut my eyes. *Home.* It wasn't my home, of course. It was one of Remington's many houses. But being away still managed to fill me with a painful sense of homesickness.

I talked to Elle for the next hour, unsure if she could hear me or even knew I was there. It was sort of like being in a confessional with a priest, not that I'd ever done that, but part of me wanted to.

"It's hard to believe it was only a few weeks that Hale and I were together," I said softly, massaging her arms. "I mean, I've been home that long. What happens if I'm here for months?"

Elle always had answers for me, so I asked her questions. If she could hear me, she might wake up with all the answers.

"If Hale and I are apart longer than we were together, will time start subtracting from itself?" I laughed sadly, still processing the fact that I, Calamity Rayne, had a living-breathing boyfriend.

"If you could have seen him the night I told him we could have sex again. It was right after I found out about his daughter and I'd been avoiding him for days. He was so eager he cut right through traffic and mauled me in his driveway. That was some *good* lovin'."

How was he making do without me now? I'd been carrying this strange weight for the past few days and coming to recognize it as doubt, but I hated admitting that I had doubts —even to myself or my comatose friend.

The problem with working for Remington was he told the truth even when it wasn't what you wanted to hear. The night before I'd returned home, Remington made a comment about men wanting everything. He said Hale was *his* son and implied that I might be better off keeping away from him due to my radical opinion that men should be monogamous. But Hale was also Naomi's son and that woman had done well. Hale wasn't a scoundrel like his dad.

Hale had a lot of Remington's qualities, but he'd dodged a great deal of his father's negative traits. Hale knew how to apologize when he was wrong, say please and thank you, and we were finally getting to a point where he'd let down his guard in private. His father did none of those things.

"I miss him so much," I whispered.

Sighing, I placed Elle's hand on the blanket. Her fingers were getting thinner. Emotion choked me as I stared at her arm, thinking it too fragile.

"Please wake up, Elle. I don't know how to make sense of anything when you're not here to tell me what to do. Should I go back? What if he can't do long distance? What if what we had only felt like love, but it was really some sort of infatuation? Maybe he doesn't miss me at all. And what if you opened your eyes and I missed looking into them for a split second? I miss both of you so much."

I rested my head beside her arm, my voice shrinking with every painful word. "This is so hard. I don't want to lose him, but I can't leave you here like this. You have to wake up. I need you."

When she didn't respond I wasted no time on disappointment. Elle didn't choose this. She'd want to be awake. Her entire existence revolved around living and milking life for all it was worth.

As I drove home I considered my new reality. It was really just a matter of perception, each person drawing their own unique conclusions from personal events.

It was getting harder to recall the way Hale and I were together. We were so new, just beginning to explore this incredible chemistry we shared when the rug was pulled out from under us.

My life went from ordinary, to exciting, to stagnant again. But his life had always been fast-paced and now he had a newborn daughter keeping him busy on top of everything else. I was probably an afterthought at the end of each day.

What seemed like years, actually happened in the span of weeks and suddenly felt like a ridiculously short time to put so much emphasis on something as intangible as love. All I treasured seemed to be slipping through my fingers and no matter how tightly I closed my fists, nothing could hold those tender feelings in place. I needed to find a pause button on life until everything returned to normal.

Perhaps I was placing too much weight on our connection. Maybe this was one of those love affairs people looked back on fondly, but never revisited. Was this where phrases like *it just wasn't the right time* came from?

I debated the mercy of shooting a horse with a broken leg. Perhaps our relationship was a hobbled horse waiting to be put out to pasture. Maybe it would be better to call it what it was and not drag it out into something ugly and painful. Just shoot the poor, damn nag so this suffering could end.

Hale called just as I pulled into my mom's driveway, so I sat in the car for a bit of privacy.

"How was your day, baby?" His voice always undid parts of me.

I'd never met someone so capable of calm. Sometimes his apparent tranquility freaked me out, but I'd seen him lose his shit once and that was enough. On the outside, Hale was a perfect gentleman, but on the inside, he was full of passion, an uninhibited, fervent man who needed to let go. He told me I was his escape from the pressures of life. I loved being that for him.

"It was fine. I miss you," I whispered. It felt like that was all we ever said to each other.

"I miss you, too. You okay? You seem a little down."

I'd been down since leaving Florida, but today was really getting to me. "I'm just worried."

"About Elle?"

"Yes, her and ... us."

He was silent for a beat. "What about us?"

"I've been gone for almost four weeks, Hale."

"Believe me, I know."

"I've been back in Oregon almost as long as I was in Florida."

"So?"

"I just... How long will we be able to keep going like this?"

"We'll go as long as it takes, Rayne. Not having you here is killing me, but every day your absence reminds me of why you're so important. It reminds me how much you mean to me."

"I know. Me too. I'm just worried, that's all."

"Well, try not to worry, baby. Elle will get better eventually."

But she wasn't. The doctors were starting to drop terms like "assisted living" into subtle conversations and Tyler could hardly bear the hospital anymore, his visits dwindling down to less than an hour a day. Part of me believed Ty had to force himself to go, knowing I'd want a full report while I worked my shifts at the bar.

I wanted to feel something aside from terror, so I searched my heart. "Your dad got her a nicer room."

"I heard. He misses you. You know he'd do anything for you."

But even Remington Davenport had limits. He was no more capable of saving my friend than he was of saving his wife who'd passed away a few years ago.

We talked for a while, seeing as I hadn't spoken to him in some time. It helped, hearing his voice and his confidence that we'd pull through, but it didn't erase all of my doubts.

When I said goodnight I could tell my mood worried him, so I tried to fake cheer. "I love you."

He hesitated. "Rayne, don't let circumstances get you down. This isn't how it will always be. You have to stay hopeful."

I wasn't a cynic, but that was a tall order, staying hopeful. Thirty years of running from my problems had not prepared me for one as

big as this. This was very different from my ordinary drama. This left no room to escape.

"I will."

As soon as I made it inside the house I went right to bed without changing out of my clothes. My mind played over Hale's last words, now hearing a strange catch to his voice I wasn't sure I'd made up or missed when he'd said goodbye.

Something in his tone filled me with worry. He hadn't just reassured me. He was reassuring himself. Maybe he was sensing the same pres-sure, but still in denial of the threat.

Everything was too real. This long distance relationship was taking its toll on both of us. The ache in my stomach, the one I'd been fighting back all day, finally had a name. Fear. I was terrified.

4

"Rayne, David's going to be late. Can you grab the guy at table nine?"

Fucking David. That guy hadn't been on time for a single shift since I met him. He was my replacement, so I couldn't suggest they fire him because if anything changed with Elle I'd be leaving again and David would be necessary.

"Sure. Let me just run this tray of burgers over to my other table."

Wedging two Mai Tais between the plates filling my order, I carefully balanced the tray and headed to the back of the restaurant. It was Saturday, so the bar was filling up early. The owners had added some patio seating off the street, which had tripled the number of patrons I was used to and my feet were feeling the effects. But it kept me busy enough not to dwell on other things.

Waiting for the woman blocking my way to *move her ass,* I patiently smiled and held my tray above my shoulder.

"Oh, sorry," she twittered.

"Take your time." *I hate people.*

She finally scooted into a chair and as I turned the corner my body jolted and my head did a double take. A tingle of excitement churned rapidly through my belly and then drained into numbness only to surge back up with the force of a tsunami, much like when a person *almost* falls down a flight of steps but catches themselves in the last instant.

The sound of dishes shattering barely registered as breath sucked deep into my lungs and my eyes stung with the shock of tears. Mouth agape, I watched him rise from the booth, broad shoulders perfectly filling out the cut of his tailored jacket, eyes so intoxicating I was drunk on the spot. It had to be a dream.

Am I hallucinating?

A startled grin curved his full lips. An ocean of concerned faces stared, but I only had eyes for him. The next thing I knew I was running like a Barcelona bull through a china shop and throwing my body into mid-air. *"Hale!"*

His strong arms caught me as my legs

wrapped around him, wrenching a grunt from deep in his chest. My catapulted body suctioned to his like an octopus on the attack. My lips peppered his neck and jaw as I cupped his face and laughed.

"What are you doing here?"

Sliding my body down his front, he looked into my eyes and smiled. "I told you I missed you."

I laughed and shook my head. "Where's Elara?" How could he just leave and come here when he had work and a baby?

"She's around the corner. We're staying at the Heathman."

"We?" I couldn't stop touching him, my hands roaming over his fancy suit shirt like a pickpocket on the hunt for his soul. *He's here!*

"Me, my brother, and my mom."

"Oh, my God! I could pee my pants I'm so happy!" Not used to smiling, I touched my cheeks, which were already sore. I glanced at the rubbernecking patrons, uncaring that I was making a scene. "This is my boyfriend! *My* boyfriend."

Those who knew me would appreciate that tidbit, being that I never dated—by choice—before Hale.

"You dropped your tray," Hale murmured,

angling his chin toward the disaster left in my wake.

I waved a hand. "I'll get it cleaned up. How long are you staying? Can we go see Elara? I've missed you so much. Oh, my God, you're going to meet my mom! I swear she thinks I made you up. Ha! I'll show her!"

He chuckled. "Take a breath, baby. I'm here for a while and I'd love to meet your mom. As soon as you're finished I can take you back to the hotel to see Elara."

I spun in a circle like a dog seeking a resting spot. I needed keys and—damn, there was a serious mess on the floor. "Where the fuck is David?"

"Who's David?"

"A waiter. I'm done my shift, but he's late."

His lips compressed and I grinned, because he tried so hard not to show any sign of impatience, but he couldn't hide his emotions from me. What I once believed to be the world's greatest poker face now seemed as readable as a Dr. Seuss book. Ha. He really did miss me.

Carrie Ann, my boss, appeared with a broom.

"I'll be right back," I said to Hale, smiling and dragging my hand down the front of his pressed shirt. "Don't go anywhere." God, I loved his fancy ass.

Returning to the slopped tray on the floor, I panted, already out of breath. "I'll get that, Carrie Ann."

I made quick work of cleaning up the mess. My gaze pinged back to Hale, way too over-dressed for our little hipster town.

Not only did he *not* have a beard, he was wearing a suit jacket. But he totally pulled it off in a *don't you want to touch me?* sort of way. I kept glancing over my shoulder at him because he was mine and somehow he created the pos-sessiveness of a monkey over a cupcake in me. Mine. *My precioussssss...*

I dumped the broken dishes in the trash and quickly remade two of the shittiest Mai Tais to ever exist, adding whatever was in front of me into the glasses. "Mel, I need you to re-make that order."

Our overweight, moody chef grumbled. "Already on it... You a walking calamity, girl."

I smiled at him through the kitchen win-dow. "My boyfriend's here."

"That's great." He flipped the burgers on the sizzling grill.

"It *is* great. He flew in from Florida to sur-prise me! He loves me."

Mel didn't seem to care, so I delivered the drinks to the table. "Your burgers will be up in a minute. My boyfriend surprised me." They didn't seem to care either.

I skipped over to Hale's table as he greeted me with a silent chuckle and an amused glint in his devastatingly gray eyes. I was petting him again because I couldn't resist. "David should be here any minute."

"We have time."

My gaze gobbled up every inch of him, from his strong shadowed jaw to his broad shoulders to his cufflinks and back up to those fascinating silver eyes. His lips looked extra full today and I was going to bite them soon. I sighed. He was so dreamy.

I, on the other hand, was a Velma. I'd always wanted to be a Daphne, but the truth was, I was born to be the awkward sidekick, sort of like an afterthought to the feminine part of the species. But this Velma was totally going to bang the Fred. To further illustrate my point, I was sitting here fantasizing sexual acts with Scooby Doo metaphors, while Hale was likely scouting over facts and figures in his brain and coming up with filthy grown-up words I couldn't utter without giggling.

Oh, he had a magnificent vocabulary. Naughty, sinful words had whispered across those luscious lips as he dragged them over my skin. So self-assured, so devastatingly sexy. *Annnnnd* my nipples were hard. *Rut-roe.*

"I remember that look." The slow rumble of his voice sent chills up my spine as the back of his knuckle teased the line of my jaw.

My finger made little swirls around the button of his jacket. "So ... this hotel. Do you have your own room?"

Eyes heavy, he slowly nodded.

My heart tripped into double time. "Maybe you could show me before we see your family."

"I'm planning on it."

Cha-*ching!* Momma was cashing in on some lovin'. Cagney and Lacey—otherwise known as my boobs—were totally getting some action tonight!

"Rayne, order up!"

Still smiling, I pivoted and raced back toward the kitchen. "I'll be right back."

As I rushed to the bar a few customers tried to stop me on my way, but there wasn't time for that. I grabbed the burgers and ran them over to the hungry table. "Can I get you anything else?"

"Can we have some ketchup?"

"Sure." I went back to the bar and found Carrie Ann. "Hey, what are the chances I could get out of here before David gets here? That's my boyfriend over there, the tall sexy one in the designer suit, and he came all the way from Florida to surprise me."

Carrie Ann rolled her eyes. "Go."

"Thank you!" I stripped off my apron and stuffed it under the bar.

As I passed the tables, the guy with the burger looked up expectantly. "Ketchup?"

I paused and reached over the customers to my right, stealing their bottle and plopping it on burger boy's table. "Here you go."

Returning to Hale, I rocked on my heels and preened. "Ready?"

He stood, his utter composure at total odds with my spastic energy. My eyes rolled back in my head as his hand rested on the base of my spine and he escorted me out of the bar. I was prouder than a mutt marching through a pedigree dog show. *My* boyfriend!

When we reached the parking lot I scanned the vehicles. "Where's your car?"

"I have a rental." He led me to a Lexus and opened the passenger door.

We both stilled as the world silenced around us. A thousand shivers chased over my skin as he leaned down and brushed his lips against mine. Divine. Luscious. Panty-drenching lips....

Wrapping my arms around his neck, I slipped my tongue into his mouth and hummed, pressing my breasts against his chest. His hand caught the back of my neck as he took over the kiss, gentling my frantic need.

Before Hale, I didn't have much practice with the opposite sex, so I was never really sure what was appropriate and what bordered on *Animal Planet*. I had very little self-control around this man.

A gravelly chuckle rumbled in his chest as he eased back. "Easy, baby. Let's get to the hotel."

"Oh. Right." My insides zinged like the needle of a lie detector hooked to a politician, zipping and clanging wildly without restraint.

Once we were on our way I reached for his hand and bounced with excitement. Hale was here, and we were going to his hotel. The sex was happening. Thank God, because while I'd once been convinced good sex was an over-glorified lie women told, Hale had proved me wrong and now I missed the sex very much.

I glanced at my lap and bit my lip. When was the last time I shaved? Last week? No, that wasn't right. Two weeks ago? Hmm. "Can we stop at that pharmacy up there?"

Briefly taking his eyes off the road, he glanced at me. "Is it something we can get later?"

"Um..." I lifted the cuff of my jeans and

found a miniature jungle spiked with over-growth. "I'll be quick."

He pulled into the pharmacy and I got out of the car before he could open my door. As he touched the handle I blurted, "I can just run in. I only need a few things."

"I'll go with you." He was big on escorting me and I was in a rush, so I didn't argue.

His hand returned to mine as soon as he rounded the car and in we went. I snatched a basket and casually sniffed my armpit through my shirt, which smelled like a deep fryer and Bud. It wasn't great, but I had just finished a shift at the restaurant and that was what wait-resses smelled like.

Shooting down the aisle with personal hygiene products I grabbed whatever might improve my sexiness. Deodorant, mango-scented lotion, shaving cream, a new razor. I even found nail polish and remover, but that wasn't for me.

Hale's lips twitched as I stocked up. He was laughing at me in that composed manner that was tough to detect, but I recognized the familiar twitch of a budding smile.

Slipping down the last aisle, I grabbed a toothbrush. "Okay, I think I'm good."

Rolling his eyes, he smirked and took my basket, placing it in front of the clerk at the register. She totaled my items and Hale swiped his card.

"I would have paid for that."

He said nothing as he opened the car door and I slipped inside.

The Heathman was probably one of the nicest hotels in our town. I'd never stayed there so I was excited for an excuse to see inside.

Hale was staying in the Warhol Suite, which had several original works of art created by Andy himself. I didn't care about any of that as we made our way up to his floor. My mind was too focused on getting the stench of fries off my skin, the wool off my legs, and the sexy man naked beneath me.

Fisting my bag from the pharmacy, I followed him to his door and announced, "I need to use the bathroom real quick before we ... do anything."

He glanced at me but didn't object. The door opened and... Wow. This was nice. There was a living room slash office, a little kitchenette area, and—bingo—bathroom. "I'll just be a minute."

Hale removed his jacket and draped it over a chair. "Don't take too long."

Nodding, I slipped into the bathroom and shut the door. I dumped my purchases on the counter and ripped open the toothbrush.

Hale's belongings were neatly put away in a black leather travel case—so adorably Hale. I found his toothpaste and got into a vigorous brushing while I nosed through the other items in his bag. Ooh, condoms. That was good. I giggled when I saw he'd packed over a dozen.

We had discussed me going on the pill, which was supposed to happen, but everything with Elle sort of took us on a detour. There had been a few times we might have been a tad irresponsible, but I didn't like to think about that, especially since I was in no rush to have children and Hale already had one. So yeah, condoms were good.

"You almost done in there?" he called from the other room.

"Thirty seconds!" I yelled, rinsing out my mouth. I stripped off my jeans and hissed at the sight of things. "Christ, I have man legs."

"You say something?"

"Can you make me a drink? Or order one?" That would take up time.

Shoving my items aside, I sat on the counter and made a complete mess. Shaving cream dripped off my legs in glops and water went everywhere.

"Fuck." Sliding off the counter, I abandoned the idea that I might have any ladylike skills in the vanity department and took off my shirt as I started the shower.

Hale knocked at the door. "Rayne? Are you *showering*?"

"I'll be right out!"

It was the speediest bathing experience of my life. I'd never been handy with a razor, so rushing to shave three weeks' worth of hair wasn't the best idea. Once I dabbed up the blood, I slathered my legs with the mango lotion.

"Oops! Too much." I was slicker than a newborn rhino. And now I was sweating, which was creating some sort of slather-mango-goo in my knee pits.

I grabbed the towel and buffed off some of the excess lotion. Ten minutes ago my skin had been drier than the Serengeti, but now I was like a human slip and slide. Hale was going to glide right off of me. I threw on some de-odorant and wrapped myself in a towel.

Oh, condom! Right.

The bathroom was annihilated, but I was clean and ready for the sex. I opened the door to find Hale reclining on a chair, finishing a cocktail. Oh, he was fine. His collar was un-done and his sleeves were rolled to his elbow. He raised an eyebrow. "You *did* shower."

"Trust me, it needed to happen."

He grinned, taking the last sip of his drink and placing the glass aside. "Come here."

Breath filled my lungs as I sashayed over to him, resembling a cross between a drunken hooker and a newborn calf. This was why I needed him. I had no game in the boudoir, but Hale liked being in charge. I liked that he liked that very much.

I stood before him and he parted his knees, inviting me into his hemisphere. Taking hold of the towel, he tugged and I was naked.

"Oh, my."

His gaze moved over me hungrily. "Fuck, I told myself you couldn't be as beautiful as I remembered, but I was wrong. You surpass my memory."

I preened happily because what girl didn't like hearing that from a sexy man? "Yes, more talk like that, please."

He sat up and pulled me onto his lap. My legs wedged between his hips and the chair as our mouths collided in a hungry kiss. Hands glided to my neck and pulled me closer as my hips ground against his hardening body.

"Jesus, Rayne," he growled, catching my nipple in his mouth.

I arched and pulled at his shirt, those tiny, little buttons always making trouble. His fingers reached between us. Once his shirt was open my palms rode over his warm flesh, savoring every square inch of muscled, male flesh.

The first brush of his fingers between my legs had me trembling. I rose on my knees, granting him access. He pulled my mouth back to his as a finger slid deep into my sex. "Oh, God..."

He wasn't gentle as he pumped his hand between my legs, but I'd have it no other way. Panting, I rode his touch and bit at his shoulder as he sucked hard on my nipple. My fingers pressed into his back where muscle tightened like twisted rope. A moan broke from my throat as the first trembles of an orgasm took hold. It was intense and quick, but we were far from finished.

Slithering down his lap I dropped my knees to the carpet and quickly unlatched his belt. Hale was a big man, and right now he was hard as a rock, so it was no easy task getting his pants off. In all of my excitement, I fell back trying to remove his shoe, but I quickly righted myself and grinned.

Hale steadied me with a hand and smiled. "My agile lady of grace."

I smirked, hearing his adoration buried in sarcasm. Then my focus returned to his dick. "Oh, Prince Everhard, we meet again."

Hale chuckled and brushed a gentle caress

down my cheek. Never in a million years would I have thought I'd take pleasure from doing this to a man, but there was something to be said about doing it to Hale. I loved the way he watched me, held me, and lost himself when I took him into my mouth. Leaning over his lap, I winked and got to work.

He hissed in a breath and cupped the back of my head, pressing me down. Heat stroked over my tongue as I used my lips to add suction. My scalp tingled as his fingers knotted in my damp hair and then I was moving.

My hands slipped between us, cupping and massaging. He groaned as the muscles in his stomach and thighs bunched and flexed. "Christ, baby, don't stop."

I was terrible at dirty talk, but Hale had a way of making me say absolutely anything. One time I'd even yelled out *ranch dressing* during sex. I don't know why. Who knows how my brain works? He was always so good with the naughty words, I think I just wanted to add something.

"Enough," he slurred, pulling me back. "I need to be inside of you. *Now.*"

Before I could stand, he lifted me off the floor and tossed me onto the bed. His rock-hard body blanketed mine, his flesh scorching hot. My legs wrenched apart as his tongue trailed up my inner thigh and found my money spot.

Arching, I cried out as his lips closed over my clit and his fingers filled me. He was a man possessed. His mouth was everywhere, biting, sucking, licking. And those fingers, slick with my arousal, slid deep until I was coming again.

He crawled up my trembling body and—Yup, that was his penis. My eyes went wide as he sank into me and I moaned long and slow. "You forgot a condom."

Catching his breath, he rested his forehead on my shoulder. "Just give me a minute here. I'll put one on."

I didn't want him to pull out anyway. For over three long weeks, I'd been horribly de-pressed and he was finally here. Something about having him inside me... It was like finding my anchor in a rocky sea of confusion where my life had shipwrecked.

My hand brushed over the back of his soft hair. "I love you."

Lifting his gaze to mine, he leaned forward and kissed me tenderly. "I love you too, Rayne. God, I missed this—us."

The slight shift of his body as he brought his lips to mine buried him deeper and we groaned through a kiss, the passion reaching an agonizing tease of pleasure. Slowly, he drew back and cursed. Neither of us wanted to interrupt the intimate reunion.

My fingers dug into his shoulders, holding him on the brink of his withdrawal. My heel pressed into his ass. I didn't want to stop. Again, I knew we should, because condoms were good, but he felt so incredible where he was.

"I should put on a condom."

My mouth pouted. My brain so addled I couldn't recall where I was in my cycle. Damn it. Stupid math. "Fine."

He withdrew and was back a second later. When he slipped back inside of me I gasped. That wasn't so bad. I was definitely going on the pill though because there *was* a difference. He thrust, and my worries about birth control and other nonsense rushed out of my head as I clung to him.

His long, chiseled body rocked over mine, pressing me into the bedding as I breathed out little, needy moans. Muscles bunched under my fingertips as he penetrated deeper. His mouth teased over my throat as my chest mashed to his, delicious friction that had me clinging tighter to his broad shoulders. No matter how I tried, I couldn't get close enough.

"More," I cried, and he caught my knee,

lifting my leg to his shoulder as he pounded into me.

The bed banged against the wall as he took me relentlessly. My cries built in a crescendo of pleas begging him to never stop. At one point I might have suggested he move into my vagina, forward his mail, and build a fort there.

I mentioned I wasn't good at the sexy talk.

Sweat slicked our skin as it went on and on. I swear, a ballistic missile could have hit the bed and we would have kept on fucking. It was a hell of a way to go.

He'd made me come countless times and I was shocked he still managed to hold out. When his gaze finally found mine he slowed, his face a picture of devotion with love and affection banked in the depths of those silver eyes. That was Hale. No matter how intensely he came at me, no matter how raw we were, when he finished he always made sure I was looking at him so I could see the love in his eyes.

"I love you, baby." He thrust deep and shivered.

My hands slid down his back and I let out a long exhale as his weight settled over me. "Wow."

Lifting his body, he gently kissed me and slowly withdrew. "Shit."

That didn't sound right. "Problem?" I slurred because words would soon be beyond my ability.

"The condom broke."

And there went my post-coital bliss. I eased up on my elbows. Hale was already standing. "Are you sure?"

"I'm sure. Damn. Are we ... safe?"

"Uh..." My head tried to do the math, but all my little brain minions were lounging around in silk robes, smoking cigarettes with sex-glazed eyes. "We should be fine." No sense in worrying. Later, I'd look at a calendar and check for sure.

He disappeared into the bathroom. "What the hell did you do in here?"

"Girlie things. Shut up."

He returned and fell onto the bed, pulling me into every nook of his long body. My butt nestled into his hips and I sighed. There was nothing like being held by Hale.

I was feeling rather sexy until my stomach rumbled. "Sorry."

"Are you hungry?"

I laughed. "You know, I actually am. I haven't had an appetite in weeks."

"I can order room service."

"What about Elara and your family?"

"They can wait a while. My mom's fine and Barrett probably went out."

I was a little surprised his brother made the trip. Barrett was whom Elle referred to as *The Hot One*. Not that she'd ever met him in person, but the Davenports were on television all the time.

Hale had originally been deemed *The Other One*. Of course, that was before I actually met him. Although he wasn't very photogenic, in person he had a devastating presence, the kind that shot right to the nipples and rendered women speechless.

Barrett... Well, he was so seriously hot he probably outranked Hale, but in a dangerous way. I much preferred Hale to all the other Davenports. There was just something mysterious and authoritative about him, something Barrett lacked.

Barrett knew he was good looking and never failed to flaunt it. He was an underwear model for crying out loud! Sometimes he was hard to look at, like the sun. Once I looked at him for a full ten seconds, and I think I hurt myself.

Hale was devastating in a whole different way because he didn't boast openly about his prowess or sex appeal. But it was there. Oh, it was there.

"What do you want to eat?" He gave me a little nudge with his nose as his lips pressed into my shoulder.

"You."

He chuckled. "You had me."

"I want you again." I nestled my bottom against him and his hand cupped my breast, massaging gently.

"So you don't want food? That's not like you."

I wasn't overweight. I mean, I had fluffy parts, but my metabolism usually kept me pretty fit. However, I loved food, especially sweets, but lately, my life had been so chaotic I'd been surviving off vending machines. "I wish you'd brought Laurent." Laurent was Remington's chef and his food was to die for. *I'd give anything to eat one of his beignets right now.*

"What's good in Oregon?"

"We're known for fruit. I want something a little more savory than that."

His smile curved against my shoulder. "Are you feeling like a carnivore?"

"Mmm. Yes."

While Hale ordered dinner I cleaned up my mess in the bathroom. My lady bits were delightfully sore and I loved traipsing around the hotel room naked.

"Make it two baked potatoes," he told the person on the phone.

I peeked out the curtains and gasped. All of Oregon was out there. We should totally do it against this window. I was pretty sure we were high enough that no one would recognize me.

"Thank you. Just leave it outside the door." The phone clicked as he laid it back in the cradle. "There was a time you couldn't bear being naked in front of me."

He grinned and folded his arms behind his head, his legs stretching across the rumpled bedding—dick just dancing in the wind. Hale had never been shy about nudity.

I turned and pushed my butt between the curtains. "I'm totally mooning Oregon right now."

He laughed. "Get over here."

Prancing to the bed, I jumped and landed on my knees. "I can't believe you're here." Leaning in, I kissed him. "Your dad has his cast off. How's that going?"

"It's going. He's in Maine right now."

"Maine? What's he doing there?"

"Checking on things. I expect he'll be traveling for a while. By the end of those six weeks, he had severe cabin fever."

"Well, he better take it easy. He's still got some healing to do."

Remington was old, but he had the energy of jarred lightning. Still, he *was* old and shouldn't push too hard too fast. I worried for the old bugger.

"You try telling him that." Hale pulled me to his chest and I snuggled into him.

"I love hotels. I don't know why, but they always make me happy. I think it's the fresh towels and room service."

He made a sound that he'd heard me, but no other response came. Hale had gotten that sort of luxury treatment all his life. Even at home, there was a wait staff and turn-down service.

His soft lips teased my temple. "Did you have plans tonight?"

I did, but they changed the minute I saw him. "I was going to go to the hospital for a bit."

"How long do you usually visit?"

Not that I thought he would mind the long hours I sat at Elle's bedside, but I didn't feel like getting another lecture about not taking care of myself. Tyler and my mom already reprimanded me for not getting enough sleep or eating regularly. "I usually go for a few hours after work."

"When do visiting hours end?"

Visiting hours didn't apply to me. They

should, but those nurses never got me out of there by eight. Some nights I slept on the loveseat, despite being told I had to leave. "They're not real strict."

"We can take a ride over after dinner."

I pressed a cheek to his chest and smiled. Hale had never met Elle, but he knew she was important to me. "Thank you."

After we ate I changed into my clothes and grabbed the things I needed to take with us to the hospital. Hale made a quick call to his mom to check on Elara and told her we'd be back in an hour. I tried not to panic over his timeline, but an hour wasn't enough Elle time.

It's Not About Me

5

The moment we stepped into Elle's room I sensed Hale slipping on a mask. I suppose it was a bit jarring, seeing a woman in such a state. All the tubes and wires hardly registered with me anymore. I no longer came to this place with expectations, only with the hope that I might add a little sunshine to my friend's long, quiet days.

Putting my belongings on the loveseat, I turned and faced Hale who waited at the door, expression blank. "It's okay. You can come in."

His eyes were watchful as he took those first steps. I moved another chair beside the one that I usually sat in.

"You can sit."

He lowered himself into the chair as I rummaged through a drawer. Once I found Elle's hairbrush, I carefully combed out the tangles that remained on the side of her head and dusted my fingers over the short spikes that had started to grow. Her stitches had been removed and her little sprouts were coming in nicely. Hale watched silently as I gingerly tucked her blonde strands behind her ear and grinned.

"We're both struggling," I told him. "Elle's been in charge of my hair since I was fifteen. I'm desperately in need of a trim, but I promised her long ago she was my forever hairdresser."

When he smiled, it didn't reach his eyes.

"That looks good," I told her. "I brought you something."

Tucking the brush away, I went to my bag and retrieved the nail polish remover. Swiping a few tissues from the box on the counter, I sat beside Hale and got to work. He watched as I removed the polish from her thin fingertips, but said nothing.

"I got you this pretty blue-green. It's called *Teal the Cows Come Home.*"

Carefully untwisting the cap, I held her fingers and I dragged the brush over her nails. I was terrible at keeping the paint off the skin, but Elle never complained. When I finished the first hand, I rested it on a tissue and moved to the other side of the bed.

"You're quiet," I said to Hale as I rubbed the polish off.

His gaze lifted, but his expression remained utterly blank. "I don't know what to say, Rayne."

My throat got tight, but there would be no crying today. Hale was here and it was a special night I didn't want to ruin. Drawing in a steadying breath I smiled.

"Hale's here. Remember Hale, the guy I told you about?"

The last awake conversation Elle and I had was right after I found out Hale was going to be a father. Elle told me to pack up shop, but I didn't listen.

"He had his baby. We're going to see her after this. Her name's Elara and she's the tee-niest little thing, Elle. You'd love her."

I blinked because sometimes my *allergies* got to me in this room. Voice tight, I said, "Hale surprised me today. Isn't that sweet?"

Forcing out a breath, I decided not to talk for a while, because my throat was getting really tight. After I finished her manicure, which looked like a two-year-old did it, I lifted her covers and gave her a leg massage. Her legs looked like mine had a few hours ago, but that was okay. At least her blonde hair wasn't as no-ticeable as my dark fur.

After an hour of taking care of her, I sat and held her hand. Hale was a silent statue the entire visit. I hadn't known what to say at first either. It took me days to have a full conversation with her and I wasn't sure if that was because she'd been so battered and unrecognizable, or if it had to do with my own self-consciousness. Now, I talked to her all the time. Tonight, I was actually holding back on account of Hale.

When an hour and a half passed I felt pulled to leave. I didn't want to go because it wasn't nearly enough time to be with her, but it wasn't fair to keep Hale there.

Fixing her blankets, I leaned close and pressed a kiss to her cheek. "I'll be back tomorrow, sweetie. I love you."

My chest hurt as we walked out of the room. I should have painted her toes. I'd do that tomorrow.

We waited for the elevator and I glanced at Hale who still wore a blank expression. Maybe he got weird in hospitals. He'd seemed okay when Elara was born, but that was the maternity ward. Sometimes medical things made people uncomfortable.

His fingers brushed mine as we stepped into the elevator and I found my hand wrapped in a tight grip, but he remained silent. As we drifted to the lobby I contemplated his silence, assuring myself it was the situation and not me. But there was a curious tug in my chest that warned Hale was worried. About me, Elle, or something totally unrelated, I wasn't sure.

I tried to think of something to say to break the ice but drew a blank. His questionable silence worried me. What if he was too detached from the situation to see the logic in me staying here? I needed him to not just accept, but agree that I was doing the right thing.

The longer his silence went on the more anxious I became. Deep down I knew what he saw, a girl so damaged she was in no condition to wake and bounce back into life. Elle was in trouble and she would be for a while, which meant I'd be here ... for a while.

He opened the car door, but caught my arm and as I moved to get inside, startling me as he pulled me into a tight hug. "Oh."

His face pressed to my shoulder as he squeezed tighter. "I'm so sorry, baby."

Condolences were for death. Elle was very much alive in there. "It's okay. She's just building up her strength."

His arms tightened even more and I patted his back. I didn't realize seeing her would upset him. When he released me I was a bit confused.

We rode in silence back to the hotel, but as

we neared the building, he finally asked, "How often do you visit her?"

"Every day. Sometimes a couple times a day."

"Does anyone else visit?"

I'd told him about Chris and that her parents were gone. "Sometimes Tyler comes by, but he doesn't go every day anymore. Just the days I have to work and can't be there until later."

His brow furrowed. "And you stay for over an hour every time?"

I shrugged. I usually stayed all night. "She's there twenty-four-seven. I don't want her to get lonely."

His mouth flattened.

"Is something wrong?"

He shook his head. "I just can't imagine doing that every day. I knew you've been visiting her regularly, but... I guess I wasn't thinking what that actually meant."

My head tipped back against the headrest. Yes, it was tough. Some days it was downright brutal. Once I'd started talking to her I tried everything. I pinched her, tickled her, I even yelled at her, but she never moved.

Elle had always been so pretty, so feminine. Next to her, I was a walking disaster, but she loved me anyway. I knew the nurses would meet her medical needs, but someone had to meet her emotional ones, so I took care of her as best I could.

But Hale was right. Others should be there. Elle deserved a room full of people caring for her. But at the end of the day, the most she had was me. Sometimes I blamed myself, believing if I wasn't such a codependent person she could have gone off to do whatever she wanted in life.

That might be misplaced blame, but it existed all the same. For all of my awkwardness, Elle had twice as much elegance. She was smart and funny and graceful in every sense of the word. She stayed in Oregon because Tyler and I were here, but she'd been the first to encourage me to leave when my boring life got to me. I should have encouraged her as well. She was meant for bigger things. She could have worked at an upscale salon in New York or gone to Hollywood to work on movie sets. But as long as I stayed in Oregon, she stuck by my side. Loyal. And then I left.

All of my life I'd been terrified of losing the one true friend who put up with me. And now I might have lost her. The guilt gnawed at me, too shameful and unflattering to speak.

Elle had to get better because she had to get out there, chase her *biggest* dreams, fall in love, and stop worrying about me. Those opportunities were still out there. And maybe I was bartering, but if she could just wake up and return to her old self, I swore I'd never hold her back again.

When we reached the hotel, Hale checked his phone. It was late and I wasn't sure if I'd see Elara tonight. "Am I staying here with you?"

Tucking away his phone, he faced me. "Isn't that what you want? I'd hoped you would."

"No, I do, but I should let my mom know where I am." Otherwise, she'd think I was sleeping at the hospital again.

On the way up to his floor, I called my mom and told her Hale had come to visit. I don't think she believed me. Ending the call, I huffed.

"What's wrong?"

"Nothing." I pursed my lips. "It's amazing how many people think I made you up. Is it that hard to believe that I could have a boyfriend? Jeez."

I mean, I knew I'd always rolled my eyes at the whole coupling thing and never showed much interest, but it wasn't like I was *that* awkward.

He laughed. "We'll prove I exist tomorrow when I drive you home."

I snickered. Then she'd see. I *could* have a boyfriend if I wanted to. I just never wanted one before.

"My mom's going to keep Elara overnight. I'm going to run down the hall and say goodnight to her. Do you want to come?"

It was after ten and I was a bit drained, but the thought of missing a chance to see Elara... "I'll come with you."

His smile was gentle, his eyes sympathetic. "I know you're tired, Rayne. She'll be sleeping. No one's going to judge you if you wait until tomorrow to say hello."

And that was why I loved him. "I'll see her in the morning. Tell your mom I can't wait to catch up."

"I'm sure she can't wait, too. Go get ready for bed. I'll meet you there in a few minutes."

After washing up, I stripped down to my T-shirt and crawled into bed. Hale took longer than expected, but I heard him come in a while later. The television played softly as he moved about the room. I thought he might have made a phone call, but I couldn't be too sure, as I kept drifting off. Sometime later, I felt him slide behind me and kiss me goodnight.

Moms and Dads

6

I awoke the following morning to the sound of cooing and Hale having a pretty intense conversation about a missing bootie. Rolling to my side, I watched him through the doorway as he held Elara and searched the sitting room for a missing baby shoe.

"Be still my heart," I whispered, smiling to myself.

So the whole baby thing, it sort of came out of nowhere. I wasn't a baby-crazed woman. I was an *avoid children at all costs* kind of gal, and usually cheated in Rock-Paper-Scissors at the bar when families sat in the restaurant section. Kids were messy and babies were fragile on top of the messy. But Elara was so cute I gave her a pass.

Still, I had to constantly remind myself that

she was Hale's and not mine. Not that I was thinking about kidnapping her or anything. Seriously, what would I do with a baby? I still wanted to enjoy the newness of us, but that newness included an infant who stirred up all kinds of nonsense where my ovaries were concerned.

I accepted his fatherhood status, maybe even fell in love with him a bit more once I understood what he'd done to become a father, but I wasn't here to be a mom. I was here to be a sex goddess.

I slipped into the bathroom and washed up before heading into the sitting room. "Good morning."

Hale turned, smiled, and sauntered over, not stopping until his lips brushed mine. "Good morning, beautiful."

Elara slouched in his arm, kicking her little cricket legs, one bootie still missing. I grinned and held out my hands. "You come to me, little peanut. I've missed you. Have you been keeping your daddy busy? Oh my, you've gotten heavy."

She cooed as I carried her back to the bed and gently laid her on her back. "So tell me, have there been any other pretty ladies around the house?"

"I heard that," Hale yelled.

"Mind your own beeswax. We're girl talking."

Elara looked up at me with bright eyes and smiled. My heart melted as I examined her tiny toes and little knuckles.

"You really are too beautiful, peanut. One day your daddy's gonna have his work cut out for him."

She babbled pleasantly as I ticked her thighs and blew raspberries on her belly.

"Yes, he is. He's going to have to chase all the boys away."

Once Hale found the shoe, he took Elara down to his mother's room. I showered and dressed because I needed to get my car, go home, and get fresh clothes. Hale and I grabbed breakfast in the hotel then we were off to my house where he would officially meet my mother.

My mother was a sweet woman. I had nothing against her on any level. She'd always supported my hopes and dreams and done her very best to be there for me. That was a hell of a lot more than I could say for my father. I didn't even know what that man looked like.

"This is it," I mumbled as I led him to the door and chuckled nervously. "Not quite a Davenport estate."

"Stop."

I paused and gave him a shaky grin, but accepted his edict. Hale was far from pretentious and I was making an issue out of nothing by illustrating all the ways our upbringings differed.

"Sorry. I'm just nervous." I drew in a deep breath as I stepped into the house. "Mom? I'm here and I brought my *boyfriend*."

Okay, I was a little immature about the whole boyfriend thing, but everyone, including me, seriously assumed I'd die single. "Boyfriend" was a new vocabulary word for me and I flagrantly abused it.

My mom came around the corner and jerked to a stop. "Rayne..." Her wide eyes took in Hale and she smiled, her shock obvious. *I knew she didn't believe me.*

"Hello." Her hand lifted slowly as if she might frighten him away.

I grinned, pulling Hale to my side. "Mom, this is Hale Davenport. Hale, this is my mother, Penny."

"It's a pleasure to finally meet you," Hale said, reaching forward to shake her hand. My mother was instantly flustered, not used to such formality. Yeah, the acorn didn't fall far.

"Please, come in. Can I get you some coffee? Have you two had breakfast?"

We followed her to the kitchen and

squeezed in at the table. I smiled, watching Hale look totally out of place in our little home.

Leaning into him I whispered, "I was sitting in that chair the first time I heard your voice." I'd also been so nervous I acted like a telemarketer and he hung up on me. I'd never expected to see his penis.

"You have a lovely home, Penny."

"Thank you, Hale." She glanced at me and grinned. "Such manners."

Once the coffee was made, she joined us at the table. "So what brings you to Oregon?"

"Your daughter. I couldn't keep away."

My mother grinned widely. "Couldn't keep away. Have you ever heard such an adorable thing? My goodness, I can see why she fell for you. And so handsome, too."

"Mom."

She totally ignored me. "So what is it you do, Hale? Ray tells me your dad's into oil and stocks."

"I have shares in all his companies and own a few of my own."

"Hale's looking into solar energy, Mom. And water turbines." Remington was old school and not yet onboard with clean energy, but Hale was open-minded enough to see the necessity of change.

Her brow lifted, impressed. "Oh, wonderful. I'm a big fan of keeping the world green."

My mother's inquisition lasted nearly an hour. Hale could have said he robbed little old ladies and she would have been just as infatuated. I couldn't blame her. He was just that charming.

She asked about his daughter and insisted he bring Elara by to meet her. She also inquired how Remington was doing. And of course, she brought up Elle.

"So sad. Elle was such a sweet girl."

"She still is, Mom." I hated when people talked about her like she was gone.

"I hadn't realized how badly she'd been hit," Hale commented, his mouth compressed with worry as his hand gave mine a squeeze.

"Thirty stitches, was it, Ray?"

"Thirty-two," I grumbled.

"They say if she wakes up, she might never be the same."

I stood and dumped my coffee, all the *ifs* and past tense talk of my friend who was very much alive turning my stomach.

"I'm shocked her brother hasn't been home to visit."

"That's because Chris is an asshole, Mom. The last time he was here he robbed Elle and their neighbors. She's better off without him."

"Such a sad situation."

My gaze met Hale's and I gave him a look telling him I was ready to go. He stood and poured his coffee in the sink. "Well, it was lovely meeting you, Penny."

My mother smiled. "You too, Hale. You come by again. Bring your daughter next time you visit."

"I just have to grab some clothes," I announced, leaving Hale to follow.

Once in my room, I grabbed a bag from under my bed and stuffed it with clothes. As long as Hale was here, I'd probably be staying with him. He stepped into my room and glanced at the pictures on the wall.

"Your mom's nice."

"Usually."

He watched me for a long moment. "People don't always know the right thing to say in situations like Elle's, Rayne."

I counted out socks. "I know. I just wish they'd stop talking like she died."

He stepped closer to the bed. "Hey. Don't get upset."

I stuffed the socks in my bag and wiped at my eyes. "I'm aware every day that passes her prognosis gets worse, so people can stop worrying that I'm kidding myself. I hear the doctors and I know she probably won't be the same when she wakes up, but she's my best friend. What am I supposed to do, leave her there alone until she opens her eyes?"

He slid the bag out of the way and pulled me into his arms. "No, of course not. No one expects you to forget about her."

I sniffled and pressed my cheek to his shoulder. "They're starting to talk about putting her in a permanent care facility."

"Well, you know I'll help you with whatever you need."

My stomach hurt because I wanted to give her the best possible care, but she was just a hairdresser who had about as much savings as me. "I don't know how she'll ever pay for this."

"Don't worry about that. We'll figure it out."

By that, he meant *he'd* figure it out.

Never in my life had I been concerned with money. I worked to support my needs and I made do. We were thirty. We weren't supposed to have problems of this magnitude.

"I can't let you do that, Hale. I need to talk to a lawyer or something. Elle has a house, but her brother owns half of it."

"Look at me." He pressed my shoulders back and lifted my chin. "I have an attorney and I have the money to help your friend. I'm not going to argue about this. For now, she's at the hospital and no one's moving her just yet. You do what you've been doing and everything else will work out."

There was that god complex again. Hale had a habit of thinking he had power over things outside of his control. But, maybe in Elle's situation, he did.

I had to ask, knowing he was here on borrowed time and had countless responsibilities waiting for him on the other side of the country. "What will happen to us if she doesn't get better? You can't stay here forever."

He turned away and his lips flattened. "All of my homes are on the east coast. That's where my businesses are. I'm not totally restricted, but I can stay in Oregon for a bit."

And that was what happened when you fell in love across the country. Why couldn't he have had companies on the west coast? We had stuff.

"But we have the world's biggest barber pole here. Don't tell me that doesn't tempt you."

He chuckled. "I'm here for now. Let's not jump too far into the future."

That didn't make me feel better. I mean, I was glad he was here, but what happened next? Would we continue to do the long-distance thing?

"Maybe you could rent an apartment here or something." Maybe I could move in with him if he got a place here. No. Wait. That was way too fast. "Sorry. I just like having you here."

Hugging me, he pressed his lips to my temple. "I like being here with you. We'll figure it out."

After I finished packing we went to the hospital. I painted Elle's toenails and gave her another massage to keep her blood flowing. Hale disappeared for a bit and returned with a slice of pizza. I wasn't hungry, but he insisted I eat.

"What's your work schedule?" he asked on the way back to the hotel.

"I work on weeknights and Saturday afternoon."

He nodded. "Every weeknight?"

"Yup."

"Then we should do something tonight."

"Like what? I didn't pack any fancy clothes."

"We should do something fun."

I hadn't had a drink in weeks. I could handle some fun. "What about Elara?"

"There's a reason I brought my mom, Rayne. I'll be with Elara while you're working. This is my week off. I needed a break, too."

Wasn't he just the cutest with all his dad stress and what not? "I'm up for anything, so long as you remember what I'm like drunk."

"We'll start you off slow," he joked, taking my hand. "But I plan on taking full advantage of you once you've hit your limit."

"You have my consent."

To Pee or Not to Pee

7

Typically, when drinking with friends, we would meet at local breweries, which Oregon had plenty of, or we'd venture down to my work and abuse my discount. All other alcohol encounters usually revolved around a dining room table, the latest flavored vodka, and a deck of cards.

The Davenports did things differently.

Talk about responsibility. Hale had a limo service pick us up and arranged a private room curtained off from the rest of the club. And by club, I mean one of those establishments with a stuffy bouncer in a suit and velvet roping to keep those who want to get in, out. With Hale, however, I was suddenly VIP.

"How did you even find this place? I've lived here all my life and I've never heard of it,"

I asked as I settled into our private room-booth thing between Hale and his brother.

Barrett had been scoping out his prey since the second we entered the club and boy, were the ladies noticing him. I snickered. The man never stopped.

Scooting around the low glass table, I sat closer to Hale on the black leather couch.

Hale lifted a bottle from the ice bucket—because, yeah, he'd arranged bottle service. That's how he rolled. "I had Miles look into it."

Aw, Miles. I got a little *verklempt* at the mention of Remington's other assistant. "How's he doing?"

Hale gave me a sidelong glance as a well-dressed waitress dropped off a Manhattan with a backup shaker. "He's adapting well, I suppose."

"Did he go to Maine with your dad?"

Again, he assessed me, his silver eyes somewhat shrewder than usual. "Yes."

Hale could be very territorial. My theories on territorial men were evolving. First, if a guy was territorial, he better earn it. That meant being there to meet his woman's every need. Then he'd earn the right to be possessive. If not, it was just petty jealousy. Hale was good to me so I let him get away with the territorial stuff, but when he tugged the leash too hard I wasn't afraid to bite back.

I had a very novice aptitude regarding the psyche of the opposite sex, but I was getting better at understanding the subtleties of dating. Hale was a very doting boyfriend. As a matter of fact, *I* was the one with commitment phobia in the beginning. Now, I was like a stage five-clinger, always wanting more Hale.

I was overcoming my commitment issues and he was working on his jealousy issues. It was understandable why he was the way he was. I mean, come on. His dad got Hale's ex-lover pregnant, thus Elara.

Me, on the other hand... My dad abandoned me the day I was born. I was so terrified of rejection I never wanted to love anything enough to risk having that love ripped away. Yet ... I loved Elle. And knowing how rare that was, she promised to never abandon me. *Damn. There was that guilt again.*

My attention pulled to our company as the long-legged waitress lingered at the door to our private room, fluttering around Hale's brother like a bee hovers over a flower.

"You're such a flirt, Barrett," I said as he finally let the waitress get back to work and re-joined us at the table.

"The world is my oyster." Barrett lifted his

drink and Hale passed me whatever he'd concocted out of the bottles on the table. "To a great night."

We clinked our glasses. "To a great night."

Tequila tinged the flavor of pineapple as my first sip worked its way down my throat. Ah, yes, the fruits of the devil.

The music was awesome. People passing by looked in on us curiously, maybe wondering if we were some sort of royalty. Hale loosened up and laughed freely, a perfect date even if we were with his younger brother. Barrett was full of jokes and soon enough I was full of tequila.

"We should dance!" I yelled, envious of the people letting go on the floor below.

"I thought you only danced to *Thriller*," Barrett commented.

"Sober. I only dance to *Thriller* sober. I'm not so sober right now." I nudged Hale. "Do you want to go down there and check it out?"

He finished his Manhattan and stood, holding out a hand. As I rose to my feet, the ground wobbled. Oh, yeah, those drinks he'd been feeding me had definitely done their magic.

We took a spacious set of stairs down the to the dance floor where colorful strobe lights pulsed to the beat of the music. Once we found an open niche, I started with my typical John

Travolta moves, circa *Saturday Night Fever.* The music was recognizable rock but revamped with techno overlays.

A remix of Avicii's *Wake Me Up* came on and Hale stepped behind me, holding my hips and swaying his body against mine. I lifted my hands, twirling my wrists, my arms stretching high above my head. His hands glided up my ribs, cutting it close to my boobs and making my nipples hard. I swung my butt, pressing into him seductively and there was really something to be said about dancing with a guy you were also sleeping with.

It was like sex on the dance floor, right there in front of the natives. He turned me and his penetrating stare held me so still my breath froze in my lungs. Jesus, just like fucking, we were suddenly making love. He pulled me to his front, possessively touching me, fingers sliding along my curves as his hungry eyes swallowed me whole. I was totally turned on.

The song switched to *Cake by the Ocean* and the liquor in my system acted as a love potion for my private parts. My gaze never left his face as I moved in what I hoped was a seductive sort of salsa. Skin damp from exertion, hair falling around my face in sloppy waves, I held hard to my clean record and reminded myself it was illegal to fuck in public places. But boy, did

I want to maul him right there on the dance floor.

As the song ended, I caught my breath. "You're a sexy dance partner," I shouted over the pulsing bass of something new.

"What?" he yelled.

"You have hot moves!"

"*What?*"

I laughed and rolled my eyes. "I have to pee!" I pointed in the general direction of the bathrooms and saw that he understood.

He escorted me to the restrooms but, of course, there was a line. The music was muffled now that we were in the back of the club.

"You don't have to wait with me," I said, being that he was the only man in a line full of horny drunk women.

They all needed to put their eyeballs back in their sockets. I threw out a dirty look, but I don't think it struck anyone as intimidating.

Hale scanned the nearby area. "I'll wait for you at that table."

"Okay." I grabbed his arm as he made to leave. "Wait."

He tilted his head in question and I lifted to my toes and pressed my front to his, licking across his full lips.

His hands tightened on my ass. "Mmm." With a promising look, he squeezed, and let me go. I, along with every other woman in the vicinity, watched him walk.

I turned back to the line and grinned. *That's right. My Hale.* Maybe we all had a little possessiveness in us.

As the line snaked into the bathroom I considered this new territorial side of myself. I never really cared before if a guy I was with looked at other women, but I cared with Hale. I never really cared about guys, *period.* Dating was utterly unappealing until Hale. Now, I was a monogamous motherfucker, wiping my scent all over him to mark my territory.

But Hale didn't look at anyone but me.

A stall opened and I stepped inside. Jesus. What the fuck did women do in here? Gathering a wad of tissue, I shoved the door closed and twisted the lock. As soon as I unbuttoned my jeans the door drifted open again. "Damn it."

I kicked the door and gave the lock another hard shove. Squatting, I did my business, drunkenly floating in the open space without touching anything. I lifted my foot to the lever and flushed. Once I righted my clothes, I wadded up more toilet paper and turned the lock. *Come on.* I jiggled the lock again. *Damn it.*

The stupid door was jammed. Gripping

the top of the door—a place I hoped was free of Ebola and other public restroom nightmares —I jerked the door hard. It didn't budge.

"Hello? Can someone help me get out of here?"

Toilets flushed and faucets ran as women chattered and cycled in and out of the restroom. I analyzed my predicament. The floor was not an option, wet and totally littered with disgusting trash. Seriously, what did women *do* in here?

After another few minutes of trying to unlock the door, kicking it, and pounding my elbow against the side of the stall to get anyone's attention, I accepted I was stuck and no one was coming to my rescue.

I was going to have to Indiana Jones this shit.

As everyone continued to move about on the other side of the wall, completely oblivious to my turmoil, I caught the top of the stall and stepped on the toilet seat.

"So help me God, if I fall into a public toilet I'm bleaching off my skin."

Not having great balance to begin with, I wobbled onto the seat, my shoes holding tight, as I caught my hand on the top of the wall. Then I just balanced there, like a Spiderman stunt reject.

"Can anyone hear me? My door's stuck and I've been in here for a really long time. Any help would be great..." When no one responded to my polite plea, I grumbled, "Are you fucking kidding me?"

Transferring my hands to the top of the door I—*oh shit!* The distance was farther than I thought. Feeling my weight shift, my feet left the toilet seat and my body slammed into the door, which of course swung open with ease.

"Oh, gross." My body flattened on the sheet of metal germs as I hung there. The door glided over the floor and smacked into the next stall.

"Rayne?" And that would be Hale.

Releasing my death grip, I dropped my feet to the floor and brushed off my hands. This sort of shit only happened to me, so I really had no explanation. "Hey."

He frowned as women shuffled around him. "I came to see what was taking so long—"

"Just using the bathroom." He looked at me like I was crazy, which, to a certain degree, I was. "I'm going to wash my hands."

He nodded. "I'll be right outside the door."

Being that none of these bitches offered any help, I hogged the sink, not caring that I was taking an extraordinarily long time to disinfect my hands and arms. This was exactly why I always strove not to break the seal. Nothing good came from drunken bathroom visits. *Nothing!*

Irritated with myself, I dried my hands and went to find Hale. He'd been warned about my predisposition toward calamities since day one and witnessed plenty of signature Calamity Rayne moments since, but sometimes it got tedious being a walking disaster. Especially when someone as perfect as Hale Davenport was my boyfriend.

I looked at him, with his designer pants and nice shoes. What the hell sort of starch did he use on his shirts to keep them so crisp and wrinkle-free? I hadn't ironed anything in a decade. And that was just his clothing. His face was the picture of a Greek god and his body was something from pornographic fairytales.

"You good now?" he asked as I approached.

Feeling utterly stupid, I forced a grin. "Sorry about that. I had some trouble."

Hello, my name is Calamity Rayne and I can't use a bathroom without assistance.

Once we were back upstairs, Barrett was preoccupied with his newfound company. By company, I, of course, meant *three* women who were making out with various parts of his body at the same time. I didn't know where to look, so I sat down and finished my drink.

The waitress approached and spoke directly to Hale. The longer their conversation went on, the smaller I felt. I wasn't sure how he made my drink, but I still had ice left, so I poured some tequila over that and sipped as I snarled in my head at Waitress McLongLegs.

He was awfully chatty tonight. Was this what he was always like in social settings? Because our relationship started at sea on a boat with only his father and the crew, I didn't really have a point of reference. There had been his sister's party. That was a mixed setting, but that was also the night Elara was born, so it wasn't anything remotely normal.

When the waitress finally left—*the flirt*—I was slouching in my seat, sipping my tequila ice and pouting.

"You okay?"

"Fine."

He eased back and nudged me with his shoulder, chuckling. "When a woman says she's fine it's never good news for the man."

I didn't know what was wrong with me. Maybe I'd had too much to drink. My feelings were sticky and unflattering. Even I recognized their presence as bad news, but I couldn't sweep them away. "Have you gone out since being in Florida?"

He tipped his head. "Here and there."

And I was sure the women gawked there just as much as they did here. "Who did you go out with?"

"Barrett."

I glanced at his brother who had his hand fed into the back pocket of one woman's jeans as her friend whispered in his ear. It was like a fucking harem. My molars locked and I scowled at the dancers below.

"What's the matter, Rayne?"

"Nothing."

"Another unfavorable word." Hale glanced at his watch and to Barrett. "It's almost one." He leaned forward. "Barrett, we're leaving. You coming with us?"

Barrett laughed as one of the women straddled him. "No. I think I'll get a cab."

Hale stood and held out his hand. I was done anyway. I was embarrassed and jealous and sulking and drunk. Time to call it a night.

Once we were in the limo, he watched me carefully. "Did something happen that I missed?"

Uncrossing my arms, I huffed, because I really disliked girlie feelings and there had been a lot of them since meeting Hale. "No. I just had too much to drink."

My insecurities ganged up on me during

the silent ride back to the hotel. By the time we entered his room I wanted to cry.

"I'm going to take a shower." Without waiting for a response, I grabbed a towel off the shelf and locked the door.

I hated feeling this way. I didn't distrust Hale, but other women made me nervous. They were so brazen about looking at him and flirting. It was like I was invisible.

Being the train wreck that I was, it would only be a matter of time before Hale noticed how much more sophisticated other women were. And with me on the west coast and him traipsing up and down the east coast, there would be plenty of opportunities for him to meet some of those sophisticated women.

I didn't believe Hale would cheat on me. That wasn't the issue. Although his father believed every man cheated, Hale held a very favorable view of monogamy.

I could still recall Remington's warning. I really didn't give a shit about power plays at the moment. I wasn't going to bend over backward to stroke a man's ego just to ensure he'd be faithful. No one stroked my ego and *I* was faithful.

I stepped out of the bathroom and found Hale sitting in a club chair watching the bathroom door.

"Feeling better?"

I nodded and dug my brush out of my bag. He observed me closely as I combed my hair.

"I'm not a mind reader, Rayne. You can either tell me what's bugging you or let it go."

"I'm fine."

"Bullshit."

Slamming the brush down, I pivoted to face him. "Fine. You want to know what my problem is? I'm a six on my best day and you're a freaking eleven on your worst. You're going to leave again and I'll be here and women don't care that you're mine and it pisses me off."

His eyes narrowed as he stared at me. "You're more than a six."

I scoffed. I didn't know how to do my hair in anything but a ponytail. I bit my nails. I didn't wear makeup and I was short. "You're biased."

"Maybe I am. It doesn't matter. You're the woman I want. And as far as being apart, yes, I'll eventually go home, but I've given you no reason to question my loyalty."

Though his expression was blank, I sensed he was insulted. I wasn't accusing him of any-thing, but the implication slipped out in my drunk and jumbled explanation.

"I'm sorry. You asked. I'm just feeling a little irritated and insecure at the moment."

"Is this a fight we're going to have?"

Feeling guilty, I quietly lowered myself to an empty seat. I didn't want to fight with Hale. Our time was precious, but something happened tonight. Maybe it was the sight of that waitress coming onto him or the fact that every woman we passed tried to get his attention. Or perhaps it was seeing the Davenport DNA in full effect as his brother had a freaking ménage five feet away from us.

None of that was Hale's fault, but it still hurt. "I don't know how to compete with other women."

"There's no competition."

I rolled my eyes. "You talked to that waitress for almost ten minutes."

"And you talked to Barrett even longer."

"He's your brother. It's different."

"Is it?"

I thought about what his father had done, how his betrayal had scarred Hale, damaged the special relationship they had in irreparable ways. I'd never recover from that sort of betrayal and I was stuck here in Oregon while Hale was flitting off for one social hour after another.

"I don't like the way other women look at you."

The side of his mouth hitched in a cocky

grin. "I don't like the way other men look at you. And they do look, Rayne. You just don't notice. That waitress was giving me the name of her boss because I recently purchased an old mill that I could possibly make into an upscale nightclub. I was merely making a business contact. It had nothing to do with her."

I lowered my head. "I'm not used to feeling jealous."

"Me neither. But for the record, I am *yours.*"

Keeping my head down, I glanced at him. "You are?"

He nodded. "I have no interest in other women. As a matter of fact, I'm so obsessed with you, I'd..." He paused, seeming to choose his words carefully. "Let's just say I'm probably willing to move faster than you can handle, but I'm being patient because I know you have a lot going on right now. But I have plans."

I exhaled and shifted to the sofa, closer to where he sat. "What do you mean?"

"I don't want to scare you."

And I did scare easily. All of my life I'd avoided any sense of commitment, finding it intimidating and restrictive.

There was a reason I blew off my degree and aborted the whole plan for my career in education. It was the same reason I didn't own my own home or make large investments. I liked freedom and hated feeling tied down. But now I had Hale and I didn't want to share him. I wanted to know we were secure.

"I won't get scared."

He gave me a measured look. "Okay. If I had my way, we'd live together."

Mmm, that would be nice—and terrifying. "I can't leave until I know Elle's all right."

"You don't want to leave and I respect your reasons. I'd never ask you to walk away from Elle, but she won't be in the hospital forever. She's either going to wake up or they're going to move her into a long-term care facility. Either way, her recovery isn't going to be quick."

Which meant this long distance relationship could last much longer than I could handle. How did people send their lovers off to war? It had been four weeks and I was dying.

On top of that, we'd only been together for a little over a month, so the need to be around him constantly was still there, making things a million times more complicated. "Maybe we should take a break until we know what's going to happen."

His jaw twitched. "That's out of the question."

He still hadn't told me how long he was actually staying. I wanted to clarify, so I'd be emotionally prepared for that goodbye. But I feared his departure might be sooner than expected. Either way, watching him leave would rip out my heart.

"I didn't expect this to be so hard," I confessed.

He moved to the sofa and pulled me onto his lap. "Listen to me. I know this isn't easy, but it's where we are at the moment. I've watched you for two days, going to that hospital and fighting back tears as you took care of your friend. You've lost weight, you're exhausted, and I see how much this situation is tearing you apart. There are other options, but I don't want to overstep."

What other options? Elle was here and I wasn't leaving her. His work was on the other side of the country. As much as I tried to deny the negative outcome, something inside of me knew this would only get worse before it got better.

Elle wasn't going to just wake up and jump back into her usual routine. The doctors had run extensive tests and there had been more than external damage. Even if she woke up tomorrow, I wouldn't be able to leave.

"I don't know what other options we have," I said sadly.

He drew in a slow breath. "There are great

hospitals on the east coast. We could have her moved to live near us, Rayne. And if she needs therapies or around the clock care, I can afford the best for her. I could hire a live-in nurse, have her in one of my homes—not some facility but my actual home. There wouldn't be visiting hours and you and Elle could be as comfortable as possible. If you'd let me take care of everything, you wouldn't have to work so much and you could be with both of us."

I frowned. "But..."

"Look, just think about it. I don't want to pressure you. But I do love you and now that I've found you I don't want to waste time waiting for my life to begin. I want to be with you. Not every couple of weeks when I can get away, but every day. I want to wake up next to you. I want your face to be the first thing I see in the morning and the last thing I see before I close my eyes at night."

That did sound nice, but there was so much to consider. "Where would we live?" I wasn't agreeing, but I was curious. Hale had several homes.

"We could stay at my home in Florida or we could go to Georgia. I have four houses, so it would be up to you. But I'd still have to travel for work."

I frowned. "How do you plan to do that with Elara?"

"Well..."

Oh no... I'd feared this conversation since the moment I learned of his situation. And now, more than ever, I sensed its approach.

"If you were there, you could help me."

No kids. It had been a constant slogan in my head since I walked away from my teaching career and killed my third goldfish and umpteenth houseplant. And since Elara came along, it had been a daily mantra. Even when I played with her and missed her, I constantly reminded myself there was a reason she wasn't mine.

"I'm not good with little people."

"Yes, you are. I watch you with her and you're a natural. I wouldn't suggest it if I had any doubts."

"I've dropped three watermelons in grocery stores, Hale. Not one, but *three*. And I wasn't goofing around either. I was just carrying the thing and the next thing I knew watermelon guts were all over the floor. Three separate times that's happened to me. I don't want to drop your baby."

"Neither do I, but I worry about the same stuff. I trust you with her, Rayne. Most of the time I'd be there, and we'd have nannies for her, but when I have to leave for business I'd be much more comfortable knowing you're there."

"What about your mom?"

He sighed. "She's been a huge help over the past few weeks, but her life's in New York. And as much as I love my mother, I've been on my own for too long to go backward. I'd rather have you by my side."

He'd rather have me than his own mother helping him? That was so sweet—and intimidating.

"Would I be like a nanny?" Maybe if it was a job I'd feel less guilty living off his money.

"No, it would be a partnership. Elara has a nanny lined up. You'd help, of course, but this is more about us than my situation as a new dad. I'm in love with you, Rayne. My daughter's a part of me and I need her to be a part of you, too, if we want any sort of future." He glanced away. "I'm not making it a condition, but you have to realize if we stay together, I'll eventually want more."

"*Children?*"

"More of you. Rayne, someday, I want a wife."

Oh, boy. Me. Marriage. I wasn't so sure those things should ever go together in a conversation. "Maybe we should see how things go."

"Like I said, think about it. I wasn't going to say anything right now, but you brought it up."

"You're asking a lot, Hale. Not of me, but of yourself."

"I've never made an offer without carefully considering all angles."

That was true. He'd once told me he wouldn't do anything he didn't gain some level of satisfaction from. And his entire family had made reference to his meticulousness. Even where Elara was concerned, he'd made up his mind and did what he felt was right.

"I'll think about it."

He nodded. "Good. You let me know when you've made up your mind. Whatever choice you make, I'll be ready to act."

I pressed my forehead to his and sighed. "I'm sorry I acted like a jealous cow tonight. I do love you though." I just wished so many other women didn't.

"Part of me likes knowing you're protective of me." His lips brushed mine as he gently tugged me closer. "I love you, too."

Emergency Exits are to Your Left

8

The following days passed faster than I would have liked. My mornings revolved around Hale. We made love as the sun came up, played with Elara, visited the hotel restaurant for breakfast with Naomi and Barrett, and then I was off to see Elle followed by a quick trip back to the hotel, a short frolic in the sheets, and off to work I went.

I excused Hale from joining me at the hospital because I needed to talk to my best friend. I told her about his proposal that we all live together and I wished more than anything that she could give me some sort of sign to help me figure out what to do. All of my life I'd depended on Elle's support for the big decisions. What Hale was asking was *huge* and it didn't just affect me. It concerned Elle, too.

It had been over a month since her accident, which meant bills were due. On Thursday, I gathered my courage and drove to her house.

As I waited in the car, staring up at her home, I wondered who I could ask to cut her grass. Tyler had emotionally withdrawn. I was pretty sure he hadn't gone to the hospital in almost a week and I couldn't push him. It was damn hard seeing her so unchanged. But maybe he could help out in other ways.

Making my way up the path, I lifted the flowerpot and found the hidden key. As expected, mail littered the floor on the other side of the door. I gathered up the numerous envelopes and left them on the hall table with my purse.

The house smelled unlived in, but there were signs of her everywhere. Her shoes sat in the hall where she'd kicked them off after her last run. The afghan was still unfolded on the couch. And her bread on the counter had grown fur.

The trash reeked in the kitchen, so I bagged up what rotten food I could find and tied it off, leaving it by the door to go outside. I gathered the few dishes that had been sitting around and took them to the kitchen.

She was almost out of dish soap. Maybe I

should start a list. Turning to find a notepad, I
—"*Jabberwocky!*"

"Calamity. Rayne. I wasn't expecting to see
you here."

"Jesus Christ, Chris! You scared the shit
out of me. What are you doing here?"

He shrugged, drawing my attention to the
scars on his arm. Were they tracks? His beard
was full and his hair looked dirty, in some sort
of dreadlock mess. "I came to check on the
house."

I frowned. Last time he'd checked on it
he'd robbed the place. "Have you been to see
Elle?"

He leaned against the fridge. "I stopped by.
She's a vegetable."

My mouth compressed as my eyes narrowed. I fucking hated him. I'd stopped liking
him a long time ago for all the stress he'd
caused Elle, but over the past few years that dis-
like corroded into utter loathing.

He was an unredeemable piece of shit and
he had no business being in her home. "Are you
staying here?"

"It's my house."

"It's your sister's house."

He glanced around, exploiting the vacant-
ness. "I don't see her. And I'm pretty sure she's
not coming back."

"You don't know that," I snapped.

He gave a gruff laugh. "Come on, Calamity. Grow up."

My anger seethed as my breath labored in and out of my chest. "You can't afford to stay here. She has bills."

"Don't be so dramatic. I could go nine months without paying the mortgage before anyone stepped in."

I didn't know if that was true. I'd heard Remington talk about the corruption of banks in this country, something about loans defaulting faster than the economy could handle and some sort of housing bubble. But I didn't know what that meant. All I knew was Elle had good credit and she'd worked hard to keep her score.

I'd been working under the subconscious assumption that I could ask Hale to help keep her in the black, but ... there was no way I could do that with Chris here. So I lied. "We're renting the house out."

"Who is?"

"Me and Tyler. It's what Elle would have wanted."

"Going to be awfully cramped here, with me, the new tenants, and all my sister's shit. Unless you meant *you* were renting the place.

You and I could probably figure out a way to share."

I was going to vomit. "Chris, you can't stay here. Last time you were here you stole the stove."

He shrugged again. "It was my stove."

I wondered if I could call the police. There had to be some sort of squatter's law he was violating. I went back to my lie because it actually made a little sense.

"We need to rent out the house to pay the hospital." Or maybe it didn't make sense. Someone still had to pay the mortgage and that would be the point of the rent. "She needs income right now and this house is more hers than yours."

"That may be true, but I'm certain it's more mine than *yours,* Calamity."

"She needs money. Her medical bills alone will be—"

"I'm not paying them a penny. Let the guy who hit her take responsibility."

Like that was going to happen. Irritated, I snapped, "You have to leave. This isn't your house anymore."

He laughed and sighed. "She's gone, Rayne. Don't you get it? She's fucking dead. I could walk in and tell them to shut off all the machines and they'd have no choice, because like it or not, I'm her family. You're nothing. The house is in my name and I'm not leaving. It's only a matter of time before my fifty percent becomes one hundred."

She wasn't on a breathing machine, which showed how out of touch and what an asshole he was. "You stay the fuck away from her!"

Pushing past him, I gathered my purse and the mail on the way out. I shivered with rage as I raced to my car, determined to get to the hospital and tell the doctors never to listen to him. I was so upset I couldn't catch my breath.

Once I drove to the next street I had to pull over around the corner to calm down. Tears of fear blurred my vision. My hands gripped the wheel as I glared out the window and ground my teeth.

Not knowing what to do, I called Tyler. I could have called Hale, but I knew he'd tell me to go with his plan and move in with him. Right now we needed to focus on getting Chris away from Elle.

"Hello?"

"Ty, it's me. Chris is at her house."

"Fuck." He sighed into the phone. "How long's he been there?"

"I don't know, but he's not leaving."

"Goddamn it. By the sound of your voice, I'm guessing he's not clean."

A derisive laugh barked out of me. "Not at all. His eyes were wrecked and his stink is still in my nose. Who can we call?"

"No one. The house is as much his as it is Elle's."

"We have to be able to call someone." I tilted my phone as my call waiting beeped. Not recognizing the number, I ignored it. "He's not going to pay the bills and she'll lose everything."

Tyler sighed. "With everything else, Ray, she might not be able to afford to keep the house anyway. Hold on. I have a weird number calling me."

"But—" He put me on hold and I waited. Maybe Hale could make him leave. The line clicked and I jumped right back into the conversation. "We need to talk to someone, Tyler. I might be able to get a lawyer."

He was quiet.

"Ty?" Maybe he was still on the other line.

"She's awake."

My entire body went cold as I tried to fathom his words. "What?"

"That was the hospital. She opened her eyes about ten minutes ago. I'll meet you there."

"I'm on my way."

I drove faster than I'd ever pushed my little

car. Thank God for Seri, because I needed my eyes to get through traffic. "Call Hale."

"There is no hail in the forecast today. Currently, it's partly cloudy with a high of ninety-one—"

"Seri, shut up! *Call* Hale."

"I'm sorry. I don't have anyone in your contacts under that name," the robotic voice responded.

"Damn it." I shook my head. "Seri, call Big Dick Davenport."

"Calling Big Dick Davenport," the voice politely replied as the phone began to ring.

"Hey, baby."

"She's awake! She opened her eyes a few minutes ago. I'm heading to the hospital now."

"Drive carefully. You sound like you're rushing."

I eyed the speedometer and dropped it back from seventy, to a safe sixty-five.

"I can be there in twenty minutes."

My heart was beating a mile a minute. "Okay. I'll see you when you get there. I love you."

"I love you, too. And Rayne, don't speed."

I nodded and ended the call. When I pulled into the hospital parking lot I didn't bother to read any of the signs and took the closest spot to the entrance. I darted through the automatic doors and raced to the elevators, jamming my finger into the button like a woodpecker going at a tree.

As soon as I was inside the lift, I pushed the button for the doors to close. "Come on," I growled as they slowly came together.

When they opened at Elle's floor I ran as fast as I could to her room and stumbled through the door, gasping for breath. I looked at my best friend, sitting up as a nurse did something with her IV. And then I burst into tears.

"You're awake," I sobbed. "I can't believe you're awake." I rushed to the bed and grabbed her hand, touching her legs and arms as I stared into her wide blue eyes. "I was so scared, Elle. I don't know what I'd do without you."

Wiping my eyes, I drew in a shaky breath and smiled at her, waiting for her to say something. She frowned and pink stole over the whites of her eyes as she started to tremble.

In a voice so raw and unused, she whispered, "Why are you here?"

I shut my eyes and wept, lowering my head as her words washed over me with such reassurance. I'd been terrified she might die in this room or wake up as someone else.

"Ty?" she whispered and I turned as our friend, wearing a mask of utter shock, staggered to her side. He glanced at me and then gently pulled Elle into a hug.

"You have no idea how happy I am to see you awake," he rasped. As he eased back, I noted the tracks of tears on his face.

Elle, still frowning, looked over his shoulder. "Hello."

Relief punched me in the gut as I saw Hale and Barrett standing in the doorway. With trembling fingers, I caught her hand and squeezed. "That's Hale."

She continued to stare over Tyler's shoulder. "The Hot One's here. Am I high?" she whispered and I laughed.

The moment was interrupted as the doctors came in and we all had to exit in order for them to speak privately to their patient and run some tests.

"We'll be right out here, Elle. Don't shut your eyes," I insisted as Hale pulled me with the others into the hall.

She just woke up and I was already leaving. I wanted to stay, but the hospital staff insisted and Elle, who seemed to choose her words with extra care, didn't object.

We went to a family waiting room and sat in silence. Hale stoically kept to my side as I continued to weep tears of joy, relief too intense to keep bottled up. I'd never been so happy in all of my life.

There were no words for those long minutes we waited, no accurate description for the uplifting emotions I felt. Tyler was there, equally moved. Together, we stared at the door wiping our eyes.

"Rayne Meyers?"

"That's me!" I stood and faced the nurse.

"Elle's asking to see you."

I nodded and glanced to Tyler, feeling guilty he wasn't asked. Maybe there was a one person at a time rule. "As soon as I figure out what's going on I'll send for you."

He nodded and I left him in the waiting room with Hale and Barrett. An unexpected fear took hold of me as I approached her room. What did she think of all this? What did she remember about the accident? How would she be different? I gently knocked on the door and stepped inside the hospital room.

She sat in an upright position holding a cup in her hand. Such a simple thing, but so monumental. I went to the chair beside her bed and slowly sat. "I can't believe you're awake."

"I was hit by a drunk driver," she said, her face telling me she had no recollection of the accident.

"He's in jail."

She frowned. "Who was he?"

"A guy named Buck Malhorne. He has a wife and two sons." I hated that he had a family because it filled me with guilt every time I hoped he'd rot in prison.

Elle slowly nodded, her brow tight. "You're not in Florida."

I shook my head. "I came home the minute I heard."

"Where's my car?"

It seemed strange that these were her worries, but I guessed there was so much confusion in her head there was no time to prioritize her questions into any sort of order. "It was totaled."

She tilted her cup to her mouth and ice crunched between her teeth. Her hand brushed over her ear. "My hair..."

"It'll grow back."

She continued to frown, two divots forming between her eyebrows. "They showed me a..." The little grooves of confusion deepened. "Thing."

"Mirror?"

She nodded. Her fingers slowly lifted to her face and traced over her eyebrows where little rogue spikes had grown. She glanced at her nails. "Did you do this?"

I nodded. "Could you hear me talking to you?"

Her head shook slowly. "What color is this?"

I smiled because Elle always appreciated clever makeup names. "*Teal the Cows Come Home*."

"No... What ... color?"

"It's blue."

"Right. Blue." She wiped her nose and sniffled. "What color?"

My worry doubled. "Blue. Well, bluish green. It's teal."

"Blue." She looked at me and her anxiety became a tangible thing between us. "Blue?"

I nodded. "It's only been an hour," I said, assuring both of us that she needed time to adjust. Swallowing, I confessed, "I have so much to tell you."

"Where's my mom?"

Oh, my God. My chest tightened.

"Elle, your mom and dad passed away."

Her gaze skittered to the side of the room as a tear slowly trailed down her cheek. "That's right. I knew that."

I hated saying it, but I wanted her to have everything she needed. "Your brother's at your house."

She looked at me and I recognized true uncertainty in her eyes. "My brother?"

"Chris."

Her breathing turned labored and the monitors chirped faster. A nurse came in and checked the machines. "We're going to need some privacy for a few minutes."

Elle suddenly resembled a frightened version of her younger self. I took her hand and squeezed. "I'm not going far. Let them help you. I'll be right down the hall with Tyler."

She nodded, but nothing would ever erase the memory of that uncertain look in her eyes. That wasn't the Elle I knew.

We were in the waiting room for almost an hour. I told the others that she was still a little confused. Hale and Barrett, the least attached, assured us that was probably typical in these sorts of situation.

I'd expected a nurse to send for me when they were done, but a doctor showed up. We all stared at him as he explained that Elle requested he speak with us. She was resting, which terrified me. She'd slept for weeks and I worried if she shut her eyes they might never open again.

"We believe Elle is suffering from slight retrograde amnesia. While she's able to tell us the year and her address, she gets very distressed when asked to recite the alphabet. Over the next few days, we'd like to run some more tests as she acclimates."

"Will she get those memories back?" Tyler asked.

"This isn't a loss of memories, per se, but a loss of information. It's better explained as a disconnect. Think of it as little files she's temporarily misplaced. Her retention should rebuild over time."

Was that why she kept asking about colors? "But she remembered us," I said, trying to recall her exact words when we arrived. "She remembered that I was supposed to be in Florida."

"Yes. She knows who she is and what her life was like, but her information is scattered at the moment. While she might remember how to make a bag of popcorn, she might struggle with using a microwave. It's a matter of reacquainting her brain with what it's misplaced."

"But she can relearn those things," Barrett said, surprising me with his attentiveness.

"Absolutely."

"Will she be able to return to her daily life?" Hale asked and the doctor hesitated.

"In time. I can't ethically grant her permission to operate a vehicle at this stage, but as she returns to her life and adapts, her skills will increase."

Everyone was silent so I finally asked, "Can we see her?"

"I think it's best she rests for a bit. We've removed her catheter and a physical therapist is helping her, but she's very weak and struggling to move around. She's disoriented and understandably confused. You're welcome to stay, but if she's sleeping I wouldn't suggest waking her."

I nodded and once he left I sank into my seat.

"You said she forgot about her parents?" Tyler asked.

"Yeah, but she remembered as soon as I told her."

"Are her parents gone?" Barrett asked and Tyler and I nodded.

Hale took my hand and squeezed. "We'll stay."

I blinked up at him and smiled, relief tunneling through me. "Thank you."

I called out of work and Tyler did the same. Barrett went on a mission to find food and returned with boxes of local dishes. It seemed the Davenport way to not just survive when visiting a hospital, but also feed the doctors and nurses. It made us very popular among the staff.

Elle woke up a few hours later and Tyler

and I went to speak to her. I felt guilty that Barrett and Hale were stuck in the waiting room even when Elle was awake, but they never complained.

I was amazed at how resilient Elle appeared, although obviously still weak. She ate food, albeit with trembling fingers, and drank pop and even made a few jokes, but there were moments in between when I recognized her internal struggle. Sometimes she couldn't remember basic words, and she'd totally forgotten Tyler was no longer engaged. She knew I'd gone to Florida to work for Remington Davenport, but didn't recall any of our conversations about Hale.

"But you recognized them," Tyler said.

"Well, more like I noticed them. And I know who the Davenports are."

She'd always called Barrett *The Hot One* and Hale *The Other One* whenever the Davenports showed up in the tabloids. I no longer agreed with those labels, but that was how she'd referred to them whenever they appeared in the public eye, which was quite often.

Her hand lifted to her shorn hair. "I can't believe they saw me like this. I look like Frankenstein."

"You do not look like Frankenstein."

Elle sighed. "I feel gross."

"You were in a coma," Tyler reminded.

"You're a guy. You wouldn't understand. Ray, can you bring me some stuff from home?"

"Whatever you need."

I'd make Hale go with me because I wasn't dealing with Chris again. God, going to her house meant her brother would find out she woke up. Maybe that would get him out of there. He was worse than a termite infestation.

"I need clothes and some toiletries. Grab my..." She pointed to her eyebrows.

"Tweezers?"

"Yes."

I made a list and promised to have everything back in an hour. Tyler stayed with Elle and Barrett stayed with the food. It was a strange comfort having Hale's brother there. Sweet that he didn't mind keeping Hale company when Tyler and I were with Elle. Plus, he could call if anything changed.

The day felt a hundred years long and it was only seven o'clock. As Hale drove, I rested my eyes.

"You okay?" he asked, taking my hand in his.

I nodded and turned my cheek to face him. "Never in a million years would I guess this was how the day would go."

He smiled. "It's a great day."

Yes, it was. The GPS directed him toward Elle's. "You know how I told you about Elle's brother?"

"Yes."

"Well, he's back. I saw him this morning when I went to check on her house."

"Why wasn't he at the hospital?"

"Because he's Chris. They don't talk."

It was no wonder Elle had a difficult time remembering him. Chris had segmented personas we all recalled. The man he'd become was totally different from the person he was as a child.

I watched Hale's face carefully as I explained more. "He's staying at her house and he doesn't plan to leave."

Hale was a problem solver, very solution oriented. He'd know how to get Chris out.

His face remained blank as he focused on the road. "Does he have a legal right to be there?"

"It's fifty percent his, but Elle threw him out years ago."

Chris had wanted his share of the property, but she was in no position to buy him out. That was part of the reason he felt entitled to take whatever he wanted and why no charges had ever been filed when he robbed the place.

"There's nothing we can do tonight, but

tomorrow I'll give her bank a call and see what's what. She has no authority over him so long as his name's on the deed."

"I just wanted to give you a heads up that he might be there. I don't expect you to get involved." That was sort of a lie. I didn't want to involve him, but I hoped he'd tell me how to fix this.

He gave me a sidelong glance. "She's your friend, Rayne. It's no problem for me to help."

But to what degree? I couldn't keep leaning on him to fix all my problems, let alone my friend's. I'd much rather he guide me in the right direction because right now I felt like a clueless child doing very grown-up things.

I wondered if this changed his offer about living together. Now that Elle was awake, she'd likely have something to say about it. Her life was here in Oregon. Mine was divided. I'd have to talk to Tyler about helping her out because she was definitely not her usual self. Either way, I wasn't ready to leave.

When we entered Elle's house it was quiet. I didn't announce myself because part of me hoped no one was home. But life didn't work that way. Chris was sleeping on the couch, an overflowing ashtray wedged between cups and plates on the coffee table. Hale arched a brow and stepped closer.

"Don't wake him up," I whispered. "It's better if he's unconscious."

He reached over the table and lifted a little baggie full of what looked like meth. Great. Hale tossed it back into the mess and quietly followed me up the stairs. "He looks like a real winner."

"He's the best of the best when it comes to bleeding people dry." That applied to both emotional and financial bleeding.

I opened the closet and picked out a few of Elle's favorite clothes. Then I went to her vanity and filled a shoebox with personal items. I didn't wear makeup or know how to coordinate colors, so I grabbed a little bit of everything.

Chris never moved while we were there and we left the house as we found it. When I returned to the hospital a nurse was helping Elle in the bathroom. She emerged dressed in a fresh hospital gown, her hair slicked to one side.

"Look at you walking around," I said, chest tight with pride.

"I'm so weak." She eased into the bed and the nurse left us. Once she was situated, she studied me. "I'm sorry, Ray. I can't imagine what this must have done to you."

"Please don't apologize."

She gave a sad smile. "I'm so foggy. What's going on at my job? Have any of my co-workers been by?"

"Cassandra visited a few times." That was her boss. "And the other girls sent flowers."

She frowned. "My clients probably went to someone else."

"I'm sure they'll come back to you when you're ready to return."

She folded her legs and I sat across from her on the bed.

"Elle, you can talk to me about what you're feeling. I'm here."

Her lashes spikes as her eyes glazed with tears. "Talking's hard." She reached for my foot, which was under my knee. "Like these..."

"Shoelaces?"

"Yeah." Releasing my laces she turned. "I know what they're called, but I can't say it or think it. I don't know."

"The doctor said your words might be misplaced for a while, but you'll get them back."

"I want to go home."

"You will." I hesitated, not sure if this was the time to bring up her brother, but I wanted her to be prepared. "Chris is at the house."

"Okay."

That wasn't the response I expected. "I don't think he plans to leave."

"Ray," she whispered. "How old is Chris?"

Worry tightened my stomach. "He's thirty-six, I think."

"Why can't I remember him past high school?"

I sighed. "Because you hit your head and he's changed a lot."

I could tell she was trying to piece everything together by the way her gaze flicked around the room but never really focused on any specific item. "Why isn't he here?"

"Oh, Elle."

I spent the next hour telling her about her brother and how he'd changed. She cried but accepted the truth. There was little consolation, with a brother like that. The asshole didn't even care she'd been in a coma, but I didn't tell her that.

When she laid down, I lingered but knew she was emotionally exhausted, so I let her sleep. I didn't want to leave the hospital, but Hale insisted I needed rest as well, promising we could come back first thing in the morning. It was my goal to be there before Elle awoke.

We didn't talk much or make love that night, but he loved me in a different way. He was there, a solid wall of strength for me to lean on as I tried to sort out my thoughts and discard the worries that no longer applied in order to make room for the new ones.

The next morning I returned to the hospital and Elle was wearing regular clothes. It was so wonderful to see her walking around. Her steps were slow, but she was able to move without much assistance, which was good.

Word got out that she'd opened her eyes and people came to visit. First my mom, then her co-workers, followed by some other friends, but never her brother. I didn't mention Chris again, because why bother? There was plenty of time to think about that later.

Over the weekend, Barrett and Hale kept the hospital staff well fed and my appetite slowly returned. The doctors ran a slew of tests and Elle continued to stress over her hair.

Every few minutes I took note of some deficient part of her mind. These weren't things the doctors would recognize, but Tyler and I often passed worried looks. Elle was a hairdresser, but she didn't know what a curling iron was called and despite requesting tweezers, she couldn't figure out how to use them.

She was put on a certain medication to help with her anxiety, which stemmed from her frustration at not being able to recall simple things. Sometimes she got moody, asking where we'd been when we specifically told her we'd be back in a few minutes.

"This isn't good," Tyler whispered when Elle had gone to use the bathroom.

"It'll get better with time." That's what the doctors had said, what I wanted to believe.

"How is she going to go back to work or take care of herself, Ray? I don't trust her not to burn the house down."

"It's not that bad." But it wasn't that great either.

The bathroom door opened and Elle stilled. "When did you guys get back?"

Okay, it was that bad. Leaving Tyler with her for a bit, I went to find Hale who had gone to speak to the billing department about having Elle discharged. He recognized my worry as soon as I found him.

"She can't stay alone," I told him. "It's not just missing words or forgetting little things. It's like she has Alzheimer's."

"They said that might happen on occasion. This is overwhelming for her."

I nodded, but deep down I knew this wouldn't resolve any time soon.

The following day was discharge day. I rode with Elle in the back of Hale's rental as he and Barrett took up the front. Elle kept smirking and mouthing dirty things about Hale's brother to me. Her libido clearly wasn't affected by the accident.

When we reached her house I unlocked the door as Hale carried in her bag. She stepped inside and stilled. "What's that stench?"

Chris was obviously still here. "Smoke. Your brother's here."

"He smokes?"

"*You* smoke."

She drew back. "What? No, I don't."

Well, there was a bonus. She'd been struggling to quit for three years. This was much easier.

She scoffed and walked into the living room, coming up short when she saw her useless pile of shit brother lounging on the couch. She staggered back a step and my hand caught her weight.

Chris watched his sister but didn't hold enough concern to put out his cigarette or even stand up. "Holy shit. You're alive."

Elle continued to frown. "Chris?"

His brow lifted, mocking her inability to recognize him. "Yeah?"

"You can't smoke in here."

He scoffed and took a long drag of his cigarette. "Really?"

Barrett stepped forward and plucked the cigarette out of his mouth and chucked it into a bottle of beer. "Have some respect," Hale's brother snapped and quickly returned to our side. He immediately went up ten points in my book.

"Who the fuck are these guys?"

I just stared at him, but Hale leaned close to me and whispered, "Why don't you help Elle get settled while we have a talk with her brother?"

Unsure what they could possibly have to say to him, I nodded and shuffled Elle into the kitchen. "We can get you some food once you're settled. I think there's some soup in the cabinet. Are you hungry?"

When she didn't answer I turned and found her staring at the cabinets from the doorway of the kitchen. "Who painted the walls yellow?"

"We did."

"They're supposed to be blue."

I was glad to know her colors were coming back, but in the absence of one issue came another. "Why don't we eat and then we can go to the store?" I couldn't leave her there with Chris.

She sat at the table as I heated up soup. When Hale and Barrett came into the kitchen they looked irritated.

"Can you sit with her for a few minutes?" I

quietly asked Barrett, who nodded. Taking Hale into the dining room, I whispered, "What happened?"

He grimaced. "He's not going to leave, Rayne. And he has every right to be here. I don't think she should stay and I don't like the idea of you being around a guy like that."

"I can take her to my house."

I was sure my mom wouldn't mind if Elle crashed for a few days. It wouldn't be permanent. She could sleep on the couch. But who would watch her when my mom and I went to work? What if Tyler was right and she burned the place down? I couldn't risk my mom's home—or Elle's safety—like that.

Hale's eyes creased with worry. "I think you need a better plan. I think it's time to start considering what she needs long-term—what we all need."

There comes a moment when the road of life forks and you know you have to make a turn, but I just stood there.

Call me Cleopatra, because I was queen of d'Nile and I refused to accept we had no other choice but the two *huge* decisions before me.

"You want us to go back to Florida with you?"

"I honestly think it would best for everyone, baby."

My head lowered. "I can't make her go."

"Ask her."

"She won't want to. Her life's here."

But where did that leave me? I was trapped between two worlds, my heart ripping in two. And no matter how much I wanted to deny this was my only option, there were no other solutions jumping out at me.

"Just ask and then we'll see what's best."

Sighing, I returned to the kitchen. Elle was smiling as Barrett told her a story about sailing along the coast of Spain. It was the first time I saw her truly happy since waking up. I sat at the table and listened as Barrett finished his tale, in no rush to interrupt the moment.

Chris could be heard shuffling around the house, but he never bothered us. As I watched Elle's captivation with Barrett, I realized I had a weapon at my disposal.

I didn't like manipulating people, but Hale was right. Getting out of here was for the best. At least right now. When she was more equipped to deal with regular life she could come back—if Chris didn't blow up her house in the meantime.

"Elle, how would you like to come back to Florida with us, take a little time to recuperate? Hale and Barrett will be there."

Her lips pursed as a flush worked over her

cheeks and she shyly said my name. "Ray…"

Barrett glanced at me, his expression confused. I'd explain my logic to him later. I just needed to borrow his potent sex appeal for a minute to get Elle to agree. I didn't want him to do anything. That would be a huge mistake. Elle was fragile. I just needed him to keep her interested enough to follow us back to Florida.

"Would I stay at Remington's?" Elle asked.

"You'd stay with me," Hale explained.

"We all would, you, me, Hale, Elara, and Barrett."

Barrett frowned but kept his mouth shut. He'd been staying with Remington, but now that his father was in Maine, there was no point in him being at the other house all alone. Or maybe there was. I didn't presume to tell a man in his thirties where he had to sleep.

"For how long?" Elle asked.

"Until we're ready to come back." I might only be able to keep her there a few weeks, but she couldn't return to work or stay on her own until she was back to her usual self. "It'll be like a vacation."

She glanced at Hale's brother and back to me. "I might be confused, but there's no way I'd give up that chance." She nodded. "Show me how the rich and famous live."

And we had lift-off.

Who doesn't like Bon Jovi?

9

All of my life—it didn't matter where I was —if Bon Jovi came on I was halfway there. Can I get a *whoa-oh?* Because I was living on a prayer. But apparently, those rules didn't apply to today, as Elle flipped off my stereo and submerged the car in silence.

"You don't want to listen to music?"

She frowned and folded her arms over her chest. "That's just noise."

I gaped at her. "You *love* Bon Jovi."

"Who?"

Right. Another familiar part misplaced and severely missed.

Distressed, I tried to comfort myself and muttered, "We got each other. That's a lot." But Elle didn't get my joke.

When we reached my house I left Elle with

my mom so I could pack. Once again, I had no idea how long I'd be gone, but this time I wasn't messing around. I packed *everything*.

On my last trip to Davenport headquarters, I'd had a little mishap with the luggage department, but Hale was having our things sent ahead of time, so there would be no tedious interactions with baggage claim. Good thing, too, because I had way more than the seventy pound limit of luggage.

My mom was taking all these changes in stride. I knew she was sad to see me go, but Oregon no longer felt like home. Florida wasn't home either, but Hale... Hale was where I wanted to be.

I'd contacted the restaurant and picked up my last paycheck. This time was a little more emotional than the last because I didn't know if I'd ever work there again. My bosses were good peeps and they'd always been there for me when I needed them, so it was hard to say goodbye. Even Mel, our grumpy chef, gave me a hug.

Barrett came to pick up my car and drove it to wherever one drove that much stuff to be shipped. Hale was having dinner with Elara and his mother, who was returning to New York rather than joining us on the trip home. Okay, yes, I'd started calling Hale's place home, but only in my head where others couldn't hear, so it didn't count.

Since we were leaving in the morning, I told Hale I was going to spend the night at my house so I could have some time with my mom before our trip. I also needed to keep an eye on Elle. But once they fell asleep, and it was just me awake, I couldn't ignore the thoughts running through my head.

I was nervous. This was a bigger move than any of us were willing to admit. I was going to live with Hale, like, in his bed and have a drawer—many drawers—in his house. I couldn't talk to him about why this made me nervous because it would come out wrong and I didn't want to hurt his feelings.

I wanted to go back to Florida and it made sense to go, being that this was the only way I could afford to look after Elle, but maybe those were the wrong reasons to move in with Hale.

I googled the time difference between Oregon and Maine and finally gave in and called the one person who I knew could help me figure things out.

"Meyers, I wasn't expecting to hear from you," Remington answered.

"I'm sorry to call so late."

"It's not that late. Hold on a minute." I heard some shuffling and the distinct sound of a woman's voice. Hale's father had obviously gotten his strength back. "Okay. I wanted a drink. Talk to me."

"We're going back to Florida tomorrow."

"That's what I hear."

"I won't be able to go back to work right away."

He made a gruff sound. "We won't be back in the area for a few days anyway."

"I... I'm going to live with Hale."

"I'm not surprised."

"Am I being stupid, Remington?"

"We all do stupid things, Meyers, but if this gets you back where you belong, so be it. You outgrew your childhood home and waitressing some time ago."

An unsteady grin twitched on my lips. For some reason, Remington believed I was cut out to be something impressive. Maybe I was, but I didn't have his instincts.

"When will you be back?" I missed him. Though he was a big pain in the ass, I couldn't deny the sense of confidence his presence brought.

"I have a few meetings tomorrow, but my business here is winding down."

"I ... miss you."

He gave a gruff laugh. "Get your emotions

in check, Meyers. This isn't daytime television."

I smiled, because, despite his prickly temperament, every cactus had a soft side. "I'll see you soon, Remington."

He was quiet for a moment. "I'll see you soon, sweetheart. Have a safe trip." And there was the Remington I knew.

When I hung up the phone I was less afraid of what might come and more prepared to face my future head on—for the most part.

The next morning Hale picked us up and we rode to the airport. It was absolutely adorable seeing him push Elara in a stroller, but the adorableness stopped when she started to cry and shit herself right in the middle of our security screening. Flying with a baby no longer seemed like a fun idea.

Once we were on the plane, Hale got her settled. Elle buckled up and flipped through a magazine, but I wasn't sure if she read a single word. I occupied myself by checking out all the luxuries that came with flying business class.

Rather than sitting side-by-side like the passengers in coach, we each had our own little, sectioned off pod area. Each chair altered directions, so we faced one another, Hale and Elara on my left, Elle and Barrett on my right, an ocean of floor space between us. My legs had plenty of room to stretch between my seat and a personal desk *with* my own private television.

As I explored, Hale fed Elara and Barrett and Elle chatted quietly.

I found a little bag filled with airline swag. "Did you guys see the fanny pack of goodies we get? Ooh! A blindfold!" I turned to Hale. "Do we get to keep this stuff?"

He chuckled and I played with my seat, which could recline to a flat position.

A flight attendant came around to take our drink orders. We had six hours to pass so I figured we should make it fun. "Can I have a beer? No, wait, how about a cosmopolitan?"

She nodded and disappeared behind a curtain by the cockpit. Hale smirked. "You'll be smashed before we take off. Don't forget it'll be just after lunch when we land."

Day drinking was always fun. A noon buzz was better. I waggled my brows. "Wanna join the mile high club?"

He laughed and glanced at Elara, who was now sleeping in his arms. Yeah, there wouldn't be plane sex with a baby.

My drink was delivered and then came breakfast.

"This is real silverware," I gasped, unrolling my fork from the linen napkin.

Everything was so fancy. Croissants and

Canadian bacon, quiche, and a little parfait. It was a five-star meal. No bags of airplane peanuts here.

After breakfast, everyone decided to nap. I tried out my handy-dandy blindfold, but then I was just staring at darkness. I wasn't tired.

Playing with the remote on the desk, I figured out how to get to the movies. *Yes! True Lies.*

When lunch rolled around, I was onto *Caddyshack* and super excited for the food. The drinks were included, so I ordered another Cosmo. I was totally crushing the upper-class version of Rayne Meyer. She was awesome, like Fergie in the *Glamorous* video.

Spreading my napkin on my lap I preened and sipped my cocktail, whispering out the lyrics, *"G—L—A—M—we're flying first class—popping champagne..."*

"I've never seen someone so happy to travel," Hale said, eyes squinting with amusement.

"This is fabulous, darling," I gave him my rich person eyes, full on Betty Davis pre-*What Happened to Baby Jane.*

His laugh told me he totally understood and accepted I was the way I was. "Are you enjoying your lunch?"

"Absolutely. Did you get the kettle corn? I

got both, the corn and the Dove chocolate. They said I could have both."

He laughed again. "You can have whatever you want."

My lips pursed. I wasn't at the right angle to give him a shoulder bump, which was like a secret I love you handshake, so I tapped his knee with my socked foot. "You're nice."

"So are you." He pinched my toes. "Where did these come from?"

"They were in the little fanny pack thing. Didn't you get socks?"

"I'm sure I have a pair."

I glanced at Elle and Barrett, who were both passed out. They even supplied pillows and blankets. Elara was curled up in Hale's arms like an Anne Geddes portrait. I checked the time on my phone. "We're halfway there."

He arched a brow. "Living on a prayer."

I stilled. "Did you just quote Bon Jovi?"

He laughed. "Yeah. Cheesy. I know."

If it was possible, my love for him doubled. Elle no longer liked Bon Jovi, but apparently, my other half did. "It's not cheesy at all."

It was a sign. And I knew then and there... *We'd make it... I'd swear.*

10

The moment the limo pulled up to Hale's house in the Keys a sense of rightness took hold of me. This was where I'd left off and exactly where I wanted to be.

I smiled as I slid out of the backseat and waited for Elle. Alfonse, one of Remington's employees who had picked us up from the airport, earned a bear hug the moment I saw him, which might have overwhelmed the man, but I was a hugger.

"Wow," Elle muttered as soon as she saw Hale's home.

"I know. You should see his dad's place."

We followed the men inside and something was immediately off. Lights were on and the television played softly from the kitchen—Hale had TVs in every room. Glancing around at the

155

tidy living space and catching the slight scent of food, my nose twitched.

Excitement took hold as I looked at Hale. "Is Marta here?" Marta was Remington's maid, who I adored.

"No, she's with my dad."

"You made it," a feminine voice called from the stairs and I frowned. What sort of fresh hell was this?

A young twenty-something woman came to greet us, and my body physically shrank into itself. Her hair was lavish, literally *lavish,* waves of white blonde reaching halfway down her back like a slow-motion shampoo commercial. She wore cuffed denim shorts and a white dress shirt with no sleeves that accentuated her tanned, trim arms.

"Let me see my little angel," she cooed, reaching for Elara. My gaze followed her as she took Elara into her arms and kissed her pudgy cheek.

My baby.

Hale didn't seem to care that this strange woman was manhandling his child. Okay, this was not what I expected.

"Rayne, Elle, this is Brynlee."

Brynlee? Oh, that was just the perfect name for her. I stared, too shocked to move or speak.

"Hi," she chirped, retaining her familiar hold of Hale's daughter.

"Who are you?" I finally asked because she seemed to be kidnapping Hale's kid right before our eyes.

"Brynlee's Elara's nanny," Hale explained, not at all on the move to send out an Amber Alert.

I frowned. Naomi had been helping Hale and he'd said all that stuff about me being there when he had to go away on business. I hadn't fully agreed with the idea, and help seemed like a great idea, but where were all the boy nannies? Elara struck me as the type of infant who would prefer a babysitter with a name like Russ or Bob.

"Oh," This was so unexpected I didn't know what else to say.

"I made some sandwiches and a pie, figuring you'd be hungry after your flight. God knows airplane food isn't real food." She giggled and Hale grinned.

This chick cooked, too? Wasn't she a little young to be operating hot stoves? I mean, could she reach the pantry? And I *liked* airplane food.

"I think Elara needs a change," Hale said.

Yeah, change in nanny...

Brynlee smiled like the kid's diaper hid diamonds. "I'll take care of her."

"And you can unpack this in her room."

"Thank you," she sort of said, but it came out more as a chirped *think hue*. Who thanks someone for telling them to clean up poop and unpack?

We were definitely going to discuss little Miss Pie Pants as soon as I had a minute alone with Hale. Turning to Elle, I said, "I'll give you a tour of the house."

We left the guys there with Elara and the chick from *The Hand that Rocks the Cradle* and went upstairs. "This is Elara's room and down there is Hale's room." As soon as we were out of earshot I hissed, "Did you see that girl? She was totally coming on to Hale."

Elle laughed and glanced to the stairs. "No, she wasn't."

I scoffed. "He didn't say anything about having a nanny." Or did he?

Damn him with his distraction tactics. He'd definitely used the word nanny, but that was the same conversation that included red flags like *living together* and *future* and the words *I eventually want a wife.*

"Well, he's a single dad, Ray. How else is he going to do it?"

"His mother!" I said, wondering why I was the only person who found this unacceptable.

"I think you're overreacting."

If only Elle could remember how I got here. It was like every worry and insecurity I expressed during the hook-up stage was gone from her memory and I had to constantly remind her that I was a perpetual teenager with irrational insecurities. To Elle, there was Hale and there was me, and we had a lot of sex in between. Oh, and he had a baby. I wasn't used to my best friend not jumping on my side.

I want my biased friend back!

Irritated, I walked her down the hall. "This is the room you'll probably take." I pushed open the door and stilled. "Or not." Little lotion bottles sat on the dresser and a pair of woman's sandals rested by the bed. "Is she fucking *living* here?"

Now, Elle was getting it. "Oh, I see the issue."

I gaped at her and whispered, "How long has she been here?"

Of course, she didn't have an answer. But Hale was going to give me one. That was for damn sure.

I took Elle to the next bedroom and she was just as happy to claim that one. She'd been pretty sharp today, but still a far cry from her usual self.

All nanny business aside, I was actually feeling a bit relieved until Elle whispered, "So what's the deal with Hale's brother?"

Everything inside of me went on high alert. "No, Elle. He's a serious manwhore. I mean, he's nice and everything, but you need to stay away from him." What if they did stuff and Elle wasn't ready? She might not remember his reputation. "Barrett will sleep with anything with a pulse."

"Well, Meyers, that's not entirely true."

I spun on my heels as Barrett filled the doorway. *"Vampire!"*

He smiled, gushing all that Davenport charm with his carved dimples and sexy man bun and shredded abs that tinted shadows through his fitted white t-shirt. For God's sake, Elle needed to roll her tongue back in her mouth. Everyone needed to calm down!

"I draw the line at sheep and men," Barrett joked. Then as if nothing happened, he said, "I'm heading back to my dad's. I just wanted to say I'd see you later."

Elle smiled, but it was her flirty smile so I stepped in front of her and blurted, "Bye."

He gave me a questioning frown but nodded. When he was gone, I turned to her. "No.

You cannot get mixed up with him. You're ... fragile."

She rolled her eyes. "Get a grip, Ray. We're on vacation."

But it wasn't vacation. I mean, it was for her, but this was my life and these were *my* Davenports. Things couldn't get more complicated than they already were. I left Elle to get settled and found Hale unpacking in his room.

Shutting the door, I asked, "Why didn't you tell me about Brynlee?" I really disliked saying her name.

He frowned. "What about her?"

"Um ... that she's living with you."

He closed a drawer. "Marta hired her. She's getting a degree in early childhood education and has been a huge help with Elara."

"But your mom was here."

"Yes, and that was never permanent." He approached me, his brow creased. "Is something wrong?"

She's too young and pretty. And why the fuck is she baking you pies? "I just don't understand why you need a live-in nanny when I'm here." God, she was such a hypocrite. But rational logic had never been her strong suit.

"You're my girlfriend. I need someone to watch Elara when we go out."

Well, didn't he just have an answer for everything? "What was wrong with Marta?"

"Marta works for my dad, Rayne. What's the issue? Babies need daycare and I have a demanding job. Do you not like her?"

No. I didn't like her. "I just figured you would've told me about her."

"I thought I did."

"No." Definitely did not mention the name *Brynlee*.

"Well, we've been a little preoccupied with getting Elle situated, and the move."

"She's living in the next room, Hale."

"Only because my mom was in the guesthouse. She'll move her stuff out there this week."

I continued to scowl, in no position to tell him whom he could and couldn't hire. "Well, I don't think she should be baking you pies."

His eyes creased as he stepped closer, his lips hooking up in a cocky grin. "Are you jealous of the nanny?"

"No," I scoffed.

His hands rested on my hips, pulling my body close to angle against his. "Liar."

I glanced away because I couldn't deny the other woman's presence threatened me on some level. Hale's fingers massaged through my jeans as he whispered close to my ear, "She's ten years younger than me, baby."

And so were all of Remington's wives.

"She's not my type." His lips pressed to my pulse and my body partially relaxed.

Maybe I was being a tad too territorial. "I just wish you would have warned me she was here."

"An oversight."

"We should probably help her move her stuff." I mean, no sense in wasting time.

"Not yet." His hands fit under my shirt and teased my skin. I squirmed because I was still irritated and I didn't like knowing another woman was in his house—Elle didn't count.

His mouth trailed to my shoulder, drawing my nipples to attention. "Relax, Rayne. The only woman I want is you."

I gave him a brooding stare, but he just chuckled and pulled me toward the bed. "I haven't had you alone in days." His fingers plucked my jeans open and slid down the zipper.

"Elle's by herself—"

"She's fine. She's unpacking."

"Elara—"

"Is with her nanny. See how convenient that is?" He stripped off my shirt and un-latched my bra.

Bending in front of my body, he pulled my nipple into his mouth and I caught his shoulders. Feeling myself fall under his spell, I swayed a little, my eyes turning heavy.

"I love your body," he whispered, breath teasing my flesh.

Okay, maybe having a nanny wasn't such a bad thing. My hands roamed over his chest and worked their way into his pants. Hale groaned and toppled me to the bed.

I giggled as he pulled off my jeans, the denim going inside out and catching on my flip-flops. He got them off with a yank.

"You're mine," he growled, irrefutably claiming all that was his to have.

Distinguished Arrogance

11

"I can't believe you gave this up to come home for me," Elle said as she basked in the sun on a lounge chair next to mine. We were at Remington's pool because I liked it better than Hale's.

"This isn't exactly how I left things. Before I was working." Which I missed very much. There was something to be said about the value of independence.

"Still, this is the life. It's so peaceful here."

Another reason why Remington's pool was better than Hale's, it was far away from Brynlee. I was glad to discover she didn't dine with us, but she sure made Hale a lot of sandwiches. Like that was hard. I could make a sandwich.

I'd come to admit the girl was good with his daughter, but I wasn't ready to say it out loud. Having a nanny made our evenings easier and assured Hale and I had plenty of time to date like a regular couple.

She was available for babysitting and tended to Elara during the workday, leaving Hale in charge overnight and in the mornings. I was really impressed with how easily he woke to feed his daughter and how naturally he took to things like dressing her. On the weekends Brynlee was only around if we went out. So, fine, I might have overreacted.

Elle had adapted well to a life of luxury and I was grateful Barrett hadn't been around much. When he did pop up, Elle took notice. She was very self-conscious about her hair, being that half her head was just past bald. If she spent too much time in front of mirrors she got upset. Most distressing was the day I suggested she give me a trim, thinking it might help her confidence.

She stared at my hair for a solid ten minutes while I waited in the chair. Finally, she put down the scissors and cried, claiming she wasn't in the mood to give me a haircut. I knew that wasn't the problem. I'd watched her try to put on makeup and pluck her eyebrows. These were skills she'd misplaced and I was useless when it came to refreshing her memory.

When I told Hale how upset she got, he

made an appointment for Elle and me at a spa. Our appointment was tomorrow and Elle loved the idea. I was happy to see her excited, but honestly, how could an appointment at a spa last four hours? I had no idea what we were going to have done.

Remington's house was quiet. Alfonse wasn't home and everyone else was away. I knew the codes to let us in, but it still felt odd being there alone. When I heard movement from inside, I sat up. The sun beamed off of the glass windows and the sliding door opened. I squinted, lifting my sunglasses as my breath sucked in on a gasp.

Without realizing I was moving, I stood and rushed toward the house as his silver hair came into view. He was standing. Walking! He leaned into a cane, but he looked great.

"Remington!" I squealed, prepared to tackle the man.

His gruff chuckle met my ears and then he grunted when I threw my arms around him, squeezing tightly. "You have the grace of a baby elephant, Meyers."

"I missed you!"

His hand slowly lifted, not reciprocating the hug, but patting me awkwardly on my shoulder. "It's good you're home."

I stepped back and looked at him, taking in

the noticeable changes. His skin had some new color and he looked well rested. There was no doubt his time in the cast had grated his last nerve.

"You have a cane."

He grumbled and lifted his sunglasses, raising a dark brow at my appearance. "This is a lot better than the crap you usually wear."

I rolled my eyes and quickly moved to snag my cover up off the back of my lounge chair. Elle stood and did the same.

"Remington, this is Elle."

He nodded. "I'm glad to see you're up and around." He turned and called for Marta to bring something cool to drink as he settled in at the glass table.

"I have to go say hi to Marta. I'll be right back."

As soon as I made it into the house she clapped in surprise and came to hug me. "Nena! You are back!"

Everyone was home, Remington, Miles, Marta and Raul, me, Hale, Elara. It was perfect and I never wanted anyone to go anywhere ever again.

We had lunch on the veranda and Remington told me about his latest business ventures. I teased him about getting in some *exercise*, which he defined as a healthy dose of living with a side of fornication. He didn't deny it and I loved that about him. The man had no shame and his arrogance was so distinguished, people simply accepted it.

I was having so much fun catching up, I hadn't realized how late it was. Hale appeared around five o'clock and it was hard to leave, but he'd made dinner plans for us and I didn't want to miss our reservation.

"When will you return to work?" Remington asked, cutting through the chatter at the table.

"Um..." I'd given the matter some thought but wasn't sure if my job was still available.

Hale cleared his throat. "She's taking time off for a while."

Remington waved away his son's words. "Nonsense. She has a job."

I glanced at Elle. She'd been adapting well, but I wasn't sure if she could manage being alone all day. "I'm not sure," I admitted.

"What's the holdup?" Remington asked. "You're here. Your friend's better. It's time to get back to life."

"Cut her some slack," Hale muttered, clearly opposing the idea.

Remington frowned at his son. "She wants to work. Don't you, Meyers?"

"Uh..." Being stuck between two Davenports was no picnic. "I do miss my job."

"There. Problem solved. I'll expect you here tomorrow morning. We have a lot of catching up to do."

When we returned to Hale's I showered and got ready for dinner. He was quiet and I knew the discussion about work was far from over. Once we were alone and in his car, he said, "You have an appointment tomorrow."

"I forgot about that. Maybe we could reschedule."

"Or you could tell Remington you have a life outside of his needs and he'll have to wait."

Okay, he was definitely irritated. "Hale, I came here to work for him."

"You came here to be with me."

I scoffed. "And you've been working every day. What does it matter if I'm working for your dad or if I'm sitting on the beach? I don't see you until five anyway."

"How long do you expect him to stay nearby, Rayne? This is a pit stop for him. You have to consider Elle."

He was right, but this wasn't about Elle. "Is that all you're concerned about? Elle?"

His mouth compressed. "I just got you back. I'm not ready to see you leave again."

I might be able to talk to Remington about

taking me on only while he's local. Maybe Miles could handle the rest. "Let's not worry about it now. Tomorrow I'll talk to Remington—"

"Talk to me. I'm your goddamn boyfriend!"

I drew back in my seat, startled by his outburst. "Why are you so angry?"

He pulled into a parking lot and waited for the valet. "You let him decide for you when you're completely capable of deciding for yourself."

My door opened before I could respond. We shelved our discussion until we were situated at a table and the waiter had taken our drink orders.

"Hale, I need some sort of income," I explained. "I know your dad isn't your favorite person, but you manage to work together. What's wrong with me taking back my old job? I was good at it."

Despite having no experience in the business world, when Remington gave me a project I usually knocked it out of the park. I liked the challenges and the unpredictability of the position. And I liked learning from Remington.

He paged through the menu. "I'm paying for everything you need. If there's something you want, tell me and I'll get it for you."

"I want a job."

His eyes narrowed. "Then work for me."

"As what? Your hooker?"

He arched a brow but didn't touch the comment. "We have openings in the clerical department."

I rolled my eyes. "I don't want to do that. This is stupid. There's no difference between me working at one of your companies and working for your dad."

He let the argument go. "Elle seems to be doing better."

Figuring our disagreement could simmer a while, I switched gears. Elle *was* doing better, but I didn't want to talk about her either. We ordered our dinner and I picked at my fish, a nagging sense of unease spoiling my appetite.

Something wasn't right. We'd been living together for a week and I had yet to feel the rightness I felt when we first returned and again this afternoon when Remington returned.

We held a polite conversation throughout dinner, but once we were on our way home the same lopsided awareness returned. I was pretty sure I was crazy. What sane woman took issue with living in her boyfriend's mansion, passing her days poolside with her best friend, and having incredible sex each night? Me, that's who.

Letting out a sigh, I made the huge mistake of muttering, "Maybe we shouldn't have moved in together so soon."

The air in the car chilled as Hale regarded me. "I beg your pardon?"

"Never mind." Ugh. Can open, worms everywhere. Why the hell did I say that?

He scowled the rest of the way home and wasn't it just perfect Brynlee was there to greet us at the door?

"How was dinner?" she chirped.

God, go home. I forced a smile and made my way up the stairs.

Hale got a run-down of Elara's evening and then the house was quiet. Elle's bedroom light was on, but the door was closed, so I didn't bother her. Honestly, I needed a break from her. Mostly because I was getting the sense that she wanted a break from me.

I loved Elle, but I was running on empty, the last month and a half consumed with worry for her while my life spiraled out of control in the distance. I needed to put all Elle worries aside for a minute so that I could concentrate on my personal feelings and figure out what the hell was wrong with me.

When I reached our room, I took down my hair and changed into a T-shirt. Hale entered and watched me from the door. "What's going on with you?"

"Nothing."

"Damn it, Rayne. Every time I ask you what's wrong you say *nothing* or *fine*, then we go through a tedious hour of guess the issue until we finally talk. Can we just skip the bullshit?"

I scowled at him because I didn't like feeling pressured. Sliding under the covers I sat with my back against the headboard and crossed my arms. "Fine. I want to work for Remington. I don't like your nanny. And I miss my best friend."

"None of that has anything to do with us."

I held out my hands, exasperated. "It has *everything* to do with us. Don't you get it, Hale? We're living together and everything's too easy. We skipped a bunch of steps, because of unforeseen circumstances, and I'm irritated that none of this feels normal."

"What are you talking about?" He pushed off the door and paced. "I thought everything was fine. We hardly ever argue. We're incredible in bed together. You're here. Elle's here. What else do you need?"

"I don't know!" I practically wailed, because if I had that answer I wouldn't feel so hysterical at the moment. "I've never done this before."

"This is being in a relationship, Rayne."

"No, this is being in an arrangement. Everything seems to have a solution, but nothing feels right. My days are spent taking care of Elle and making sure she doesn't break, but she's getting annoyed because I'm always telling her how to do things, which is the total opposite of how things were between us. And then you're at work and Brynlee's taking care of Elara and how the hell does everyone else seem to be adjusting to this when none of it is how things were a month ago? Am I the only person who thinks this is strange?"

"I don't know what you want."

"Well, neither do I," I snapped. There was definitely something wrong with me.

"Do you want me to fire Brynlee?"

Yes. "No."

"Then what?"

"I just don't like the way she talks to you."

"She has to talk to me. I'm her boss." He was clearly irritated and I was making it worse.

"I know! I'm being irrational and I can't stop."

"I'm sorry Elle isn't making this easy for you."

"Jesus, don't apologize for her."

"Well, what the hell do you want me to do? I'm trying to figure out a solution, but you don't make it easy. If going back to work for my dad is what it will take, fine. Go! But I'm not going to be able to follow you across the globe every time he travels!"

He'd never yelled at me before and I wasn't sure how we'd jumped from a simple disagreement into a screaming match. So much for never arguing.

On cue, Elara started to cry. Hale huffed out an exasperated breath. "I have to go take care of my daughter."

When I was alone, the sadness kept me company. I hated feeling like this. Typically, this would be the moment I called my best friend, but she had been so distant with all things involving Hale and me, I wasn't sure if she even liked him. Maybe I was being selfish, but after the last month of reorganizing my entire life on other people's behalfs, I really needed it to be about me for a second.

Hale was willing to throw whatever solution was available at the problem, but that didn't work for me. It felt too much like treating a symptom when we should really be identifying the problem. This was exactly why I was thrilled to have Remington back. He would make sense of things. And he would give it to me straight.

I heard a deep voice and frowned. Hale wouldn't talk to Elara in that tone. Sliding out of bed, I cracked the door and stopped breathing.

Did no one pay attention to a single word I said?

Barrett turned from Elle's door and stilled. "Hey, Meyers."

I'd assumed she was alone when I saw her door closed, but apparently, I was wrong.

Pressing my lips tight, I glared at him and slammed the door. And then Elara started to cry again. *Great.*

12

Being that I excelled at procrastination above all else, I texted Remington the following morning and told him we'd talk later that night. Elle and I had reservations at the spa and apparently, it was a big damn debacle for me to reschedule. So here I sat, beside my friend, while some woman named after a flower rubbed my feet.

"This is exactly what I needed," Elle sighed.

I frowned as the pedicurist labored over my calluses. "So are we going to talk about you and Barrett?" I was still steaming over what I saw last night.

Resting her head against the massage chair, she grinned and faced me. "He's so hot, Ray. You should see his abs."

The entire world had seen his abs, being that he modeled for his sister's clothing line. "Did you see them in a magazine?"

She laughed and waggled her brows. "I saw them up close last night."

I flinched as the sadist working on my cuticles clipped a little too close to the skin. "Ouch!"

The pedicurist muttered an apology and I turned back to Elle. "Do you think it's smart getting close to someone like that so soon after the accident?"

She rolled her eyes. "Look at me, Ray. The fact that he can show any interest in me at all when I'm missing half my hair and a good part of my brain is a freaking miracle. I'm certainly not going to object."

But what about the meaningful stuff? Elle had always been a little more comfortable with her sexuality than me—okay, fine, a lot more comfortable—but this was Hale's brother. "I just don't want him to complicate things."

"Nothing's getting complicated. We're just hanging out."

"Yeah, naked."

"I haven't taken off any clothes. Yet."

I faced her, trying to judge if she was joking. "Really?"

"Really."

Her gaze shifted to the mirrors across the salon and her expression turned serious. "I need to feel pretty right now, Ray, even if it's just superficial fluff. Every day I get frustrated. I still can't remember simple words and I look like I've been scalped. Nothing about my life is how I remember it and it's hard. Barrett's helping my self-esteem in a big way. I'm going to take advantage of any chance I have to feel better right now."

I sighed, feeling like a terrible person. "I understand." But a part of me still worried how this would affect the usual Davenport dynamic, as selfish as that was. I excused my guilt because I also worried Barrett would use Elle and she'd be too uncomfortable to stay. I wanted my best friend there with me and I wanted Hale's brother to keep his dick in his pants.

"What's going on with you and Hale? Did you two have a fight last night?"

My lip curled. "Yes, but I'm not even sure what we were arguing about. I don't want to talk about it."

When had I become such a martyr? Last night I'd been bitching that Elle rarely showed interest in my life anymore, and here she was asking if I was okay.

Realizing I was being stupid, I asked, "Do you think it's weird we're living together?"

"I think you care about him and your circumstances are what they are."

But I didn't want to live with someone just because of *circumstances*. I wanted to do it because our relationship had progressed and we were at that point.

"I sort of understand what you were saying about dating someone with a child now. It complicates things."

I could tell by her confused expression that she didn't remember that conversation. "Elara seems like an easy baby."

And she was, but now there were nannies involved and schedules and all kinds of grown-up stuff. "I hate being an adult."

Elle laughed. "A what?"

"An adult. A grown-up."

"Oh."

I went with a red polish on my toes. Elle chose a French manicure with a tropical flower painted on the bed of her nail. Once we had those awkward foam things wedged between our toes and wore a set of floppy yellow flip-flops, we moved to the manicure tables.

"So are you and Barrett, like, dating?"

"What? No. We're just passing time."

Naked time?

What if Barrett went out with someone else? Sometimes he disappeared for days and shacked up with random women. I didn't want to tell Elle that, but I worried she'd find out the hard way. Maybe she wouldn't care. Maybe I was the only person who got jealous over stuff like that. Well, Hale got jealous, too. Maybe jealousy was contagious.

"I think I'm going to go back to work for Remington."

"He's a little scary," she remarked.

"Not really. Once you get to know him he's just a big marshmallow."

"I don't think so. He's different with you. Why is that?"

I frowned. "I don't think he treats me any differently than he treats anyone else."

Elle snorted. "Oh, come on, Ray. He definitely does. He treats you like..."

"An employee?"

"No."

"A colleague?"

She shook her head. "Like a daughter."

I couldn't help my smile. Sometimes he did look after me and offer me skewed fatherly advice, but I was curious what Elle saw that made her say such a thing. "What makes you say that?"

"Well, did he ask *you* to join him in the hot tub?"

"*What?*" Scowling, I faced her. "Did he ask you that?"

She shrugged. "You went inside to see Marta and he made a few comments. He's a bit of an old perv, but I can see how women fall for him."

"I can't believe he said something like that to you." He would definitely be hearing about this. "Stay away from him." Jesus. And she was *passing time* with Barrett. Couldn't this man find his own women and keep away from his sons'?

"Relax. It was funny. He knows I'm not interested. He's old."

"He's a pig." I couldn't believe he hit on my friend.

"My point is, he'd never look at you that way."

I didn't know if I should be flattered or insulted, so I remained disgusted.

Once we were finished with our manicures we went to another part of the salon where we changed into robes and had tea sandwiches and champagne.

"Hale's awesome. This is nicer than any spa I've ever been to," Elle commented and then laughed. "I think."

I didn't have a point of reference when it came to girlie places like this. "This robe is nice." I shifted. "Are you wearing underwear?" They said to take everything off. I removed my underwear, but maybe they meant for me to keep them on.

Two men appeared, dressed in black. When they announced they'd be giving us a massage, I panicked. I probably should have left my underwear on. Damn it!

"I'll see you in an hour," Elle waved, following one man into a private room.

I stared at the other man. "I'm with you?"

"Yes, ma'am." He led me into a dim room with soft music playing and a very intimidating table. "Once you remove your robe, lay face down on the table and use this sheet to cover your body. I'll give you some privacy."

But there was nothing under my robe. I stared at the table.

Shit.

Working quickly, I stripped and climbed onto the table with the grace of a hippo mounting a tall rock. I rushed to cover my body before anyone came in. Fluffing out the sheet, I draped it over my back, covering my body, shoulders to my ankles, totally out of breath and sweating.

There was a light knock. "Ready?"

No. "Yes."

My face wedged into the padded hole as I heard him enter. The music was soothing but I was far from relaxed. The slick sound of oil being lathered between fingers had me looking nervously side-to-side, but all I could see was floor. *Wait...* The man's shoes came into view. *Oh, god.* He was going to touch me.

"So are you vacationing or do you live around here?" His feet disappeared and the sheet lifted off my ankles.

Oh, God. He was definitely touching my leg. "We just moved here." Well, that felt kind of nice, but I panicked when he reached my upper thigh. "Do you live here?"

Of course, he lived here. He fucking worked here. I was an idiot.

"All my life." He switched legs. "I like the color on your toes." His fingers slithered through said toes as he massaged my feet.

"Thanks?" No matter how much I tried, I couldn't relax. A man was touching me. *Stranger danger!*

He came extremely close to my bare butt and when he worked on my arms his fingers brushed my armpit. Not that the armpit was any sort of erogenous zone, but it was neighboring Boobie Boulevard. I was obviously too immature to enjoy a massage.

A cool breeze crept over my entire back as he lifted the sheet. "Turn over."

Christ! I flipped to my side, unable to see his face behind the sheet, and rolled to my back. When he covered me I screwed my eyes shut, because I never intended to look him in the eye again.

He returned to my legs and this time when he passed my mid-thigh I started to laugh nervously. "Crazy weather here," I blurted.

"What was the weather like where you're from?"

I couldn't remember, on account of him being six inches from my hooha. "Frigid."

He chuckled and moved to my shoulders. "Is this your first massage?"

"Yes."

"You seem tense." He lowered the sheet, not exposing anything, but my nipples got hard. *What is wrong with me?*

When it was finally over I was edgier than before. Elle, however, looked like she'd just had sex.

"That was incredible," she sighed, with half-lidded eyes.

I frowned because now I regretted being too in my head to enjoy the experience the way she obviously had. Still in our robes, we waited in another room as the masseuses handed us two heavy menus.

"Latisha will be right with you."

"Who's Latisha?" I whispered to Elle, who was frowning at the menu.

She closed it and put it aside. "I think I'm going to get everything. My eyebrows are in horrible shape and I don't even want to tell you what's going on downstairs."

"You mean wax?" I looked up, trying to see my brows. "How are my eyebrows?"

She glanced at my face. "You need them done. While we're here, you might as well take care of everything."

"Why? You think I need to do my lip?" Shit, was I getting a mustache?

"Not that. I mean your bikini line. I'm getting a Brazilian."

My eyes widened. "Doesn't that hurt?"

"Yes, but I'm tired of shaving every time I put on a bathing suit. Trust me, it's the way to go."

I smiled at her, momentarily speechless.

"What? You're creeping me out, Ray. The mention of my vagina shouldn't put that grin on your face."

"You remembered."

"Remembered what?"

"That you used to get Brazilians and how much they hurt."

Elle paused, her confused expression morphing into one of pleasant surprise. "Alicia waxed me. Oh, my god. She's probably wondering why I missed my last few appointments."

It was the silliest thing to get excited over, but it was also a monumental moment. I gripped her hand and squeezed. "You're getting there, girl." I was certain. All because of Elle's once impeccably maintained and well-groomed vagina.

Latisha arrived and I sent Elle back first. No sound came out of the back room while she was in there and when she returned, her brows were defined and she appeared unharmed. A little rosy in the face, but at ease.

I followed Latisha back to the room. There was a white leather chair and a little pot of hot wax.

"So what are we having done today?"

"Um, just my eyebrows."

She examined my brows, combing them into place and staring through a magnifying light. The wax was warm, but not hot. However, when she ripped that first piece of fabric away it stung like a motherfucker.

I endured the process because I was a girl

and Elle said my brows needed this. But then I started thinking about my vagina. My vagina and I had a newfound bond. We'd come to an understanding of sorts, and both benefited from my new sex life. I'd done a little landscaping before I went back to Oregon, but since returning to Florida, I'd let things go.

Hale liked when I was smooth, but he didn't complain when I had hair either. Maybe he'd like me waxed and if I got the Brazilian I might not have to shave as frequently.

"Does waxing last longer than shaving?"

Latisha applied some lotion to my brows and plucked a few strays. "You mean with a bikini wax? Yes. Are you grown out?"

I twisted my lips. What kind of question was that? "I'm regular."

Without any sort of invitation, she parted my robe and looked right at my twat.

"Uh..."

"You could use a wax."

Apparently, my curiosity was consent. She reclined the chair and shifted my legs, once again parting my robe. My eyes went wide as she slathered wax on me. There was no getting that shit off now.

Biting my lips, I frowned and held my breath, anticipating the pain to come. Why had I opened my mouth?

The strip of fabric pressed into my skin and then—

"Fuck you, you fucking fuck!" I cupped my poor vagina and glared at Latisha. *"Are you crazy?"* Fuck. I was going to pass out from the pain. Why the hell did women do this?

The sadist with the wax weapons laughed. "I have cooling gel. I'll put some on as soon as I do the other side."

"The other side!" I practically fell off the chair getting to my feet and knotted my robe. "I'm good. I'll shave the rest."

Then I frowned. My vagina was closing up. Literally locking together like some sort of sea mollusk in the deepest abyss of the darkest part of the ocean. Glancing at my pelvis, I turned and opened my robe and whimpered. Sticky shit was all over me. I lifted my leg and whimpered again.

"I haven't removed all the wax yet."

Oh, God. I was going to have to finish this or walk around with Venus flytrap pussy for the rest of my life. Reluctantly, I slid back onto the chair. As Latisha got back to work I tried to think of anything this painful that men might go through to make their genitals more attractive. There was nothing.

We women got the shit end of the stick all the way around, period cramps, childbirth, hot flashes. The next time I heard of a man complain about getting a finger up his ass for a prostate exam I was going to laugh. This girl had no sympathy for the opposite sex after this.

The strip tore away.

"Goddamn it! Fuck!"

13

That night I joined Remington for dinner. I had expected to eat at the house, but now that he was walking around the man didn't idle long. It was nice to have an evening just the two of us.

He took me to a nice restaurant looking over the ocean. Remington was fancy business and did things with old-school class. I realized this when he took the liberty of ordering for both of us. "We'll start with two dry martinis and the fugu."

The waiter nodded and left. I googled fugu. "Um, we're eating a puffer fish?" All I could think of was the cast from *Finding Nemo*.

"It's a delicacy."

"It says here one drop of poison could kill

an adult. Holy shit, a hundred people die a year from eating fugu. Are you trying to kill me?" People kept trying to hurt me today.

"Put your phone away, Meyers."

I slid my phone into my bag, unsure if I was brave enough to risk my life for food. "So…"

Remington eyed me and frowned. "You've lost weight."

"I've been under some stress."

"Understandable, but your friend's recovering."

"Speaking of my friends, could you please not hit on them?"

He smirked. "I don't think she's interested in a man my age."

"You're right. So stop."

The waiter delivered our drinks and my eyes watered as I took a sip. "Wow, that's one dry martini."

Remington sipped his without issue. "Hale doesn't want you to work for me."

"Hale isn't the boss of me."

"Are you sure?"

My lips twisted. I wasn't sure who was running the Calamity Rayne Show these days. Elle used to be my director, but then I started taking orders from Remington until Elle got hurt. Now, we were all jumbled together and

Hale wanted to call the shots, but I sort of wanted to call them myself, only not really *by* myself. Gah! I had no clue what I wanted.

"Do you think I made a mistake moving in with him?"

"Yes."

Well, that was blunt. "Why?"

"Because Hale has a lot on his plate right now and so do you."

"Not really. I mean, there's Elle, but other than that—"

"Exactly what I'm talking about, Meyers. There should be something other than your friend's prognosis directing your life. You're supposed to be looking at college courses."

"Remington, you know that isn't happening."

"I know no such thing. You made a deal with me and I expect you to uphold your end of the bargain."

The whole college thing happened when he refused to meet his granddaughter. Once he met her, I was over our bargain. Apparently, he wasn't. "I have no interest in a business major."

"Then major in something else."

I arched a brow and laughed. "So you'd be okay with me choosing something like art or philosophy."

"I would." He took another sip of his martini. "The point is to get you moving in some sort of direction. Your life is stagnant."

"I haven't told Hale you offered to pay for me to go back to school."

"It doesn't concern him."

I rolled my eyes. "This is why he gets weird about me working for you. He's your son, Remington. Stop treating him like the opposition."

"He claims to want the best for you, but he's holding you back."

"No, he's not."

He arched a brow.

"If I told Hale I was going back to school he wouldn't object."

"So why haven't you told him yet?"

"Because I haven't made up my mind about going."

Remington shook his head. "You've been drifting through life for years, Meyers. It's time to decide something."

I wished he'd ordered me something else to drink. I wanted the alcohol in my glass, but it was too strong to chug. "So tell me what you think I should do."

"You should come back to work for me. Take a few night courses. Help your friend find an apartment. And get that girl out of my son's house."

Whoa! I frowned at that last bit. "Do you have something against Elle?"

"Not her. The other one. What the hell's her name? Brianne? Courtney?"

"Brynlee?"

"Yes."

I grinned, shocked. I finally found someone who didn't immediately *love* the nanny. "Why don't you like her?"

"I don't have an opinion about her. But I know how these things work. If you think I never fooled around with my children's au pairs you're out of your mind."

All of my illogical opinions settled into something heavy and unwelcome. "Hale wouldn't do that."

"I'm not worried about Hale. She's younger, good with his daughter, nurturing, and very aware of his success. Get her out of there."

"But what about Elara?" Remington already made it clear he didn't want me playing nanny.

"There are plenty of unattractive women out there. Hire one of them."

I stared at my martini and sighed. "I don't think she'd do anything. Hale and I live together now. That would take balls to try something with me in the house."

"You're not home now."

"Jesus. Are you trying to ruin my dinner?"

The waiter delivered a plate that looked like fried licorice. Remington sliced a shard off and swiped it in a dollop of white sauce. I waited to see if he died.

"Try it. You'll like it."

Cutting off a small strip, I dipped and sent out a little prayer that, should I be poisoned to death by a cooked puffer fish, someone had the sense to erase my browsing history on my laptop. *I was curious!*

Popping the small bite in my mouth I chewed and, well, it was rather tasty.

"Do you like it?"

I sliced off another piece. "It's good. I like this sauce. What are these little orange balls?"

"Roe."

They were delicious. I took another bite. "What is that, a plant?"

"They're fish eggs."

I stilled. "Aw, man." More images from *Finding Nemo* filled my head, only now I was imagining the sad beginning when the mom and all Nemo's siblings died.

"Stop being such a pacifist and enjoy your meal. You eat chicken eggs."

True.

Remington ordered bluefin tuna for our

main course and that was equally delicious. On the limo ride home, he readdressed our earlier conversation. "You know you have a room at my house, Meyers."

"I know." But I couldn't do that to Hale. "This is the first time in my life I've committed to something. I don't want to walk away like I always do."

"Maybe you should consider if this is about proving something to yourself, or being where you want to be."

"I love Hale." I did. I loved him. We were in love. He was my boyfriend.

"Sometimes we love the wrong people."

Truer words had never been spoken from a man like Remington Davenport. He'd loved too many people, and his love came with zero reassurance.

When the limo pulled up to Hale's I thanked Remington for dinner and told him I'd think about everything we talked about. When I let myself in the front door my ears perked up.

Laughter came from the den so I went to see what was so funny. There was nothing funny about what I saw. Elara lay on her back on the carpet while Hale and Brynlee kneeled beside her, their heads so close they were nearly touching. Two glasses of red wine perched on the side table.

"Who's got a big smile?" Brynlee cooed, a little too breathily for my taste, and Hale chuckled.

"What are you guys doing?" I asked, unimpressed, since no one seemed to care that I was home.

Hale turned and grinned. "Elara's smiling. Come see."

I stepped close and my frigid mood warmed, because who could frown when looking at a smile that angelic? Then Brynlee blew raspberries on Elara's stomach and my grin fell away. That was my game.

"How was dinner?"

"Good." I paused as the nanny's blonde flowing hair fell in waves to the carpet. She wasn't a part of this conversation and someone should tell her I could see down her shirt. "I think you missed a button. I'm tired. I'm heading up to bed."

His gaze turned guarded. "Okay. I'll be up once I get Elara down."

Why the fuck was she here? I turned and went upstairs, but their laughter continued and with every echo, I grew more disgusted.

I was appalled by my insecurities, shocked that Hale acted like nothing was wrong with her being here when he was completely capable of taking care of his child after work. And I was utterly repulsed that Remington's warning about the other woman had made everything worse.

I climbed into bed and waited. He didn't come up for over an hour and when he finally entered the room I thought it would be best to pretend I was asleep.

Hale's body curled into mine and I frowned when I felt his erection. Was that a souvenir from downstairs or something he just acquired here?

"You awake, baby?" His hand slipped under my shirt and cupped my breast. "Rayne?"

"I'm sleeping." I kept my eyes closed.

A slow chuckle rumbled in his chest as his fingers found my nipple. "I want you."

I nudged him away. "I'm not in the mood."

He sighed and turned onto his back. When he didn't say anything I assumed he'd fallen asleep, but his aggravated breathing proved he wasn't. He tossed and turned for about twenty minutes, keeping me awake until he got out of bed and quietly left the bedroom.

I sat up, wondering where he was going. The sensor lights on the back of the house kicked on and I climbed out of bed. Looking down at the back patio, I watched him take a seat by the pool, obviously frustrated. Then another light flicked on and I saw Brynlee step out of the guesthouse wearing only a little nightgown.

My breath fogged the glass as it staggered past my lips. "Go back inside," I whispered.

Hale turned as Brynlee took a step closer to the pool but stopped halfway between him and the guesthouse. He looked at her and my stomach cramped. So help me God, if he touched her I'd go ballistic. When I saw she was talking I searched the window for a lock, desperately needing to hear what she said.

The window didn't open. What good was that?

I watched in horror as she took another step, but her progress halted when Hale held up a hand. My heart raced. He stood and said something and then he turned and disappeared into the house. Where did he go? Brynlee's shoulders slouched, but she didn't move. *Go back to your house—*

"I thought you were asleep."

I pivoted, all the heat leaching from my face. "I was looking at stars."

He glanced at the window and back to me.

"I saw the light come on," I confessed. *And*

then the nanny come on to you. I glanced back out the window. Brynlee was gone.

He frowned. "I was just getting some air."

For some reason, I nodded rather than telling him what I saw.

Moving slowly, I climbed back into bed and rested my head on my pillow. Hale returned to his side, but this time he didn't touch me. The longer the silence lasted the closer I came to the verge of tears.

I assumed Hale had fallen asleep, until he said, "I'll start looking for a new nanny tomorrow."

Relief should have been instantaneous, but it wasn't. My victory was muddled with unanswerable questions. I wanted to know if he was letting her go so the temptation wouldn't be there or if this was about doing something for me or if I really wasn't that crazy and something bad just happened by the pool.

But maybe she'd done nothing wrong and was only losing her job because her boss's girlfriend was a psychopath. It sucked being the crazy person in this scenario and I couldn't take the guilt.

"You don't have to fire her."

The blankets shifted and I turned to my side, facing him. His expression was unreadable and he remained silent. Sliding closer to him, I placed a hand on his chest.

"Hale?"

He caught my fingers and squeezed gently, but didn't look at me. Then he shifted, and pinned me beneath him, his mouth closing over mine as he kissed me deeply. "I want you."

I couldn't shake the horrible feeling that he was getting all turned on by the nanny each time he came on to me. "Slow down there, tiger."

His body pressed into mine as he nuzzled his way to my neck. "Why are you keeping yourself from me lately?"

"I'm not." Was I? We'd had sex a few days ago. Or was that last week?

"Rayne, I need to be with you. That connection's important."

Hearing the longing in his voice and recognizing the stress in his eyes, I nodded. I didn't want to examine my reasoning too closely because there were too many unfavorable theories floating through my head. I only knew I wanted to be the one to meet his needs, no one else.

The blankets kicked away as he removed his pants and briefs, his body sliding over mine. He peeled down my panties and wrenched my legs apart, lining his cock up to my sex, but not penetrating.

"Tell me you want me, Rayne. I need to hear you say it."

"I want you," I rasped. And I did. I wanted him all to myself and I didn't want any young women coming onto him, especially in our house.

He thrust into me and whispered, "I don't like this distance between us and I'm tired of missing you."

My body bowed against his as I moaned. He cursed and thrust again, his hands crawling over me, needy and rough. I held onto him as he fucked me hard, my cries likely traveling to other parts of the house, but I didn't care. I did wish I'd gotten that window open though.

There was something about being taken in such an impassioned way that had my insecurities scattering. His desire scared the timid parts of me into hiding and coaxed the braver sides out to play.

He wasn't gentle and he wasn't apologetic, but he was certainly demanding. He pulled me into him, treating my body to blatant pleasure as he commanded I come again and again. It was as though he were punishing me in the most erotic way, proving all of my unspoken doubts were unfounded and showing me exactly how deeply he needed me. It was as if he sensed my worry, suffered my withdrawal, and this was his way of telling me he wouldn't stand for it.

I learned the lesson well.

When he finished, we were both spent. His body collapsed beside me and then came reality. "We forgot a condom again."

Hale cursed. "I'll remember next time. I promise."

I really needed to go on birth control. Tomorrow morning, making that call was the first thing I planned to do because the last thing we needed was another circumstance taking precedence over the natural progression of things.

Hale pulled me into his body and kissed my shoulder. "Get some sleep, baby. I love you."

"I love you, too."

It's the fuzz!

14

"How's it going down there?" My eyes wondered around the uncluttered doctor's office. "Find anything interesting?"

It wasn't like I expected my new gynecologist to pull out a school ring or anything, but I was nervous, so I kept talking. I should know a person pretty well to be in this situation, but at the moment I couldn't even remember my doctor's name.

The stool rolled back and her glove snapped off. "Everything looks good."

"So can I close up shop?"

"You can sit up."

Finally. I lowered my legs and closed my little smock, hiding away my money shot with the provided paper blanket. It wasn't as nice as the airplane blankets, but it kept me concealed.

The doctor made some notes in a laptop and said, "I'm going to write you a prescription for the pill, but I want to go over some general guidelines since you've never used oral contraception before."

I nodded and paid close attention as she explained about hormones and the lining of my uterus and the hindering of sperm. It all seemed so government op, like we were staging a defense strategy at the frontlines of my cervix and Hale's sperm was the enemy. None of his little soldiers were breaching my barricade. I was very confident in her plan because Hale and I sucked at remembering condoms and anything was better than winging it.

"It's important to take the pill at the same time every day. If you start the pill today, you should use a backup method for the first seven days until the birth control takes effect."

"I'll start today."

When I left the doctor's with a sample pack of pills in hand, I swallowed one as soon as I reached the car. The pills were tiny, so I didn't think I needed a drink, but as I backed out of the parking lot I could swear the little bugger got stuck on my uvula.

I cleared my throat and made hacking noises as I drove, trying to dislodge that tiny pill stuck in my throat. Even when I was sure it had dissolved, that pill haunted me.

I was in Hale's Rolls, which he kept immaculate, so there weren't any water bottles lying around. When I saw a corner store I pulled over. Clearing my throat, I walked into the store and grabbed a bottle of water, chugging it while in the line at the register. When it was my turn, I reached for my purse and —oh no.

"Um... I think I left my purse in the car." I hoped it was in the car.

The cashier narrowed his eyes. "You pay cash."

I searched my pockets, which didn't exist because I'd worn a dress. Putting the bottle on the counter, I said, "Let me run out to the car and grab money. How much is it?"

He glanced at the bottle. "Two-fifty."

"*Two*-fifty? For a bottle of water?" What a racket. "I'll be right back."

The cashier moved the bottle aside and rang up the next customer. Back in the day, people would offer to help out a stranger, but at two-fifty a bottle, who could afford it?

I searched Hale's car and cursed when I found nothing. Not only did the man not have a single dime tucked in the cushion of the seats, my purse wasn't there either.

"Damn it." I went back into the store and faced the cashier. "I don't have any money on me, but I can come back later and pay you."

He scowled. "You pay now."

Okay, there was clearly a language barrier. "I lost my purse." The line grew and my face heated. Turning to the other customers, I said, "Can anyone help a girl out? I lost my purse."

Amazing. Every last one of them acted like I was speaking in a foreign language. Facing the cashier again, I said, "I work for the Davenports. You know the Davenports?" I figured if he knew who I belonged to he'd realize I was good for it.

He examined the bottle and pointed to the cap. "Open. No good now. You pay."

Trying for patience, I explained, "I know it's open. I'll pay you, but I have to get some money." When I saw he didn't understand, I huffed and held up a hand. "I'll be back in five minutes."

Returning to the car, I backed out of the spot. If I had my purse I'd have called Hale, but my phone was probably sitting in the little dressing room at the gynecologist's office. Plus, it would take Hale twice as long to get to me. Better to just get the purse and go back and pay for the damn water.

Not being from around there, I saw plenty

of odd things whenever I went out. Sometimes Key West seemed like a different planet. It was balmy, teeming with energy, and very colorful, but it was also foreign, seeing that I seldom ventured out without the Davenport entourage. I felt like a total idiot when I couldn't find the doctor's office I'd just left, so I continued to circle the same streets, thinking I must have just missed it.

After twenty minutes of driving, I had to pee. "Come on... Where is it?"

Coming across a road I didn't recognize, I turned the car and a moment later I realized why that was a mistake. Okay, this wasn't a road so much as it was a cul-de-sac of vendors.

Putting the car in reverse, I glanced in the rearview and... Well, shit.

A police car blocked me in and his lights were definitely flashing. I put the car in park and rolled down the window as he approached.

"You can't drive down here, miss."

I fidgeted because I really had to pee and now I was nervous. "Sorry. I got lost."

"Where are you heading?"

I couldn't tell him my gynecologist, so I smiled and tried to flirt my way out this. "If you'll just let me pass, I'll be on my way."

Apparently, that wasn't the right thing to say. He eyed the car, which reeked of wealth and here I was in my boho dress, sweating like a pig, fidgeting so I didn't pee all over Hale's leather seats, with a bag of pills to my right.

"License and registration."

I silently cursed and reached into the glove compartment. When I handed him the registration and insurance, I explained, "I don't have my purse, which is where I keep my license."

He reviewed the paperwork. "And I'm guessing you're not Hale Davenport."

"No, sir, but I work for the Davenports if that helps."

He stepped away, speaking into a walkie-talkie and eying the back of the Rolls Royce. When he returned, he said, "I'm going to need you to step out of the car."

"Look, officer, I swear I didn't steal the car. I left my purse—"

"Your plate's been reported. Someone driving this vehicle was identified shoplifting about thirty minutes ago."

"Shoplifting? I told him I'd be back!"

The door opened. "Step out of the car, miss."

Unlatching my seatbelt, I slid out of the car and hung my head. The next thing I knew I was sitting in the back of a locked squad car on my way downtown. The jig was up. The fuzz had finally apprehended me. This was a new level of calamity I wasn't prepared for and I still *really* needed to pee.

Thankfully, the officer didn't cuff me or anything so dramatic. When we reached the station he let me use the bathroom and then told me to wait at a chair beside an empty desk. I watched as he made a call and then I waited, figuring someone would eventually come rescue me.

All of this to protect my ovaries from implantation.

It took about thirty minutes for Hale to arrive and he must have entered through a different door because I didn't get a chance to speak to him before I saw him talking to Officer What's His Name.

When he finally approached me in the criminal detention zone, I looked up at him and pouted. "This is why I need a chaperone."

He smirked. "Apparently you were detained for shoplifting *and* grand theft auto. I got them to drop the charges."

"Thank you."

He laughed. "What happened?"

"I don't want to talk about it. Can we please leave?"

We walked out to the lot where a bunch of police cars were parked but I didn't see the Wraith. "What about your car?"

"Alfonse went to pick it up." He walked me to a convertible BMW and opened my door. "Get in, Bonnie Parker."

"Ha-ha," I said dryly. He was the farthest thing from Clyde. "My purse is at the gynecologist's office. But I think you sent me to some collapsible setup because I can't find the building now."

"They called. Alfonse already picked it up for you."

"Oh." I tried imagining the gardener slash chauffeur walking into a woman's facility and walking out with my pink purse. "Where are we going?"

"Well, you've been naughty."

I pursed my lips. "It wasn't my fault. These things just happen to me. I told the clerk I'd be back to pay him for the water, but he wouldn't listen. And why don't you have money in your car?"

"There's always a credit card hidden under the front seat, for future crime sprees."

"You're so full of jokes today."

He pulled over just outside of Duval Street and came around to open my door. Escorting me to a bench, he said, "Wait here. Can I trust you not to rob anyone?"

"Seriously, you're not funny."

He chuckled and disappeared into a little

shop. He returned a moment later with two popsicles. Sitting at my side, he handed me one of the sticks, which had some sort of chocolate covered fantasy on the end.

I eyed it cautiously. "What is this?"

"It's frozen key lime pie."

I took the stick and nibbled. Sweet lime flavor burst over my tongue. "You're rewarding me?"

He took a bite of his own and relaxed. "I happen to like when you're naughty."

"I've never been arrested before." I licked at the hard chocolate shell and bit into the soft lime flavored center. Holy happy mouth, this was good.

"Did they put you in cuffs?"

"No. Thank God."

He snickered. "That would have been something to see."

"It's not funny. Stuff like this only happens to me."

Turning his silver gaze on me, he grinned. "I'm not making fun of you, Rayne. I love rescuing you."

I slouched and finished my frozen pie.

"Hey." He nudged my shoulder. "Cheer up. Nothing's on your record and the store clerk's been paid."

I sucked on the wooden stick. I could eat

about ten more of them.

Hale stood and held out a hand. "Come on. Let's blow off the day and have some fun."

I finally smiled. "Really?"

"Yeah." He took our sticks and tossed them in a nearby trashcan. We didn't return to the car but rather strolled down Duval Street.

Bikes leaned against a cement wall and pedestrians rambled down roads and sidewalks. The humid air kissed my skin as a temperate breeze teased the palm leaves overhead.

The buildings were a mixture of restaurants, hotels, and cafés. A steady melody of bicycle bells rang as we wandered along the street hand-in-hand. It was the first time we'd actually ventured out like tourists and it felt so incredibly normal. I loved every second of it.

Diners' conversations spun a low hum in the background as people occupied tables shaded by large umbrellas. Though I'd never been to New Orleans, Duval Street reminded me of a tame version of Bourbon Street, something about that shameless, almost decadent, seediness that pulled a person in. Everything was so alfresco and thrumming with life.

We paused to watch a native roll a handmade cigar. A grand marquis in the distance lit and I gasped at the majestic display. "Is that an old theater?"

"It's actually a pharmacy now. But they did a magnificent job restoring it. Let's check out Mallory Square."

He led us through a more congested area of vendors and the vibe picked up. Doo Wop spilled from bars onto the street.

I gasped again. "Is that Coyote Ugly place like the one in the movie?"

He nodded. "Did you want to go in?"

Passing the door I saw several women stomping along the bar in daisy dukes and cowboy boots. "Let's keep walking." There was so much to see.

We entered an open plaza surrounded by brick archways and mobs of people. The music grew louder and switched to mariachi. Everyone we passed had a smile on their face. Vacationers traveled at an ambling pace, carrying a verve of energy that spoke of fun and day-long happy hours. I wanted to be a vacationer.

No one rushed and everyone looked cheerful. I was smiling too. The ocean lay before us, an endless puddle of blue, as we weaved through crowds and kiosks. Vendors peddled everything from popcorn to jewelry.

"I feel like we're in a Jimmy Buffet video."

Hale chuckled and shifted his arm over my shoulders as we walked along the water watching the ships come into the harbor. Key West was a very accepting place. As men and women strolled through the town, so did men holding hands with other men and vice versa.

Hale pulled me to a small wagon full of glimmering gems and silver. "Pick out something you like."

I stared at the kiosk, so many shiny things. "I don't wear jewelry."

"You don't like it?"

I shrugged. I mostly couldn't afford it. "Every girl likes pretty things. I'm just afraid I'll lose it."

He grinned. "Try this on." He cradled my hand and slid a ring onto my finger, but it was too big.

The merchant spoke with a Cuban accent. "She looks like a size six." He eyed Hale, drawing some conclusion about his pockets and slid open a drawer with a key. "You might like these better."

Diamonds twinkled in the sunlight and my eyes went wide. "I don't need anything."

"Don't be ridiculous." Hale leaned over the velvet-lined drawer and examined the selection. Plucking something with quite a sparkle from the case, he turned and I balled my hands into fists.

"What are you doing? Give me your hand."

I lifted my right hand and he slid the heavy ring onto my finger and smiled. "Perfect."

The ring was delicate, a thin platinum band with a diamond anchor running horizontally across my finger. The points of the anchor were subtle little hearts. It looked too fancy for me, but my recent manicure helped pull it off. I glanced at him and smiled. "It's really pretty."

"So are you."

He turned and paid the merchant, then took my hand as we continued to walk. His thumb occasionally ran over the ring, his eyes glancing at me every few seconds.

I wasn't sure why he picked that specific ring, but I loved that it was an anchor, because in a way that's what Hale was to me. *My* anchor.

We reached a pier shaded by umbrella-top tables and sat. Hale ordered two margaritas as musicians played from a wooden stage.

"It's so nice here." The waitress returned and passed me my drink.

"It's nice being here with you. I haven't walked around like this for ages." He reached across the table and rubbed his fingers over mine, drawing my attention back to the diamond ring. It was the nicest jewelry I'd ever owned.

"Thank you for this."

"I'd like to buy you another ring someday." He picked up my left hand. "Maybe for this finger."

Oh, boy. I drew in a breath and sipped my margarita. "Why is it getting crowded here all of a sudden?"

"The sun's about to set. They put on a show every night."

I squinted at the water and Hale excused himself for a minute. When he returned, he put a straw hat on my head, which shaded a great deal of the glare coming off the ocean. "Thanks."

"You look good in hats."

In the distance, street performers swallowed fire and juggled machetes, but the most interesting sight to see was the man in front of me. I tried to recall how stuffy he'd been when we first met, a time when I mistook his interest as irritation. Now I realized he only spoke when he had something to say and he always meant what he said.

"Why were you interested in me?" I asked.

He tilted his head. "You're different."

I scrunched my nose. "I'm weird."

"The best kind of weird," he said, not daring to disagree. Sitting back, he sighed, his mouth curving and his lashes lowering as an expression of ease took over his face. "You counterbalance my life. You make me laugh and I love seeing what you're going to do next. You're unpredictable."

Being that he was a bit of a control freak, I found it odd my unpredictability attracted him. "And that's a good thing?"

He nodded. "You always pique my interest." He sipped his drink. "Plus, you're sexy as hell in the most effortless way."

My mouth pursed. Well, that was nice. Someone go deflate my ego before it floats away...

The waitress returned and Hale ordered another round of drinks and a tray of conch fritters. As the sun dipped below the horizon we were given a breathtaking show of pink skies, as sultry music accompanied its blazing decent.

Walking back to the car, I leaned into him, holding his hand and wrapping my other hand around his. Despite my whole run-in with the law thing, it turned out to be a fabulous day.

Once we were in the car on our way home, it occurred to me we'd been gone for almost six hours. "Who has Elara?"

He'd said he was letting Brynlee go, but I wasn't sure if my near-arrest interfered with his plans.

"Marta took her to my dad's. She's keeping her overnight."

"Oh."

"Barrett took Elle out on the sloop."

"I'm sorry, the what?"

"The sloop. His sailboat."

I frowned. "Just the two of them?"

"They're adults, Rayne. They'll be fine."

"How long are they going to be gone?" I didn't know if Elle would remember to pack her anxiety medicine and I worried I might have to hurt Barrett if he took advantage of my friend.

"They'll be back sometime tomorrow."

"They're having a sleepover?" That wasn't good. However, that also meant Hale and I finally had some privacy.

What could I honestly do about Elle and Barrett anyway? She was an adult, if a confused one. However, I couldn't claim I was any different. Did any of us really know what the heck we were doing?

Elle did. No matter how much she'd changed, she was still in there. Little signs had been cropping up more and more. Just yesterday she had mentioned some celebrity gossip, impressing me with her apt recall. Maybe I was underestimating my friend's ability to make proper choices for herself. And maybe I was being too hard on Hale's brother. No. Barrett was still a slut.

The evening air cooled my skin as Hale maneuvered the convertible along the streets back to his house. "I had a really nice day with you."

"Ditto." His fingers laced with mine, his thumb once again brushing over the ring.

When we reached the house, I was suddenly nervous, which was silly, because this was Hale. It was quiet and I was happy to see my purse resting on the dining room table beside Hale's car keys. I removed my hat and took a minute to savor the lovely day we had.

Hale's hands gently touched my shoulders, which had gotten sun, and I shivered. "Do you want a drink?" he asked softly, his lips grazing the side of my throat.

"Sure."

I followed him to the bar where he poured two glasses of wine. My gaze traveled to the guesthouse, which was dark. "Is Brynlee gone?"

He handed me a long-stemmed glass. "She's gone." He clinked his glass to mine and I sipped, relief finally settling in.

"I'm sorry if I overreacted about her."

He placed his glass on the bar and studied me for a moment. "You didn't. I won't have anyone coming between us, Rayne. Especially not some kid."

As much as my insecurities got the better of me from time to time, his words startled me. "What do you mean?"

His posture was casual as he eyed me, long, fit body leaning against the bar. "I needed a nanny to see to my daughter's well-being and comfort. I don't need anyone but you seeing to mine."

"Last night at the pool—"

"Was the first and last time she made an inappropriate invitation in my home. Had she made a comment like that before, she would have been gone long ago."

"What did she say?" I was afraid to know, but at the same time, my curiosity was endless.

"Does it matter?"

It probably shouldn't. What mattered was that Hale had handled the situation the moment it became a concern. I shrugged because I didn't want to dwell on issues that no longer mattered.

"Rayne." He waited until I lifted my gaze to his. "I love *you*. I know we'll disagree and I'm perfectly aware of how stressful the last few weeks have been, but you never need to question my loyalty to you. *You* are the woman I want. Only you."

Feeling vindicated, I smiled. "I'm glad."

He removed my glass from my hand and

placed it beside his. His gaze found mine, and the air in my lungs turned heavy. Stepping closer, he brushed his lips to mine and gently ran his fingers through my hair. My mouth opened as I tilted my face and he deepened the kiss.

Rather than the usual haste I'd grown accustomed to, he took his time, kissing me and holding me close. I sighed, as his lips worked down my throat and the hem of my dress lifted, but he didn't undress me. He merely teased the sensitive skin of my thigh with slow whirls of his fingertips.

"Come with me," he whispered, taking my hand and walking me up the stairs.

When we entered his room he watched me closely as he stripped off his jacket and shirt. I wondered if there would come a time when the sight of him wouldn't take my breath away.

My eyes feasted on his tanned chest and chiseled abdomen. Broad shoulders begged for the bite of my nails. I glanced at the ring on my finger and smiled.

Wearing only pants, he stepped close and looked in my eyes. My breath held as he lifted my dress, the material slithering off my heated skin and leaving me standing in only my bra and panties. His mouth closed tenderly over my shoulder, sending quivers to my core. As he peeled away my bra, my skin puckered in the slight chill of the air. My panties lowered and his touch drifted over my hips, between my thighs.

"So beautiful," he whispered, soft caressing fingers grazing my sex.

I wanted to touch him too, so I unbuttoned his pants and pushed them to his hips. He stepped forward as they fell to the ground in a heap and the heat of his body warmed my front. My hand slipped between us, cupping and stroking him as his mouth found mine.

Backing me to the bed, he gently lowered my body. My knees parted as his weight pressed over me. He was so patient, so tender. Rolling to his back, he reached for a condom and slid it over his length. I straddled him and he watched me through half-lidded eyes as I positioned my body over his.

Cupping my hips, he held me as I sank onto him. We both sighed as he filled me and pulled me close, catching my nipple between his soft lips.

I rocked over him, swaying and moaning with each glide of his hard body against mine. His grip tightened, but there was no hurry, no rush to be anything more than together.

We watched each other as we made love. Our foreheads pressed together as our breath mingled and we held each other tight. When we came we came as one and I shut my eyes and sighed. This was everything I'd been missing. It was the quiet that held us tight, secure within our relationship and absent of all the noise from the outside world.

"I love you, Hale."

He brushed his mouth over mine. "I love you, too, baby."

We slept only a few hours before reaching for each other in the dark. I'm not sure if it was me searching for him or him reaching for me, but we found one another and made love again sometime during those quiet hours.

When morning came my body was tender and my insecurities nowhere to be found. I watched Hale sleep until his mouth curved and I knew he was awake.

"Are you staring at me?" he mumbled.

"Yes. You have tiny freckles on your nose." They were far too boyish for such a responsible man, hidden like little secrets on his tanned skin.

His eyes opened and his body stretched in a blatant invitation. I glanced at the blankets, trying to discern if he was hard. Following my gaze, he threw the covers off his body and shamelessly put himself on display.

My cheeks heated and I looked away.

"Oh, no, you don't," he rasped, catching my chin. "You can't look at me like that then turn away."

My lips pursed as I tried to hide my smile. "Don't you go blaming me for *that*." I gestured to his erection.

"Oh, you did it." He tucked my hair behind my ear and tipped his chin in the direction of his hips.

I silently chuckled, knowing what he wanted, and twisted to face the foot of the bed as I slithered down his hard body, taking him into my mouth. He sucked in an audible breath, his hands roaming freely over my legs and ass.

"Back up." He pulled my knees, placing them on either side of his shoulders as he yanked my body down.

I squeaked as his tongue swiped at my sex, his fingers massaging into my ass and holding me to him. It was hard to concentrate while he was distracting me with soft strokes of his fingers and tongue.

His knees lifted as his hand traveled up my spine, directing my attention back to his cock. It was probably a terrible blowjob, but how was I supposed to think with him teasing me at the same time?

Finally, he flipped me onto my back and

put on a condom. "I need you," he rasped, dragging his tongue up my stomach and tracing my breasts. "I want it hard." Back onto my stomach, he hitched me to my knees, lining up our bodies and thrusting deep.

My fingers curled into the bedding as I rocked forward, moaning with every thrust. He held my shoulder, keeping my body arched at an angle that sent him deep. Once I was panting and wearing out, my chest flattened to the bed, he moved his legs outside of mine, making the fit extra tight as he pounded into me.

It was hard and it was wild, but it was absolutely Hale. His body quivered and jerked as he came. We were both spent and I'd likely be walking crooked for the rest of the day, but it was totally worth it.

This little escape from others was exactly what we needed. It reaffirmed the delicate connection we shared and all the bottled-up chemistry between us.

I sighed and rolled to my back. Hale fell to my side and pulled me close. I wanted to stay there forever, in his arms. As much as we had lives outside of those four walls, I could have remained there for the rest of my life and never missed a single thing. Finally, I felt anchored again.

15

The days that followed were so perfect, I wondered if all my previous angst and worry had been imagined. It seemed the wave of anxiety had passed and all systems were under a great *woonami* warning—that's a wooing tsunami.

While Hale searched for a new nanny, I delayed my plans to go back to work for Remington and spent the days helping with Elara. Elle had become quite the first mate and every day she and Barrett sailed somewhere new. Some nights they stayed in the cabin of his sloop and others they returned home.

I asked again if something was going on between the two of them, but she said no. I wasn't sure if the new Elle would lie to me, and maybe she wouldn't, but I couldn't imagine spending that many nights with a guy like Barrett Davenport and nothing happening.

The morning before their last excursion led me to believe my best friend was back but changed, more than anything else I'd witnessed so far. I'd just put Elara down for a nap and was quietly coming down the stairs when I paused at the sound of Barrett's voice.

"Don't forget the chips."

From the landing I could see Elle in the kitchen, but not Barrett. She nodded and placed a few snack bags in her pack. It was so ordinary, yet strange to see this side of Elle. Then I saw Barrett and my breath held.

He approached her from behind, leaning around her body to inspect the bag. "You got everything." He wasn't asking but praising.

Elle turned in the space of his body and the granite counter and smiled up at him. "I'm getting good at this."

Barrett smiled, but it wasn't the expression he flashed during photo shoots or when flirting with other pretty girls. This was a genuine smile I hadn't seen often—or ever. He carefully tucked a strand of Elle's blonde hair behind her ear, but that was as far as he went. There seemed to be a subtle tremor in the air that neither of them wanted to rattle. The moment stretched and I expected to see them kiss—after all, it was Barrett—but all he did was look at her.

"You're good at a lot of things."

The look on my friend's face was a priceless show of pride and confidence with so many vulnerable undertones, I decided whatever they were doing together was just fine and good for Elle. It might even be good for Barrett, too. I couldn't quite explain it to Hale when I tried. It wasn't so much of a sexual tension I felt as much as it was a shared common interest and delicate, newborn friendship. I knew then Elle had control of the situation and I could stand down.

Besides, I was enjoying my time with Hale's daughter more than I was willing to admit. Lately, her hearing and vision seemed so sharp. I could tell she was absorbing everything I said. Sometimes she'd even babble back and we'd have a lengthy conversation about her nine-week-old concerns and my ongoing deciphering of the world.

"And that is what you call a corn dog. You'll have to wait until you have teeth to try one. I'm not sure when you'll be getting your chompers, but I'll teach you about all the good carnival cuisine when you're ready. Funnel cake is another favorite."

As I pushed her stroller down the sidewalk

I continued to educate her on the sort of food I knew she'd never experience with the Davenports. Elara stared at me from under the canopy of her carriage and smiled. Sometimes her grin would falter and she'd look at me as if questioning my sanity, but I was pretty sure that was just gas.

"Are you excited to see your Grandpop? We're going to surprise him. Yes, we are. And he's going to be grumpy, but it has nothing to do with you, cuteness."

As I turned onto Remington's property I waved to Alfonse who was washing the limo out front. I left the stroller on the path and slid the diaper bag over my shoulder before gathering Elara into my arms. Letting myself in, I smiled at Marta who briefly came over to tickle Elara's foot.

Remington's voice echoed from the back of the house so I waited in the foyer for him to finish his call. Miles, who was organizing some papers in the kitchen, looked up and waved. He seemed to be adjusting well as Remington's right hand.

Swaying, so Elara didn't fuss, I waited and listened for the call to end.

"And what did I say was going to happen?" Remington grumbled, not sounding happy.

Elara babbled, her voice echoing over the marble tile, which had her eyes widening.

"Shh, shh, shh," I gently hushed her, swishing her slowly from side to side the way she liked.

"I've said from the start, giving her that property was a mistake and getting it back would be impossible. You didn't want to listen and now look at the mess on your hands." Remington paused. "The estate's been in the family for generations, Hale. You disrupted that. I can't help you."

I frowned at the mention of Hale's name. Were they talking about the New England property, the one Hale had used as part of his settlement with Elara's mom?

Jasmine didn't want a baby, but she sought comeuppance for the pregnancy. She was currently recovering in Paris on Hale's dime, and that was fine, being that she'd signed over custody to him, though he wasn't Elara's actual birth father.

Her biological father, for reasons I still couldn't fathom, would never be disclosed to the child or the public, but that was also fine because Hale was a great dad and Remington wasn't.

"I'm surrounded by idiots. Miles, get me a drink!" Apparently, he was off the phone.

"We came to visit," I announced, stepping into the den.

"Meyers. There's something on your hip."

I rolled my eyes. "Say hello to Grandpop."

Despite his posturing, Remington took the baby into his arms and grimaced in the most loving way. It was the sort of sneer that said the verdict was still out, but something in her little face appealed.

"You sure are a pretty little thing." He perched Elara on his knee, making frowny faces at her as she cooed and sighed.

"Mr. Davenport, I have your martini," Miles said.

"Put it on the table." Looking down his nose, he studied Elara under his lashes. "What brings you by, Meyers?"

"It's a nice day. We figured a walk would be fun."

"Getting a little comfortable in your apron strings."

I smiled and plopped the diaper bag on the floor as I dropped into a chair. "I'm having fun."

"Hale have any new candidates for the au pair position?"

There had been a couple interviews, but we hadn't found the perfect person yet. I wanted someone older. Hale wanted someone certified in CPR with a background in early childhood. His requirements were obviously more logical than mine, but we were trying to compromise, hopefully landing somewhere in the middle.

"We're still searching."

"At least he got that girl out of your hair." He shifted Elara and found a comfortable position. "Your friend's been spending a lot of time with my other son."

"She's more of a seaman than me. But she says there's nothing going on between her and Barrett." I sensed that might change very soon.

He chuckled. "Either way, it gets him out of my house. I can only take Barrett's philandering for so long."

"He learns from the best." I eased back and tucked my feet under my legs.

"Watch it. You're talking in front of my granddaughter."

I liked seeing Remington with Elara. It looked right and brought out his softer sides, which were still pretty crude and jagged, but I could tell he enjoyed her.

"Classes started at the university."

And now it was my turn to surprise him. "I picked up my books yesterday."

He arched a brow. "Did you?"

I nodded. "I'm taking astrology."

"Jesus Christ," he muttered.

I smirked. "You said I could take whatever I wanted."

He rolled his eyes. "You're set on keeping your head in the clouds. I suppose it's enough to get your feet wet."

And it was. I liked looking at stars and we had a deal. This way, everyone was happy, though I knew Remington would rather see me take something a bit more useful in the real world. "You were on the phone with Hale?"

His gaze drifted from Elara to me. "There's a situation."

My stomach pinched, but nothing as severe as I was used to. The Davenports were solution-oriented and they'd figure it out. "A situation with Jasmine?"

"You should talk to Hale about it."

"Oh, come on, Remington."

"She's pissed about his counter offer. Apparently, she's attached to the idea of living in New England."

I'd never been to that property, so I clarified. "When you went to Maine this summer were you staying at the estate?"

"Yes. Hale's portion is down a ways, but I checked out the renovations. She's certainly getting paid for her time."

My stomach soured as I considered that time also included her interactions with Remington—interactions that took place while Jasmine and Hale had an *arrangement.* Remington betrayed not only his son but also his beloved wife, Rachel. It was something he carried with him because Rachel died before he could ever make it right.

Hale was alive and well, but Remington showed little interest in making apologies there. The man had an almost arrogant entitlement in terms of helping himself to what others considered theirs.

It was fucked up and I hated even thinking about it because I loved Hale and part of me loved his father. The whole Jasmine thing was icky and I wanted it to go away, which was why there had been a counter offer, to begin with. If part of her settlement was Hale's portion of the New England estate, the woman would always be near the Davenports.

Hale, being so angry with his father after discovering his treachery, hadn't cared that this would be inconvenient for Remington. But once he calmed down, he realized he'd made a mistake. Revenge was not a natural motivator for Hale and he was now trying to renegotiate the terms and offer Jasmine a different property.

"But she's still in Europe, right?" I asked, hoping Hale still had time to negotiate.

"For now. Her lawyer's stirring the pot. It's never wise to renegotiate once you've established the upper hand. It reeks of weakness." His brow furrowed. "Meyers, I think she made a..." His head drew back. "That's your jurisdiction."

I laid out the changing mat and took Elara. Remington sipped his martini while I cleaned her up. Once she was fresh, I gave her a bottle and we continued to chat, but avoided further talk of Jasmine. It would all work out.

"You're good with her," he commented as Elara closed her eyes, resting in my arms.

"I haven't damaged her yet, so that's a plus."

"I dropped Barrett once. That probably explains a lot."

I laughed and tucked the bottle away in the diaper bag. "I should probably go. It's her nap time."

He nodded. "Wrap up that babysitter search so we can get back to reality."

I smiled and carried Elara back to her stroller. On the walk home I wondered about Jasmine. There was no doubt in my mind she didn't want Elara, but I still worried, unsure how ironclad the adoption papers actually were. Though it was in Hale's favor that the biological father was close by, it wasn't anything he could disclose in the public's eye.

When I got back to the house I carried Elara to her crib. Hale was in the office and Elle wasn't home. I cleaned up the kitchen from breakfast and made sandwiches for lunch. When I knocked on the office door, Hale waved me in, still on the phone.

Placing his plate on his desk, I sat across from him and ate as he finished his call. His eyes creased with stress and his mouth was tight. "Add another thirty grand to the offer and see what happens."

My eyes widened at the number, but I kept my thoughts to myself. When he hung up he sighed. "Thanks for lunch."

"I took Elara to see your dad."

"How did that go?" He was obviously distracted.

"I heard him talking to you on the phone. He said there's an issue with Jasmine."

He chewed his sandwich, his eyes watching me closely. When he swallowed he waved a hand. "I'm handling it. We have a few months until she's back in the states."

"Was the thirty thousand for her?" We rarely discussed money, but I was curious.

"On top of the money I already offered,

and her choice of property anywhere in New York."

I didn't know much about New York, but I knew living in the city was expensive. All of this money was in addition to the initial payout Jasmine got when she agreed to take the pregnancy to full-term. "She wants to live in New York?"

"It's where her career was."

I already had a guess, but I wanted to check because maybe I was wrong. "What does she do?"

"She's a model."

"Oh." *Figured.* Ugh.

His penis had been in the vicinity of her magnificent model vagina and I didn't know why I was thinking about that, but I was now very conscious of my meal and all the calories it hid. Who was I kidding? I had zero discipline or interest in competing with that woman. I shoved the last bit of my sandwich in my mouth. So worth it.

"It'll all work out. Eventually, I'll hit her price."

But he'd already paid her off. The house in New England was the final part of the deal. All of this exploitation of Hale's finances seemed like abuse.

"What if you pulled back your offer and she had no choice but to take it?"

"I can't do that." And I knew exactly why. There was always a risk to playing hardball and that risk was sleeping upstairs in a little pink jumper.

When he finished his lunch, I took our plates to the kitchen and washed them. My shoulders were tense, so I distracted myself by folding laundry and reorganizing Hale's pantry. I typically wasn't a neat freak, but there was something about touching those household items that made me feel good, as if claiming my domain. It was like playing house, something I hadn't done since childhood, but suddenly enjoyed again.

He came into the kitchen just as I was sorting through his silverware.

"Hey," I said, closing the drawer. "I put all the knives back in that wood thing on the counter."

He smiled, but it didn't reach his eyes.

"You okay?"

"Yeah. Stressed."

"Anything I can do to help?"

He arched a brow. "What are you offering?"

I glanced at the clock. "Elara will probably

be asleep for a while longer." I shrugged. "What do you want?"

His expression relaxed as he crossed his arms over his chest, easing his weight against the counter. "You."

I smirked. Well, okay.

Prancing closer to him, I gave a cheeky grin. "How do you want me?"

He studied me for a moment and I saw the shift in his gaze. Hale rarely showed his cards, but I could usually predict his hand by a glance or the way he breathed. He was definitely stressed and in need of letting off some steam. I usually benefited from his intense moods, so I was happy to help.

His fingers grazed my jaw. "I want you on your knees."

Yes, yes, yes. This was why I absolutely understood and respected blowjobs now. Before, they seemed like an assault of the tonsils that would be solely unpleasant. But since meeting Hale, I learned they were so much more.

There was this whole power play thing about them, me submitting and giving him control until he slowly but surely lost it. Women might start a BJ on lower ground, but if done properly, a good blowjob could bring a man to *his* knees.

My eyes followed him as I lowered to the floor. "Like this?"

He gave a curt nod and unfolded his arms. Resting his palms flat on the countertop, he looked at me and waited. I loosened his belt and he was already hard by the time I had his pants open. Glancing up at him, I batted my eyelashes and he nodded.

Rising off my heels, I stroked him gently. He sighed and tipped his head back. I kissed the tip and licked up his shaft.

He grunted. "You're being a tease."

I glanced up at him and grinned before taking him into my mouth. Breath hissed through his teeth as his fingers knotted in my hair. I shut my eyes and let him direct me, using my mouth to ease his stress.

There was nothing gentle about his hold, but every time I glanced at his face I saw his love and affection. When I felt him getting close I tightened my lips and sucked harder. He growled and jerked my hair back, his control slipping fast.

Staring at me for a heated moment, his eyes darkened as his breath labored. "I need you."

He yanked me to my feet and bent my body over the counter, my feet arching and toes pressing into the floor. My dress lifted as the sound of my panties tearing rent the air. I was already soaking wet and moaned as he thrust deep, filling me to the hilt. My arms stretched over the granite surface as his hands pressed into mine, holding me in place as he thrust hard.

My cries echoed through the house, reverberating with the smacking sound of flesh. It was a relief, no longer having to waste time on condoms. Since the Pill had taken effect Hale took full advantage of having me whenever the mood struck, not that he ever really hesitated before.

His gravelly voice mingled with my pitched cries as he moaned and pounded into me. My body tightened and fluttered as he fucked me to orgasm and then filled me with his release.

I trembled as his weight gradually blanketed my damp skin. He kissed my shoulder and whispered, "Thank you, baby. I needed that."

I giggled. Apparently, we both did. "Anytime, sailor."

He smacked my ass and I jumped as he withdrew. "Sorry about your panties."

"Totally worth it," I rasped, peeling my body off the counter.

Standing, my legs were a bit shaky and he helped me adjust my clothes. The front door opened and Elle came in. Hale turned and zipped his pants, taking a moment to latch his belt.

Elle paused the second she spotted us in the open kitchen and raised a brow. "Sorry. Am I interrupting?"

Hale smiled and kissed my temple. "I have some work to finish. I'll see you in a little bit."

I grinned at Elle, sure my face was flushed. "We were just ... organizing."

"I can see that by your hair." She dropped her bag on a stool and folded her hands on the counter.

I grinned. We just had sex there. "So how was sailing?"

"Awesome," she sighed. "I really like boats. Did I used to like boats?"

"Not that I recall. How's Barrett?" Inquiring minds wanted to know...

She smiled and rolled her eyes. "He's so funny. You guys should come out with us sometime. I could show you all my maritime knowledge."

"Did he show you his ... mast?" I wasn't too savvy on the nautical terms, but I knew the mast was the big post that held the sails or something like that.

Elle snorted. "No."

I couldn't take it anymore. "Give me something, Elle. You two have spent every day together for a week. You expect me to believe nothing's going on?" *And I saw that moment in the kitchen...*

"Nothing's going on, Ray. I swear."

I frowned. That didn't make sense. Barrett always had something going on and Elle always had a sort of celebrity crush on him. "Why not?"

She shrugged. "I'm just..." Her lips pursed. "What if I do it wrong?"

"I think you have us confused."

She smiled, but I recognized true concern in her eyes. "I don't remember sex."

My eyes widened. "Really?"

She nodded. "I mean, I remember dating people, but ... as far as doing the actual deed, I can't remember much."

"Oh." Well, I could see how that might be a problem. "Maybe the guys you dated weren't that memorable, to begin with."

For a good part of my life, sex was terrible for me. But now I got it and I was sad for Elle. She was missing out on something incredible.

"I think he tried to kiss me the other day, but I got nervous and moved away."

I hesitated. "Elle, I don't know if Barrett's the right person to experiment with. He seems to only move at one speed and it's faster than usual."

"Really? I think he's the perfect guinea pig. He has plenty of experience. And as far as moving fast, he's been really patient with me."

Taking a deep breath I accepted there would be no talking her out of this. "Well, just remember to use a condom. Davenports have strong swimmers." And Barrett sailed his mast in international waters.

"Can you give me some pointers?"

My eyebrows shot up. "Me?" When she nodded I bit my lip. "Um...never stick your finger up a guy's ass without explicit permission. I did that once and the guy didn't take it too well."

"Ew! Why would you do that?"

"I heard it makes them come faster." And I was curious, which we'd already established.

"What else?"

"I don't know, Elle. Watch porn."

"What?"

"Porn. Pornography. Videos of people having sex."

Her eyes widened. "Where the hell am I gonna find that?"

"Oh, boy." I glanced at the office door and to the coffee table where I'd left my phone. "Give me a minute."

I took the baby monitor into the office and set it on Hale's desk. "Can you get Elara when she wakes up? I need to help Elle with something."

"Sure. Is everything all right?"

"Yeah, just girl stuff."

Once I grabbed my phone, I followed Elle up to her room where we locked the door. I also stole two pints of ice cream from the freezer on the way, because it was customary to have treats during any sort of theater.

"Okay. Buckle up. We'll start with an amateur search, because in reality, no one talks that cheesy."

I did a quick online search and the site I frequently visited popped up before I finished typing. "It does that because Google's smart. It has nothing to do with my recent search history," I lied and typed *amateur sex.*

"Holy shit," Elle said as a close up of a penis filled the screen.

"Well, what did you expect?" I clicked on the video, but the guy was terrible with the camera. "Hold on. I can find a better one."

For the next hour, we watched people fornicating. Elle might have seen a little too much for her forgetful, somewhat virgin, eyes. I, on the other hand, was ready to go find Hale again, but Elara was awake, so that wasn't happening.

Elle blinked, sitting back on the bed with her ice cream. "You do all that?"

"Well, not the butt stuff. I've never been to fifth base with a guy." That was still a little outside of my wheelhouse, but I'd try anything once. Those women seemed to enjoy it.

"I don't know if I can handle all that."

"You've done it before," I reminded. "Even in the butt a few times when you were drunk."

She frowned. "I did?"

I nodded. "Look, just do what you're comfortable with. It'll come back to you. I mean, look at me. I didn't have a clue what I was doing, but Hale was patient and I learned." Maybe Barrett could be patient, too.

She blew out a breath. "Okay. I think I'll just practice kissing if he tries again."

I grinned because although our roles were somewhat reversed, this felt like our old friendship. "You'll get there. Look how fast you're adapting to everything else."

She smiled. "Thanks, Ray."

That's not an entrance...

16

My days continued to revolve around Hale and Elara, and it was no surprise that Elle continued hanging out with Barrett. Our nights were peaceful, interrupted only by my weekly astrology course, which I told Hale I was taking to get his dad off my back. He laughed, knowing how much Remington likely disapproved of my concentration.

But other things remained on my mind. Jasmine's lawyer had not responded to Hale's counter offer yet, so that was always a lingering thought. But beyond those worries were other concerns, namely, my butt.

Studying for my first exam required a lot of night work and stargazing. This was fine because the best ways to look at stars was with a lover and a good bottle of alcohol. I had both available, so we made a habit of floating in the pool at night and watching the sky. And we, of course, did this naked.

As we drifted in the water, I named constellations. If I didn't know the constellation's name, I simply made it up, because let's face it, I promised to take a class, not ace it.

"That's Rhiniferous's Dong."

Hale chuckled. "It's big."

"Like all rhiniferouses' dongs are."

He paddled us to the edge of the pool and put down the bottle of wine. We drank from the bottle because glasses spilled easily and sometimes pool water got in the cups. Slipping off the raft, he disappeared under the water.

Hands shoved at the underside of my raft, rocking me as I clung to the float, but it was too late. Over I went, my scream silencing as I plunged into the heated water.

Sputtering, I broke the surface and swam after him, climbing up on his back as I tried to dunk him. He wrestled me into the water. My slick legs coiled around his hips. Laughing, we played like children and teased like lovers until we were both obviously aroused and winded.

We waded for a while, kissing me under the stars and talking about nothing in particular.

Somehow, his body found its way into mine and we stayed like that, attached, but not really having sex. Anchored.

It was incredibly intimate and I wished we could sleep like that, together in the warm pool. But drowning was bad, so I kept my eyes open, my head resting on his shoulders as he held me safely in his arms.

His hands cupped my butt and slowly massaged. I sighed, my thoughts once again returning to all the videos Elle and I had watched the other day. My curiosity had become a living thing.

I wanted answers, not just about my body, but about Hale's and where it had been and if it wanted to revisit certain places. He said he only needed me to meet his needs. But what if he wasn't being upfront about all he needed or wanted?

"Speaking of Uranus," I said, breaking the silence. "Have you ever had anal sex?"

Hale stilled and then chuckled. "Why do you ask?"

I shrugged. "Just curious."

Hale had rules when it came to discussing past relationships, so getting an answer out of him would be like getting a unicorn to introduce me to a leprechaun.

"Is that something you want to do?"

Lifting my head off his shoulder, I looked at him, trying to read his expression. But with only the moon and stars for light, I didn't glean much. "Not if you don't."

"Not all women like it."

"Well, I've never done it, so I don't know if I'd like it or not."

"I'd be gentle." That definitely wasn't rejection.

My body tightened and, being that he was still inside of me, he felt it. "I'm curious."

"We can try it," he whispered. "If you don't like it, we can stop."

I had a sense he'd done it before, but he wouldn't confirm my suspicions. "When?"

"Not tonight. I want it to be right."

I returned my head to his shoulder. "Okay."

And there started a little knot of anticipation that pulled tighter and tighter with every passing day.

A few nights later while having sex, Hale's thumb grazed my backdoor. Everything inside of me clenched, locking up like Fort Knox.

Hale grunted. "Rayne, what are you doing?"

"Not yet!"

"Not yet what?"

"Back there. I'm not ready."

"Loosen up. You're choking me."

"Oh, sorry." My muscles relaxed and he slid into me, his hand no longer by my ass. "I just wasn't ready."

"I told you, you would know when it's going to happen."

"I know, but I got nervous."

Every night I balanced somewhere between mildly relaxed and on high-anal-alert until one night after my shower I found a fancy glass bottle on my dresser. It was lube.

Of course, this didn't help me relax. I mean, I was excited, but I was also scared. So I did what I always do when unsure. I made a cocktail and googled.

I got a lot of tips about relaxing and taking deep breaths. Apparently, not freaking out was the golden ticket to paradise.

While some women loved it, others hated it. I had no idea what sort of woman I'd be, and my prior sexual encounters only enhanced my apprehension. Before Hale, there had been so much awful. So, so, so, *so* much. I remembered lying there, my boobs jiggling as some guy prodded my lady bits and thinking, *how the fuck was this supposed to be pleasant?*

Then there were the times the guy barely got it in, made a few enthusiastic groans, grunted, and it was done, leaving me wondering what I'd missed. Sometimes it was unremarkable, other times it hurt, and each time I was left underwhelmed until I decided I never wanted to have sex again.

That all changed when I met Hale. He got me. He knew I had a habit of getting lost in my head and overthinking everything, which was what I was doing now. So it didn't surprise me when his text interrupted my search.

Stay off the Internet.

I CHUCKLED AND TOTALLY IGNORED him. I didn't put down my phone until Hale walked into our bedroom and I was staring at an image online that I'd never be able to bleach from my mind's eye.

He tsked. "I told you to stay off the Internet."

"I should have listened."

He took the phone from my hand, shut it off, and placed it on the nightstand. Everything running through my head was the absolute opposite of sexy. Sporadic thoughts about Mexican food and gerbils. I suddenly wanted my drink box and crayons and nothing to do with adult matters or butt sex.

I'd definitely gone to the wrong websites.

Hale stripped out of his clothes and watched me, a promising glint in his eye, but I was of the mindset to keep to the other side of the room. He pulled back the covers and shut out the lights.

I carefully curled up on the far edge of the bed and faced the wall. "Well, goodnight."

He chuckled and yanked me across the mattress until I was flush against him. His hand closed over my chest as he kissed my shoulders. "I forgot what you're like when you're nervous."

I laughed, sort of hollow, as my fingers protectively cupped the space between my legs. He continued to kiss my shoulders gently and my body slowly relaxed, but never enough to part my legs. I wasn't braced for a dick up my ass. Why had I even suggested such a thing?

He rolled me onto my back and kissed me, his tongue stroking slowly against mine as he softly rubbed his body over my front. Okay, this wasn't so bad.

His fingers entwined with mine as he lifted my arms one by one, pressing them into the pillows. His mouth traveled to my chest, his tongue tracing the wing of my collarbone as he made his way to my breasts. My body arched, not at all listening to the warnings running through my head.

He really took his time, sucking gently as I continued to relax. My fingers ran through his soft hair, holding him to me. This was the sort of sexy time I liked, the kind that didn't make you call out obscenities. Somehow, he distracted me and managed to get his fingers between my thighs. Stroking tenderly, he teased my clit and my body—the traitor—opened for him.

Kissing down my belly, he gently probed, working his mouth against my core. When he had my legs over his shoulders I was inconsolably lost to the pleasure. I writhed and panted and called out his name as he delivered my first climax.

There was no going back at that point. Hale was a magician when it came to pleasuring me that way. It was how he'd first convinced me to take off my clothes and do other things.

He continued to explore my lower regions, petting my folds and kissing me in the most sensitive places. I sucked in a breath as his touch ventured further south. *Oh, God.*

His caresses remained gentle. Jesus, he was

really invested, because as he continued to kiss and probe, I eased into what felt the start of another climax. He coaxed and fondled and there was definitely more lubrication than my body could naturally produce. It was all really pleasant until the pressure came.

"You okay?"

My eyes held wide as I slowly blinked. "Is that your finger?"

He chuckled and kissed my thigh. "Yes."

Yeah, his dick was never fitting. That car was simply too big for this garage. Stiff as a board, I pouted. So much for that idea. Then I exhaled quickly as his little finger—feeling much larger than usual—sank inside.

I hissed in a breath. "Holy fuck."

"Give it a second." His hair teased my hip as he lowered his face and gently kissed my clit. I breathed hard as his finger slowly started to move, not just in and out of my backdoor, but another one was sliding in and out of my vagina too. My God, he was a multitasker.

Sinking my weight into the bed, I breathed as he pressed into me, driving my heart rate up until I was panting and spreading my legs wider. It actually wasn't that bad, and there was something on the horizon, something I could sense but didn't fully trust.

His fingers picked up the pace, his words

dancing over my senses as my body became a waterfall at his command. He tasted my arousal as the air thickened with the scent of sex.

"That's it, baby. So fucking sexy." Thrusting his fingers faster, the steady penetration continued, deeper, firmer, harder...

Then it hit me. My orgasm came so suddenly I practically howled. My body broke into a cool sweat as every muscle inside of me quaked under the force of my release.

Hale continued to pump his fingers and his mouth dropped to my clit. I was caught in a vortex of ecstasy as one orgasm folded into another, my body splayed beneath him, completely under his control.

He kissed over my hip and rolled me to my stomach. His tongue was *everywhere*. I was past caring because no matter how relaxed I was, my body never left the cusp of climax. He had me totally on edge in the most divine sense of the word. If I tensed, he felt it and brought me back down. And soon I was on my stomach.

Gripping my ass cheeks, he pulled them apart and slick heat coated my skin. My brow tightened as the blunt tip of his cock nudged me. His fingers pressed in, stretching the muscle and spreading oil around and then came the pressure again.

I sucked in a deep breath when it seemed

too much to bear, but he didn't ease back this time. Everything inside of me locked as he kept going, slow and steady, until I was breathing faster than Zul in *Ghostbusters* as if waiting for the Keymaster. And then everything stopped.

My breathing slowed and my hearing muffled as he held himself buried inside of me. "Breathe, baby."

I let out a gusty breath and realized I was white knuckling the duvet, but nothing in the world could make me loosen my grip. Hale drew back by the slightest degree and pressed in again. I groaned, because, well, there was a big cock rammed up my ass.

There wasn't any sort of burning, per se, but there was extreme pressure. I actually believed I couldn't move without his help. I suddenly understood why people said this was so intimate. He truly had absolute and total possession of me in that moment.

His weight shifted as his legs brushed against mine. His flat stomach and hard chest warmed my back as his lips traced the slope of my shoulder. "You still with me, baby?"

I nodded, but only slightly.

His voice was gravelly, thick with arousal and desire. "This is as strong as trust gets in the bedroom."

He slowly withdrew and pressed in again,

nothing like what they showed on pornos. The moment was not a side dish lost in the midst of some sexual smorgasbord. It was *not* an appetizer. It was the main fucking course. The *piece de resistance* of the menu, the delicacy with the highest price tag. And it couldn't be rushed. It had to be savored.

There was absolutely nothing casual about anal sex and I couldn't wrap my brain around how anyone could see it as otherwise. The butt hole was now, and would forever be deemed, the *trust hole*. It was the entry into things I hadn't fully considered when I suggested we try it.

"Hale?"

He held himself still and rasped, "Yeah, baby?"

"I love you."

I could sense his body relaxing into mine as his lips curved against my skin. "I love you, too, Rayne. So much."

His lips pressed to my neck as he guided my body and moved slowly, deeper, and the pressure transcended into sensations I couldn't begin to describe. With all of my anxiety and worry, I'd never considered how incredibly beautiful this could be. Hale held me close, whispered softly into my ear as he caressed and kissed my skin.

"My beautiful Rayne. Where was I before you? Lost." His touch was so reverent. I couldn't imagine giving this part of myself to anyone else.

And then ecstasy took hold, deep and penetrating. My body collided with his, naturally, riding one wave of pleasure into the next without ever letting go.

In the end, I felt changed, altered in some unnameable way. It was as if this act had somehow reaffirmed our connection, emphasized our trust in one another and strengthened the foundation of everything we stood on together.

Hale was so gentle with me, not just during, but after. He pulled me close and cuddled me. I assumed he'd always owned a part of me, being that he could touch pieces of my soul others had missed. But tonight I felt claimed and nothing inside of me wanted to pull back. I felt safe and secure and cherished in a way I'd never known before.

"Are you really okay?"

Startled by his question, I rolled to my side to face him. "What do you mean? Of course, I'm okay. That was lovely."

He nestled his face close to mine, his breath teasing my ear. "I demand a lot of you in bed. But you always go beyond satisfying me, Rayne. You're different ... from other women."

My chest warmed as his words sank into my soul. "I'll always give you what you need, Hale. I don't want you to ever feel like you need to look elsewhere."

"I never would. I only want you, baby." His lips found mine in a slow and drugging kiss. Sleepy, we eventually eased apart, me resting on my back, my head cradled in the crook of his arm while he shut his eyes and wore a face of absolute contentment.

Hale demanded a lot outside of the bedroom as well, but he wasn't an irrational person. Everything he did had a logical reason behind it. I envied that about him, so much so, I no longer resented his stubborn side. Deep down I believed everything Hale did in terms of our relationship worked toward a happy future that included him and me.

Staring at the ring on my finger, I rested against him and sighed. My mind ventured farther than I typically let it stray as I considered his words the night we watched the sun set in Mallory Square.

Perhaps it wouldn't be so bad wearing a ring from Hale on my left hand. It actually might be nice to have a token of his love, one that openly laid a claim, showing the world my heart belonged to him and his to me.

For the first time in my life, the idea of commitment didn't scare me so much. It called to me. I was very much in love with this man and I couldn't imagine letting him go.

Shoes everywhere...

17

After a trip to the local college campus to pick up another book, I entered the house and heard Hale speaking quietly. Assuming he was on the phone, I went about my business, but then I heard another voice.

Frowning, I peeked into the den and blinked. Mrs. Doubtfire was sitting on our couch. Literally.

"Rayne, I want to introduce you to Tilly Nesbit."

Was he kidding me with a name like that? Her name was perfectly charming and appropriately dated to match her appearance. Wearing a floral blouse complete with a bedazzled chain that held her glasses, a woman of about a hundred and seventy looked at me, wearing enchanting church-grade makeup.

Well, isn't that special... One of the minions in my head said in perfect Dana Carvey Church Lady voice.

"It's nice to meet you," I greeted, leaning in to shake her hand.

She smiled with a mouth full of dentures, the scent of floral talcum powder teasing my nose. "I've heard a lot about you, Rayne. It's nice to put a face to the name."

My smile was shy. "You have?" I glanced at Hale, my cheeks heating. "Were you talking about me?"

He shrugged and winked. "Just telling the truth."

Mrs. Nesbit chortled, the sort of laugh only old women could nail. "He was telling me how wonderful you are with Laura."

"Elara," I quietly corrected.

"And how much little Laura adores you."

My chest warmed and I tried not to get too full of myself, but it was too late. He thought I was good with his daughter, who *adored* me.

"Well, thank you. She's a great baby," I told Mrs. Nesbit. I seriously wanted to check if she was wearing Robin Williams' foam bodysuit under that getup.

I gave Hale a look that I hoped told him, *you say nice things about me, I'll give you whatever you want.*

He stood and hid a smirk. "I'm sure we'll have an answer for you by the end of the week, Tilly. I'll be in touch."

The woman rose and nodded. Her hands clutched one of those change purses that had a two-ball silver closure. I didn't know they still made them.

"It was nice meeting you, dear."

"You too." I watched as Hale escorted her to the door. When he returned, I grinned. "Is that the new nanny?" There was no chance of flirting with respectable old Tilly Nesbit.

"Possibly. I still have a few more interviews. I'd like you to be here when I meet them. Another one's coming by tomorrow."

"Okay." I wanted to meet them, too, being that I'd really been bonding with Elara lately. Speaking of which... "She called her Laura."

"She's old."

"If it's just an unfamiliar name to her, that's fine. But if it's a forgetful thing, then we probably shouldn't leave her in charge of the baby."

He grinned and kissed me, his hand squeezing my hips. "I like when you say *we* in reference to Elara."

I hadn't realized I'd said we. I meant him. Or we. Whatever. "I just mean—"

"I know what you mean." He kissed me

again. "I won't hire anyone who can't remember my daughter's name."

I relaxed as he moved to collect some paperwork off the table. "Good."

All of this concern for another person's wellbeing was really overwhelming. It would probably be easier if I just did the job myself. "You know, I could keep watching her."

He glanced over his shoulder. "I thought you wanted to go back to work for my dad."

I shrugged. I wanted both. Couldn't I somehow manage to have both? "I'm just saying, it's no big deal for me to spend a few hours with her each day. As far as babies go, she's not so bad."

He chuckled. "We still need a sitter. I like my adult time."

True. I liked that, too. "Okay."

"But we have a little wiggle room. My dad's heading back to New England this week."

"He is? But he just got here." Why hadn't he said anything?

"I think he's keeping company up there. He'll probably be back and forth quite a bit."

"Keeping company? What is that, code for *old people sex*?"

He laughed. "Don't bank on the other person being old. They're usually about our age."

My nose scrunched. "Ew. Your dad's a pervy old man."

"You don't have to tell me."

I heard Elara waking so I went upstairs to get her. Once I had her changed and fed, I walked her down to Remington's. Hale was right. He was leaving.

"Will you be gone long?" I asked, rocking Elara in my arms.

"I should be back before you multiply again."

"Multiply?"

"Every time I see you there's a human hanging off your hip."

I scoffed. "I am *not* multiplying." I was on birth control. I was probably the only person alive to get arrested because I was in such a rush to take the damn pill and prevent ... multiplying.

"Just watch yourself. You have baby fever."

I scoffed again. "I do not."

His eyes narrowed. "There's a pacifier clipped to your shirt."

"The baby likes it!"

"I think *you* like it."

Why was I even debating this? "So what if I do?"

He arched a brow. "Everything slows for women after children. Their careers, their education ... their sex drives. Pace yourself before you get pinned down."

"I'm not going to get *pinned down*, Remington. Jeez!"

"Am I interrupting?"

I turned to find Miles standing in the doorway. "No, we were leaving. I just came to wish you a safe trip."

"I'll be back in a few days, Meyers," Remington called as I collected the diaper bag.

Like I could get knocked up that fast even if I wanted to. *Gah! Why am I defending my ovaries to him—even if only in my head?* I was on the Pill! He was an idiot and I did *not* have baby fever.

"Have a safe trip." I gathered Elara's things and left.

When we returned to the house, Elle was debating going with Barrett for a race along the Gulf. I was still unsure about her spending so many consecutive nights at sea with him. "This is a long trip."

"It's five days, Ray."

"Can you tolerate that on a sloop?" I'd spent almost two weeks on *The Lady Parr,* Remington's luxurious yacht—one of them— and that was enough for me. I couldn't imagine being stuck in the ocean on some rinky-dink sailboat. No, thank you. I'd be talking to Wilson volleyballs by my second day in the sun.

"That's not what I'm worried about," Elle said, biting her lower lip. She had a perfect beach tan from so many days at sea.

I knew she wasn't worried about getting seasick, but it would have been my first concern. Elle was clearly still hung up on her lack of intimate memories.

"So just don't do anything with him," I suggested. I had been celibate for nearly a decade. Surely she could manage five days.

"It's not that easy. Sometimes I want to, but I freeze up."

"Okay, so pack a lot of sunblock and condoms. I can't decide for you, Elle."

She moaned and fell back on the bed. "I know. I'm being ridiculous."

"No, you're not. I waited years until I found the right guy who I could actually share chemistry with." But that probably wasn't an issue with her and Barrett. "When you're ready, you'll know it."

So off she went. Barrett was gone, Elle was gone, and once Remington and his entourage left it seemed a little too quiet at the house. Alfonse was still at the big house, but he wasn't the most talkative chap. I studied and passed time with Elara while Hale worked.

Around noon the next day, the doorbell rang. A man in jeans and a dress shirt was on the other side holding paperwork. This must be the next nanny candidate. "Hi."

"I'm looking for Hale Davenport," he greeted with a casual smile.

"Come on in. You're a little early, but that's fine. Hale?"

Hale stepped out of the office. His surprise at seeing the nanny guy was quickly disguised with a welcoming smile. "Thanks for coming out." He shook the man's hand.

"Hale Davenport?"

Hale nodded and the man handed him what was likely his resume.

"You've been served."

Hale's smile disappeared and the man's words clicked. I frowned as he let himself out of the house. Um... What the hell just happened?

Hale tore open the envelope and cursed. I glanced at Elara, who was playing happily, lying on her back. "What is it?"

"Jasmine. She's *suing* me."

"*What?*" How could that be? They were in negotiations.

He read over the paperwork and dropped into a chair. "I was afraid this would happen."

"What exactly is she suing you for?" My

stomach knotted as I glanced at Elara. We could run. We'd take the sloop and get fake identities and live off the land. Elara could learn to read from Aborigine tribes.

I was getting way ahead of myself. There was no way this woman could take Elara. My body started to tremble. Elara was ours. No one could threaten that. Right? Oh God, I was going to throw up.

"She's going after me for *intentional infliction of emotional distress*." His brow creased as he turned a page.

Okay, that wasn't as bad as a custody suit. "She's suing you because you hurt her feelings?"

He sighed, his mouth creasing with stress. "Our agreement was intended to make this easy on her. I guess my counter offer violated our initial agreement."

This was my fault. I was the one who told Hale to try to get his portion of the estate back and give her something else. Everything had been finalized before Elara was born, but Hale made the mistake of offering Jasmine something too close to his family.

"This is a fucking mess," he groaned, rubbing his forehead. "I'm being subpoenaed to a district court in Maine." He stood, not looking at me and mumbled, "I have to call Clayton."

Clayton was Hale's attorney. I moved to the carpet and picked up Elara. Keeping my voice low, I whispered, "Everything's fine. Everything will be fine."

But everything wasn't fine. Hale had two days to prepare and he wanted to get there early so he could meet with Clayton and go over some things in person. Marta and Miles were with Remington who was also in Maine.

"Why does the hearing have to be in Maine?" I asked as Hale packed a suitcase.

"Because the property's in Maine."

Elara dropped her pacifier so I washed it off and put it back in her mouth. Returning to the bed, I asked, "Can you just give in?" If this was about the property dispute, maybe it was better just to go back to the original agreement.

"I'm not doing that. I've been very accommodating and she's been paid fairly. I offered her an additional ninety thousand and something just as valuable in exchange for the estate property. She's taking advantage and if I show any sign of weakness, she'll only take more."

"You sound like your father."

He raised a brow and sent me a look that said he didn't appreciate the comparison. "I'm going to see about getting an extension with the judge. If I buy some time and talk to Jasmine, I can probably convince her it's in her best interests to take the counter offer."

I frowned. "Do you think it's smart to contact her?"

This whole thing was about the stress he'd caused in the first place, not that Hale had put pressure on her. He was right. He'd been more than accommodating.

He scowled. "This isn't her. This is a greedy lawyer getting in her head and convincing her she's been misled."

"Do you want me to come with you?"

He sighed and sat on the bed. His hand brushed over Elara's hair. "I'd rather you stay here. I had to postpone the interviews, but we really need to have someone available. I'd like you to reschedule with the candidates and then, if I get tied up in Maine, you and Elara can come there with the best choice."

Part of him seemed to be preparing for a long, drawn-out process, which made me nervous. "What if I hire the wrong person?"

"You won't. I trust you."

Ugh. The pressure of expectations. Although, there was something nice about having his confidence. But still scary. I didn't want to let him down. "But you'll look at whoever I suggest, right? You'll have the final say?"

"I trust you, Rayne. You'll make a good choice."

Since learning about Jasmine and the pregnancy and Remington's part in everything, I'd been quietly waiting for the other shoe to drop. I'd expected it to be loud when the shoe fell, but this was all very hush-hush big money, with lawyers and faceless players and some hokey claim about feelings being hurt. It was bullshit.

The longer I thought about it, the angrier I got. Hale was a good man and a good dad, and he'd been the only person to step up to the plate in a shitty situation when everyone else—the *real* people responsible—wanted to turn the other cheek.

I should be grateful it wasn't a custody suit, but one accusation didn't rule out the threat of another. If Hale exacerbated things, Jasmine might go in for the kill. And it would destroy us to lose Elara.

She was his daughter. She was our baby. Well, not mine, but I was here and I loved that little, pudgy-faced angel and I'd seriously go Cujo on anyone who tried to take her from us.

When Hale left for the airport my worries suffocated me. I'd tried to contact Elle and Barrett, but it seemed they weren't getting my texts at sea. Why didn't the Gulf have better cell towers? Damn it.

I made it about twenty-six hours unsupervised before I freaked out. Elara sensed my stress and added to it, not taking her bottle and being particularly fussy.

It was no surprise my anxiety landed me in the bathroom with cramps because that's what I did when I worried. Elara, a girl after my own heart, did the same and went through several diapers.

She hadn't napped and I really needed a break, so I did my best to tire her out. Because I couldn't stop sweating and Elara had puked on my dress, I changed into one of Hale's dress shirts and a pair of socks.

"I think you're ready for real food," I told Elara. "We're going to have a talk with Daddy about getting you on some baby cereal."

She continued to cry as I mixed up another bottle. Hopefully, this one would stay in her stomach.

Crying was a funny thing. Sometimes it was quiet. Sometimes it was ugly. But when a baby cried for hours on end it was enough to make a person question their sanity and jam an icepick in their ear.

I went to the stereo and sorted through Hale's playlist. "Ugh, your dad's selection of music is abysmal." Seriously, what kind of man bought the *Les Mis* soundtrack?

"This might work." I cued up Bob Seger and Elara looked around curiously as the music filled the house.

It was enough to stop the crying. If I could get a bottle in her and tire her out, I might be able to trick her into a nap. She took the bottle, but then she was all bright-eyed and bushy-tailed, ready to party.

I put her in her bouncy seat and threw my weight into the couch. "Why aren't you tired?" I groaned. Then I arched a brow as I had an idea.

Glancing around the house, I sat up. "You want to party? Okay. Let's party."

I grabbed the pewter candleholder off the sofa table and went to the stereo. "Prepare to be dazzled by my incredible dance skills."

Cranking up the volume, I spun on my socks and slid across the floor in front of Elara when the piano keys pounded out the most memorable riff Bob Seger had ever created.

I twirled, in perfect timing with the chord progressions, and Elara's eyes widened. *"Take those old records off the shelf!"*

I was so *Risky Business* it wasn't even funny. I fist pumped. I cocked out my leg. I even did a little butt jiggle at the fireplace. My coffee table air guitar was top notch. Bob Seger really didn't get the respect he deserved.

And then everything went silent.

I stilled and Elara cooed, hiccuping a laugh. Turning slowly, I blinked at Alfonse.

Lowering my arms, I casually stepped off the coffee table—very Snoopy sliding away from Schroder's piano—and cleared my throat, placing the candlestick down.

Flattening the tails of Hale's shirt over my butt, I simply said, "The baby likes Bob Seger."

He blinked. "Mr. Hale asked me to see if you needed anything. I'm going to the store."

Moving behind the couch, so my bare legs weren't on full display, I sputtered, "Um ... yeah. Could you get some baby cereal?"

He nodded. "Anything else?"

Dignity, if they're selling it. "That's all. Thanks."

He turned and left. I exhaled and groaned as I collapsed onto the sofa.

Arching a brow at Elara, I mumbled, "See what happens when you don't nap?"

She finally passed out on my chest around four. Hale still hadn't called and I was getting squirrely waiting around. When the phone finally rang it startled me awake. Searching the coffee table, I dug it out of the mess of rattles, baby wipes, and soiled diapers.

"Hale?"

"Hey, baby." He sounded relieved to be

talking to me, which meant he wasn't having the best day.

"How's it going?"

He sighed. "Her lawyer's a real piece of shit. My father's lawyer dealt with him before. A real sleaze."

"Did you tell Remington what's going on?"

"He knows. I'm going to try to have a sit down with Jasmine before our meeting with the lawyers tomorrow."

I frowned. "She's there? I thought she was in Europe."

"Apparently, her lawyer felt it would be more favorable for her to be present. I'm trying to keep her away from the estate without stepping on her toes too much."

Because, technically, the property was hers until she accepted a counter offer. "Where are you staying?"

"I'm with my dad. I miss you. How's Elara?"

"She's good." There was no sense in worrying him. "We're watching *Little Shop of Horrors.*"

"Good. If all goes well, I should be back late tomorrow night. There's a nanny coming by tomorrow morning around ten. The other one canceled. This one's named Jason and he works for the YMCA. Feel him out, but don't commit to anything until you meet all the candidates. I should be back for the rest of the interviews."

"Okay. Why don't you get some rest? You sound tired."

He sighed again, which was very unlike him. "I love you."

"I love you, too."

I wasn't a fan of an empty house. True, Elara was there, but Hale's absence was sinking into my bones like an old arthritic ache that I felt with every breath and motion.

Jason was a nice kid—a little awkward. He was a junior at State and working toward a degree in child psychology. I asked fancy questions like why he'd consider leaving his job at the Y and I wrote down all his well-practiced answers, but I didn't feel like he formed any actual bond with Elara during the interview.

When he left, I put Elara down for a nap because her sleep bank was a little depleted from yesterday. Then I cleaned the house because it looked like a frat party came through. Fine for me, not so fine for neat-nick Hale.

I was wiped by the time I put my little bubble butt to bed that night and I hadn't heard from Hale aside from a few generic texts. I showered and changed into pajamas, and then returned to the den. Bed was boring without Hale.

Flicking through channels, I bounced back and forth between *Monsters Inc.* and *Black Hawk Down,* because I couldn't figure out what kind of mood I was in. With my knees folded under my snuggie, I watched explosions on screen and fell asleep sometime around Sully getting sent to the Himalayas.

A hand brushed over my shoulder, scaring the bejesus out of me. *"Sniper!"* I tried to jump off the couch, but my foot tangled in the fabric and I went down.

"Jesus, Rayne." Hale rushed around the couch and helped me up. "Are you okay?"

My butt hurt, but that didn't matter. "You're home!" I wrestled off the snuggie and hugged him with all of my strength.

He grunted and wrapped his arms around me. "I told you I'd be back."

My arms tightened. "I know. I just *really* missed you."

He sighed and kissed my lips. "How did the interview go?"

"Okay." I felt bad, giving him more bad news. "He's just not our guy."

Hale nodded. "We'll keep looking." The corners of his eyes wore lines of stress. "I need a shower and my bed."

I reached for the remote and shut off the television, happy to join him. When we made love it was gentle and tender. We held each other close and I savored being in his arms again.

As I laid next to him in the silence, comforted by his familiar breathing, I thought about how we somehow passed the point of being apart. I didn't like being away from Hale and I suspected I'd never live in Oregon again.

Snippets of home played through my head, the familiar roads, the nostalgic places we hung out, my mom's house, my old room. Those things, in which I'd found such security for so many years now seemed small and faded. I didn't want to go back there. *This* made me happy, if also a little sad.

Rolling my head on the pillow I faced Hale. His narrow nose and soft lips were so pretty when he slept, so at ease. Tonight I saw something in his eyes, a sort of desperation that wasn't usually there. He'd held me and whispered how much he hated being away from me, how he never wanted to let me go. At first, I thought he was lost in the moment, but now I realized he was speaking of something deeper.

My future was here, with him. Oregon was my past. Everything I wanted always seemed so blurry and uncertain, but now it was staring me in the face.

I wanted Hale. I wanted Elara. But these weren't simple wants. They were great big terrifying needs that might break me in permanent ways if I didn't get them.

I snuggled into Hale's side. Even in his sleep he pulled me close and nestled his face to my hair.

"You okay, baby?" he slurred.

I smiled. I was okay. Just a little jarred at how clear my hopes were after the last few days.

I again looked at the ring on my finger, a sense of warmth heating the marrow of my bones as I understood Hale was my person in this life. He was my permanent piece that gave me no other choice but to fully commit my heart and soul to his. It was definitely scary, but also a relief after so many years of drifting through life without an anchor.

As I realized this was where I belonged and where I would stay, the strangest thing happened. A tear slipped from my eye and trailed down my cheek. I was happy. Sometimes it was hard to realize I was growing up.

Strangely Perfect

18

Though Elara never actually said anything, I believed she, too, had missed her dad. The day after Hale returned, he avoided the office. We swam and had a picnic on the beach and Hale only took calls from Clayton who was on his way back to New York. Barrett and Elle were still at sea and Remington was staying in Maine.

As Hale adjusted the umbrella in the sand, I watched him, still reveling in his nearness. Elara slept on her boppy and I covered her legs with a light receiving blanket so she didn't get too much sun. Hale returned to his chair and our fingers naturally laced together.

"It's so beautiful here," I said, enjoying the soft breeze and briny air.

"It's one of my favorite places."

"Which of your houses is your favorite?"

He sipped a bottle of water. "Depends. When I want quiet, I like my place in Savannah. I love the verve of Key West and the hot weather. My New Hampshire home's great for fishing. And Jersey's nice right after the summer season. I don't like it when the shoe-bees are there."

"Shoe-bees?"

"Vacationers. Summer people that swarm to the Jersey shore like bees, but don't live there year round."

"What about the estate up north?" It wasn't technically his at the moment, but the remainder of the estate belonged to his family.

"That's my dad's escape. I know we all own a share, but that's inheritance stuff. I don't count it as mine like I do the properties I purchased on my own. And it's *not mine*, until I get her to sign."

Knowing he was speaking about Jasmine, I asked, "Did you meet with her?"

He nodded. "It wasn't great, but I might have gotten through to her. I'm trying really hard not to piss her off, but part of me wants to shake her for getting greedy when I did her a favor."

I wasn't sure I'd call it a favor. I was glad Hale stepped up and took Elara because I couldn't imagine a world without her, but Jasmine had been the one to carry her for nine long months. Her first choice had been to end the pregnancy at the start.

But maybe Hale *did* do her a favor. Jasmine wouldn't have to battle with the guilt that was rumored to follow an abortion since Hale stepped in and took the responsibility out of her hands. Or maybe she resented him for taking her baby. The whole thing was complicated.

"Maybe she'll surprise all of us and do the right thing," I said.

"I'm not worried."

I frowned, unsure how that was possible. He'd been so stressed over the last few days. Nothing, besides having the case postponed, was accomplished. This had to worry him to some degree. He seemed utterly preoccupied, despite his assertion.

Deciding to change the subject, I said, "We should go out to dinner tonight—the three of us."

He smiled, but his mind was clearly elsewhere. "That sounds nice."

When we returned from the beach I gave Elara a bath in the sink because that was how my mom used to bathe me at that age. Hale showered and came downstairs dressed a little more formally than I'd expected.

"Are we going somewhere dressy?"

"Alfonse is picking us up in an hour. I made reservations at Rossie's."

I raised my brow because Rossie's was one of the places Remington frequently dined and the dress code was beyond my wardrobe's scope. Thankfully, Hale's sister, Seraphina, had purchased most of Elara's clothes, so the baby looked like a pageant beauty in her ruffled socks and periwinkle romper. I wore my go-to black wrap dress.

When I came downstairs, Hale was having a drink at the bar. He appeared distracted once again but smiled at us as we approached. Tell-tale signs of stress showed in his face and in the dark circles under his eyes.

"My two beautiful girls."

There was a knock at the front door. "That'll be Alfonse." He'd likely started knocking after catching me dancing in my underwear. I grabbed my purse and slipped into my sandals.

Dinner was lovely. We were the picture of a high-class family, but for as much as the lure of luxury brought me to the Davenports, that wasn't what held me there now.

I loved everything that Hale and I were

with little Elara at our side. I would never have picked this as my version of perfect, but that's exactly what we were together.

After returning from the restaurant, I carried Elara upstairs and changed her into pajamas. But rather than lay her in the crib, I held her and rocked her to sleep in the chair.

Hale found me in the nursery sometime later. "Isn't that a pretty picture."

Looking up from Elara's angelic face, I smiled. "I love her."

Sometimes words like "I love you" were hard to say, meaningful and full of promises people weren't always able to keep. But confessing that I loved Elara wasn't difficult at all. She wanted nothing from me and never spoke of expectations. When I made her smile, my heart melted and grew—sort of like the Grinch after he made right with all the Whos in Whoville.

"She loves you, too," he whispered, coming over to run a gentle finger across Elara's cheek.

My chest filled with warmth as I stared at her, so unspoiled and dainty. Did she love me? She definitely looked to me when she needed food or wanted something out of reach. It seemed such a gift to have her faith I suddenly wanted to cry.

My lips pressed to her forehead and I whispered, "Sweet dreams, baby. I love you."

Hale lifted her from my arms and placed her in the crib. Together, we closed the door to the nursery silently and walked to our room.

Buzz Buzz Buzz

19

"Do you have to go?" Hale was once again packing for another meeting with Jasmine's lawyer and I was in charge of Elara, being that we still hadn't found a nanny.

"You know I'd stay if I could."

Biting my lip I tried not to pout as he folded his dress socks. The man was meticulous. "How long will you be gone?"

"I promise to return as soon as I can. Believe me, staying with my father is *not* something I enjoy."

Elle and Barrett were on another excursion and would be back in a day or two, but that wasn't the same. I actually considered inviting my mom to Florida for a visit, but even that thought didn't relieve the ache of seeing Hale go.

I glanced at the baby monitor in my hands. The fuzzy image on the screen showed Elara sleeping soundly. "What if you took us with you?"

Hale paused and looked at me. "It's a business trip, Rayne. I'd hardly have time to spend with you while I'm there."

"But Remington's there. We could hang out with him."

He grunted and returned to the closet.

"I promise we won't be in your way."

Laying out four suits, he sighed. "If that's what you want then you'll need to have you and Elara packed within the hour. My flight leaves at five."

A smile stretched across my face and I squeaked. Jumping off the bed, I pressed a kiss to his cheek. "Thank you!"

"Don't thank me yet. New England's cold this time of year and there isn't much to do. Pack warm clothes for you and Elara."

Despite the cold weather, New England was a spectacular sight to behold. The fall foliage dressed the land in vibrant shades of orange and gold. The coast seemed carved out of cliffs and long white beaches. History was everywhere and the countryside was breathtaking, while little adventures seemed only a short car ride away from the pulsing city sites.

Marta was thrilled to see us and I was just as happy to see her. Although I'd recently discovered my love for Elara, I was desperately in need of a break from playing nanny. Marta scooped the baby out of my arms the moment we arrived and Hale and I joined Remington and his *lady friend* in the grand parlor for cocktails.

I'd never actually met one of Remington's women, so this was a first. For some reason, I suffered such a jumble of nerves one would think I was being sized for a new stepmother.

Hale and I sat on a small settee across from the lovebirds and I found all the jewelry on the other woman's hands a distraction. That was a lot of glitter and gold.

"This is Odette," Remington introduced. "Darling, this is my son, Hale, and a dear family friend, Rayne Meyers."

I was a dear family friend! This made me think of all the other possible titles he could have saddled me with and I started playing a game of comparison in my head, wondering which label was best. Hale's girlfriend. Personal Assistant. Walking calamity. Dear family friend seemed just fine.

Odette was a redhead with lily-white skin stretched over a good deal of plastic surgery, which made guessing her age tricky. Since I was sick with curiosity, I played a little detective game to figure out how old she was.

"Where are you from, Odette?"

"New Hampshire, a little town just a ways from here. My family's been dealing with the Davenports for years."

I raised a brow. "Any deals I know of?"

"This isn't a business meeting, Meyers. Sip your drink."

I tasted my cocktail and continued to eye the company. Remington sat close to her, but he didn't touch her in any outwardly, intimate way. Hale appeared rather disinterested in the whole meet and greet.

Continuing my investigation, I asked, "Did you go to college? I've recently started taking classes again."

"I did." Odette smiled proudly with teeth too ordinary to be dentures. "I was the first female in my family to earn a Bachelor of Arts. My major was music."

"Odette has quite a singing voice," Remington commented

"Oh, Rem..." She playfully patted his knee and I curled my lip.

It was just plain weird seeing him in this tomcat light. I mean, I knew he was a hound, but yuck. I much preferred seeing him as Remington, the arrogant business shark.

He raised his brows and dipped his head. "It's true. You should hear her sing. Do a few bars for them, darling."

Well, now I wanted to hear her. And that was two times he called her darling. Interesting. "We'd love to hear you sing."

She placed her martini glass on the coffee table, which looked like an antique from the first settlers, and she drew in a deep breath. I was not prepared for the sound that came out of her mouth. We were suddenly transported back in time as this tiny woman belted out the slow, sultry lyrics of *Dream a Little Dream of Me.*

But what took my breath away was the shock of Remington's raspy voice taking up the part of Louis Armstrong. He even got playful and threw out the little *buzz, buzz, buzz* portion of the lyrics.

My lips stretched wide as I sat in awe of the two lovebirds. As they hit the last line in perfect harmony, I gaped and clapped.

Odette laughed and nudged Remington with her shoulder as he swept his martini off the table and swallowed it down.

"Remington! I had no idea you could sing!" I was beyond impressed.

"That's not singing. Odette's the one with the pipes."

Truly charmed by the woman, I asked, "Have you ever performed?"

"Oh, no, dear. It's just something I enjoy in private."

"Very well done," Hale commented.

I could sense he was impressed, but his mind was, of course, elsewhere. I wished so much that he could relax for an evening and put all his worries aside, but those worries had brought us here and it seemed he was dead set on keeping his focus on the solution—whatever that was.

He placed his empty glass on the table and rose from the settee. "I think I'll head to bed. Long day tomorrow."

"Oh." I paused, not quite ready to retire, but unsure if he expected me to join him. Chugging my drink, I stood.

"You going to bed too, Meyers?"

I hesitated, my glance bouncing between Hale and his father.

Hale waved a hand. "Stay. Enjoy yourself."

Relieved, I said, "Okay. I'll just walk you up."

He took my hand and led me up a sprawling staircase to the room where our bags had been delivered.

"This house is gorgeous." There was an almost castle feel to it. Everything was so old, but so well preserved.

"It's one of my father's favorites."

"I think Odette's his new favorite. They're totally adorable together."

He stepped into our guest room and shut the door. "Do yourself a favor and don't get too attached to my father's playthings. His taste changes often."

I was aware of exactly who Remington was and needed no reminders, but I wished Hale would cut him a little slack. "Well, he looks happy and I'm happy for him. How old do you think she is?"

"I'd say somewhere in the neighborhood of thirty-nine and working quite hard to keep herself perpetually under forty."

That was his version of a joke because the woman was definitely older than forty. At least she wasn't twenty. "Do you need anything before bed?"

He glanced over his shoulder as he slipped off his shoes then strolled slowly to the door where I stood. Caging me in with his arms, he looked deep into my eyes and whispered, "What are you offering?"

I flushed and shrugged. "I told them I'd be back down."

His fingers trailed down the side of my

body, grazing my breast through my shirt. "I can be quick."

"Hale, I meant did you need a glass of water or anything."

His fingers were at the zipper of my jeans, the button popping free with a tug. "I'm not thirsty."

A sound escaped my throat as he pulled the zipper down, tiny, little teeth separating one at a time. I glanced between us, as his fingers slipped into the front of my panties and found my clit.

"Hale."

"Shh." His fingers smoothed over my folds, teasing and sending mixed signals to my brain. Did I want to go downstairs or stay here? Decisions, decisions...

My lips parted as he easily slid a finger into my sex.

"You're very wet, Ms. Meyers."

"You did that on purpose."

"Got you wet? Hmm. I'm not sorry." He withdrew his fingers and lifted them to my mouth. "Taste."

My lips slowly parted. Gently, he fucked his fingers, drenched in my arousal, over my tongue and groaned.

"God, you have the sexiest mouth. Don't go downstairs."

"Hale..." I was torn. "I hardly ever get to see your dad when he's not working."

"I'll make it worth your while to stay." His hand gripped my ass through my jeans and my head rolled back against the door. His breath teased over my shoulder as he pinched the hard tip of my nipple through my shirt.

"They're waiting for me," I whined, no longer in a rush to leave.

His fingers fed back into my panties, sliding easily into my slit. "Let him wait. You're mine."

I gasped as he shoved my jeans to my thighs and fastened his mouth to my neck. I clutched his shoulders as his other hand closed over my breast, massaging possessively.

"Fuck, Rayne. I need you." He stripped off my shirt but left the bra. His busy hands shoved my jeans lower, bunching the denim at my knees as I tried to step out of them.

"My boots." Stupid skinny jeans were always a problem.

"Leave them."

Giving up on his quest to get me naked, he swung my body up in his arms and deposited me on the bed, belly down, ass over the edge. The clank of his belt buckle was a mere warning as he parted my thighs as much as possible, fingered my sex, and replaced his touch with the thick head of his cock.

I rose on my toes as he plunged deep, burying himself to the root. He held me there, pinned under his weight, jeans twisted around my knees, bra strap falling down my shoulder as I balanced on my elbows.

Breathing heavily, he brushed my hair over one shoulder and kissed the back of my neck. "You shouldn't have followed me up here."

"I'm sort of glad I did."

"I'm in a selfish mood," he warned, punctuating the confession with a sharp stab of his cock and rocking me deeper into the mattress.

I'd begun to notice a pattern with Hale. Whenever the topic of Jasmine or the company of his father came about, something inside of him, something a little more animalistic than the tame version he shared with the rest of the world, crept closer to the surface and unleashed a sort of Hale-beast.

The betrayal he'd suffered was a wound that would never fully heal, and no matter how entrenched we became in our own love affair, there would be times he'd always need the affirmation that I was his and nothing could threaten our devotion to each other.

When he got like that I never suffered. On the contrary, I gained. It was all a matter of me giving him permission to let go.

Looking over my shoulder, I caught his gaze and slowly nodded. "I'm yours."

Satisfied, his hand pressed to my shoulder, lowering my chest to the bed as he drew back and plunged deep. A gasp escaped at the sheer force of his thrust, but he was far from finished. Again, he drove into me, my legs slightly bound and my arms pinned beneath my chest.

His thumb pressed between my ass cheeks as his hips moved like a piston, the old bed creaking wildly. He sank his thumb into me and I moaned loudly, my mind swirling as he penetrated both my openings.

"That's it. You give me everything I need, don't you, baby?"

"Yes!"

Harder, he drilled into me, one hand pressed heavily into my shoulder holding me in place as his other hand worked my ass.

The heavy bed creaked as the slap of skin echoed in the antiquated room. Hale groaned with every advance, producing sharp moans from my throat.

"Fuck, I'm gonna come." He withdrew his thumb and gripped my hips.

I sucked in a long breath of air as he yanked me back, his release pumping out of him. My arms were practically numb as he blanketed me and shivered, leaving kisses over my damp skin.

He slowly withdrew. My lower body pulsed with the need to climax as his come trickled past my swollen sex. His lips brushed over my shoulder and he lifted my body, turning me to my back. I lay there, catching my breath as he carefully worked off my boots.

They landed with a clomp on the hardwood floor. Looking up at him through my lashes, I watched him shoulder off his shirt. The rest of his clothes were already gone.

He peeled off my jeans and panties, tossing them to the floor and then yanked my knees forward, parting them and dropping a kiss onto my throbbing clit.

I hissed, but his tongue was gentle, a soothing touch. It amazed me that he could do such a thing after finishing inside of me, but he didn't seem to mind, which made it all the more erotic. I hummed and closed my eyes as he pleasured me with long strokes of his tongue and soft pulls of his lips.

No matter how greedy he claimed to be, he always saw to my needs in the end. I came on a breathless plea, calling out his name and trembling as my skin chilled.

Rising to his full height, he stared down at me, an assessing glint to his silver eyes. "You're stunning. The most beautiful woman I've ever seen."

Such lies, but who was I to object? I smiled and held out a hand to him. He took my fingers and placed a kiss on the knuckles.

"You're sweet."

"Only because you make me so," I whispered, the house now strangely silent. "I hope no one heard us."

He raised a brow. "I'm sure they figured out why you didn't return."

I scrunched my nose. Breakfast tomorrow was going to be awkward if that was the case.

Hale unclasped my bra and folded it on the nightstand. "I have to wake up early tomorrow morning. I might not see you before I'm out the door."

He'd be meeting with Clayton and then off to try and talk down Jasmine's attorney once more. I really hoped this would be the end of all this back and forth. Though I'd never been one to rush ahead, I couldn't escape the feeling that all this Jasmine stuff was holding us back.

"I'm sure I'll keep busy. There are lots of sights to see."

He crawled into bed and pulled my body close to his. "Make sure you bring a sweater for yourself and an extra blanket for Elara. The temperature's supposed to drop."

I loved when he watched out for us like that. "I will."

A Lovely Morning in Hampshire

20

I entered the formal dining room and again had the sensation of traveling back in time. This place was seriously old school. I was expecting a pilgrim to pop out at any moment.

Remington was at the table, reading the *Wall Street Journal*, already fully dressed, and Odette was to his left wearing a silk robe that looked about as expensive as a bridal gown.

"Rayne, you never came back last night," she greeted, sipping from an antique teacup.

"Sorry about that." I poured myself some orange juice and settled in at the other end of the table. Remington glanced at me under his bushy dark brows but said nothing. "Good morning, Remington."

"Indeed."

I frowned and sipped my juice.

"Did you sleep well?" Odette asked.

"Like a log. I didn't even hear Hale leave this morning."

"Oh, is he gone?" she asked, a look of surprise on her face. "I didn't know he had an appointment this morning."

"He's meeting with his lawyer."

Remington cleared his throat. "Odette, why don't you go take a soak in the tub and give Meyers and I a moment to discuss some things."

Odette appeared a little surprised by his dismissal, but she placed her cup on the saucer and rose from the table. "Of course. I'll see you later, Rayne."

I smiled, but then frowned as soon as she left the room. "Everything o—"

"I shouldn't have to remind you some matters are private."

Startled by the censure in his tone, I drew back. "All I said was Hale went to see his lawyer."

Remington pushed the newspaper away and leveled a narrow stare on me. "One response leads to another question. Odette's an acquaintance, not a confidante. Watch what you say."

Where was the fun Remington from last

night? "Okay. Sorry. You're grumpy this morning."

He sat back in his seat and folded his arms across his chest. "Also..."

Great. What now?

"You should know that, in old houses like this, not only do the fixtures rattle, sound has a way of echoing. I'd appreciate less noise tonight."

My jaw unhinged as I stared, unblinking, at the top of his head. Thank God he wasn't looking at me anymore. "I..."

"No need for further discussion. You two are adults. But a little discretion would be nice."

The ice in my glass rattled as I placed my juice on the table. "I'm sorry," I whispered, utterly humiliated that they'd heard us.

Remington waved a hand and pulled his paper back, opening it to the next page. "What are your plans for the day?"

Small talk? Really? It seemed more appropriate to find a hole and bury myself in it.

"Well, right now I'm thinking about driving down to the beach and throwing myself off one of those tall cliffs."

"Well, pick a decent one. Surviving a fall like that would ruin anyone's day."

I scoffed. "Thanks a lot."

"Stop being so dramatic, Meyers. If you think I was unaware you and my son have a vigorous, physical relationship, you're denser than I thought."

World. Swallow. Me. Now.

"Marta," he called and the maid appeared. "Add a splash of something stronger to Meyers' juice. She's having some sort of fit."

Marta looked at me and I blinked for the first time in several seconds. "I'm fine, Marta. Where's Elara?"

"She is napping. We had a nice long tub this morning and then a big breakfast. I made her some porridge with a little sugar and she loved it."

I smiled because I bet she did love it. Worlds were opening up now that she was starting on solid foods. "Thank you. Let me know when she wakes and I'll take her for a bit."

"Of course, Nena."

As the maid left, Remington commented, "By the time she starts talking she'll be calling you Mother."

I stilled. He was really on a roll today. Reaching for a Danish, because I typically ate my feelings, I stuffed down several uncomfortable emotions. "I'm not her mother."

"Perhaps you should consider changing that."

My hand stilled, chewed up Danish soaking up all the saliva in my mouth. "I beg your pardon?" I swallowed.

"You heard me. I know you care for the baby."

"So? I also like puppies, but you don't see me adopting any of them."

"It would help my son."

Putting the pastry down so I didn't drop it out of shock, I brushed off my fingertips and gave my head a shake. "Hold up. A few weeks ago you were badgering me about apron strings getting too tight. Now, you're suggesting I adopt your ... granddaughter?"

"If you think Hale will ever let you go you're mistaken, Meyers. He's too deep to turn back now. Think of it as a business merger of sorts."

My mouth pinched as I grit my teeth, trying so hard not to snap at him. But I couldn't hold back. "Why do you always have to make ordinary things feel like acquisitions?"

He raised a brow and looked at me. "Is that what you two have, something *ordinary*? I don't think Hale would appreciate that definition."

"You know what I mean. Why can't we just

be in love? No pressure. Just enjoy it like everyone else in the world gets to."

His laughter came out so jaded I knew I'd miscalculated. "*Fucking* is pleasurable, Meyers. Love is painful. You should be aware of the difference."

Narrowing my eyes, I said, "I don't like this side of you. Why are you acting like this today?"

"Will you marry my son?"

"Answer my question first."

He held my stare for a long moment and I was certain he wouldn't answer, but then he said, "I didn't enjoy the show last night."

"I said I was sorry! Believe me, the last thing I wanted was for you to hear us!"

"Another thing I doubt you and my son see eye to eye on."

My nostrils flared as my hands folded into fists on the table. "You aren't going to make me feel cheap or make me question Hale's motives about things that are none of your business. It was an accident, Remington. Get over it." There was so much venom coming from my pores, yet he didn't seem concerned in the least.

"You owe me an answer. I answered your question, now answer mine. Do you plan to marry Hale?"

"I don't know! Jesus, can't things just move at a normal pace?"

"Not when there's a woman out there trying to bleed my son dry!" he snapped. "Open your eyes, Meyers. Davenports never renegotiate. Hale knew better than to alter the terms of his original agreement and you talked him into it anyway. If you think that woman's walking away now, when she has my son by the balls, you have no business sense at all!"

Suddenly terrified, I sat back in my seat. This was about Jasmine? "What are you talking about?"

"He's now up to a hundred and twenty thousand dollars on top of what he's already paid. I didn't teach him to negotiate like that. He's doing this to please *you* and now her lawyer has him in a goddamn vice. They know what the Davenports are worth. They're not going to stop until they're certain they've taken as much as they can get."

"Hale offered her more money?" I had no idea. He hadn't said anything in a few weeks. Today they were going to go over other options. *More* money? None of this made any sense. "How would me adopting Elara change anything?"

"What do you suppose they'll go after

when Hale finally stops giving in to their demands? They have him in a corner."

My blood ran cold, my greatest fear creeping in. "Elara."

"There's no tidy way out of the mess he's made, but presenting a wife or a mother for the child would certainly help matters when the court gets involved."

I needed to talk to Hale. I wanted to rush through the house and take Elara in my arms and run somewhere safe with her. "She can't do that."

"She can. It's her baby."

A white-hot rage rushed through me as I hissed, "And yours, Remington! You have to stop her."

He shook his head. "That baby—"

"Say her name!"

He paused, notably startled by my protective command. "*Elara* ... is *Hale's* child. If you love him and want to protect what's his, you'll do something. You're the one who told me throwing money at a problem doesn't make it go away. I suggest you give my son the same advice."

A draft teased my ankles as I stared at my half-eaten pastry. Would marrying Hale really better his situation? Would it make Jasmine back off? It might protect Elara and she was what mattered most.

For as much as I adored the Davenports, they had a way of making me sick. Mostly Remington. Pressure built in my chest and I wanted to cry.

It was so unfair to put me in a position like this. I loved Hale, and yes, I'd probably marry him, but it was too soon. All of this was happening too fast and for the wrong reasons. And I hated Remington for even suggesting such a cold arrangement in the face of what I believed was a good and true love.

"You expect me," I whispered, "to speed up my life and take the fall for something you've done."

I shook my head, feeling robbed by a friend I trusted. He was a bully and somehow I thought I had a pass when it came to playing his victim.

"I won't do it, Remington. I love your son, and I love his daughter, but this is my life. I'll marry him when we're ready and the time's right. Not a minute before. And certainly not for you. You want everyone to clean up *your* mess. If you're so damn worried, *you* do something."

With that, I rose from the table and left the room.

Sometimes I Break Things

21

I spent some time with Elara after her nap, but my thoughts were so distracted I passed her back to Marta. Grabbing my coat and a bottle of liquor from Remington's stash, I decided to take a long walk to clear my head.

The estate was enormous and there were plenty of places one could get lost, which was exactly what I wanted to do. Getting lost seemed one mature step above running from my problems, so I didn't beat myself up too badly for escaping.

Once I lost sight of Remington's house, I followed a dirt path and swigged straight from the bottle.

"God, what the fuck is this?"

I examined the label, but it was in French.

For all I knew it was wine gone bad, but it might have been bourbon. Either way, it was keeping me warm and numbing the tension in my neck.

How could he suggest I marry Hale or adopt Elara as some sort of negotiation strategy? I'd known them for *months*, not even half a year. It was way too soon to even use words that big.

Guilt stung my conscience as a small voice in my head admitted I'd been thinking such words for weeks now. But no one knew about those thoughts. They were private.

And what about Hale's opinion on everything? It was usually the guy's job to propose.

I strolled along a large section of trees, pretty sure I was still on Davenport property, but rather turned around as far as finding my way back home. Remington was a colossal dickhead. He was selfish and never put himself in any sort of vulnerable position, but had no problem suggesting his loved ones lay it all on the line.

"Dear friend, my ass," I grumbled, stumbling along the trail.

He should be the one to do something. This was *his* mess. Had he even tried stepping in and talking to Jasmine's lawyer? And what about that lawyer anyway? He sounded like a total scumbag piece of shit. Gah, I hated greedy people. No doubt he was walking away with a fat commission.

"Whoa." My feet stopped and my face lifted as I stared at an incredibly large, well-kept home. My head tilted as I recognized the familiar pillars and gable roof. "Where have I seen this place before?"

Frowning, I stumbled forward and took another sip of the bourbon wine. Somehow I knew the floors inside were honey and the windows would be dressed with custom-made shutters painted in a delicate bone white.

I found myself staring up at the mammoth house from the sprawling porch. And then it clicked.

"This is *her* house." It was Jasmine's, the one Hale had promised her, the one that started the lawsuit and was now the cause of so much trouble.

I recalled the day, not too long ago, that Remington sent me to meet with the interior designer. Another dickhead move to hurt my feelings.

Back then he'd been trying to frighten me with Hale's complicated life. Now, he didn't give a shit about complications and expected me to dive in headfirst.

My hand reached out and turned the antique knob, shocked to feel the door give way and ease open. "Holy shit."

The sun reflected off the windows and not a touch of paint was chipped. Everything smelled brand new and nothing was lacking. I stepped into the foyer, very much like the one in Remington's house on the estate, and I gaped at the untouched beauty.

Stairs, ten feet wide, flowed up the center of the house, splitting into two separate wings. It was so picturesque, so out of a fairytale, I waited for Lumiere and Mrs. Pots to come out to greet me.

"Hello?"

Of course, no one was there. I peeked inside the shade of a lamp, not at all surprised to see a light bulb already installed. Twisting the switch, the lamp turned on.

They'd taken care of everything. Even the bathrooms were prepared with linens and toilet paper.

I walked slowly through the quiet halls, peeking inside every room. Beds were dressed. Linen closets were bursting with luxury towels. Not a single corner was left unfurnished.

I was suddenly angry. What sort of woman was offered all of this and not satisfied? Of course, she had been satisfied, until Hale took this house off the table. But, still! It was so much. So, so, *so* much.

Unfortunately, there was no food in the pantry or the refrigerator. But that was okay because I had my trusty bourbon wine. I sat on a brand new sofa—one I was pretty certain I'd picked out—and I drank.

I'm not sure how the time went so fast with no television or books to read. I hadn't even checked Facebook, being that I was too drunk to remember I had a phone. I just sat there, thinking, but not really clear what was going through my head.

This woman... I never let myself judge her, but now, sitting in this incredible home staring at all of the beautiful things waiting to be claimed... I hated her. She was hurting my Davenports.

I watched my foot lift in front of me and slowly nudge a glass figurine off the table. It fell to the floor and shattered. Then I immediately felt guilty, because what if that was part of the original house, some Revolutionary War relic and cost a bazillion dollars? If Hale managed to somehow keep the home, he might want that figurine back.

"Fuck." I dropped to my knees and collected the pieces. It wasn't too bad, but there was no way it was worth anything now.

Sitting back on my heels I blew out a breath and burped.

"Whoa." I waved a hand in front of my face. Whatever I was drinking, my breath smelled flammable.

My phone buzzed, scaring the crap out of me. I gathered the pieces of the broken figurine and shoved them under the couch before I dug my phone out of my pocket. "Hello?"

"Where are you?" Hale greeted. "My dad said you've been gone all day."

I could hear Elara cooing in the background, which meant he was back at the house. Shit. What time was it?

"Um... I went for a walk."

"All day? It's getting dark."

"I was upset."

"Are you ... drunk?"

I looked at my bottle which only had a few swallows left in the bottom. "Probably. I took a bottle from your asshole dad's office."

Silence.

In hindsight, calling Remington an asshole to Hale probably wasn't my wisest choice of the day. Not because Hale might take offense on his father's behalf. He thought his dad was an asshole on most days. But letting Hale know Remington had upset me enough for *me* to call him an asshole would probably piss him off.

"What did he do?" he practically growled.

"Nothin'. Just being Remington."

"Rayne."

"I don't wanna talk about it. How was your meeting?"

"Terrible. Where are you? I'm coming to pick you up."

I could no longer hear Elara. Glancing around the pristine Jasmine palace, I bit my lip. "I can probably get back on my own."

"You can't even talk without slurring your words. Do you know where you are?"

"Umm... It's big. There are a lot of windows."

"Are... Are you on the property?"

"Maybe."

"Rayne, I'm in no mood for twenty questions. Please just tell me where you are so I can come get you before it gets dark."

"You'll be mad at me."

"No, I won't. I'm getting in the car. I need an address."

My face scrunched tight and I shut my eyes. "I'm on the estate."

More silence followed by a hissed curse. "I know where you are. I'll be there in a few minutes." The line went dead.

"Oh, that's not good." Moving back to the

couch, I slid my phone onto the table and stared at it.

Shadows lengthened along the walls as the sun fell behind the trees surrounding the house and soon enough I was sitting in the subtle light of one lamp as Hale pulled up.

"Rayne?"

"In here."

I didn't turn when I heard his footsteps, too afraid he'd yell at me for breaking and entering.

"How did you get in here?"

"The door was unlocked."

He rounded the sofa and glanced at the table. Did he know a figurine was missing? Lifting the bottle, he eyed the label. "Tell me you didn't drink all of this."

"Sorry."

He returned the bottle to the table and sat down with a sigh. We stared at the vacant fireplace between two large windows but said nothing. Chances were, he couldn't handle more Remington related frustration. And I wasn't in the mood for any Jasmine crap, so neither of us asked about the other's day.

"This place is nice," I eventually commented when the silence got to me, but there was no inflection in my voice. Being here pissed me off.

Hale gave a grunt, which could have been agreement or something else. "How bad was he? Do I need to get involved?"

Would Hale yelling at Remington change anything? "No. He was just in a mood and talking crazy."

"Are you okay? He's a thorn in my side, but you two have a special relationship. I know you care about him, Rayne."

Sometimes caring about Remington was the biggest complication of all. "We'll be fine."

He glanced at me. "Do you want to talk about it?"

"Not really."

"If you want me to say something to him, I will."

I shook my head. "There's no point. He's just Remington being Remington. Why didn't you tell me you offered Jasmine more money?"

His body stiffened. "Is that what you two argued about?"

I looked at him, wondering why he'd confide details about Jasmine to his father, but not to me. "You could have told me you were doing that."

"I hate that she's even an issue to consider in our lives. I don't like letting that stuff interfere with us. It'll all work out in the end."

"What if it doesn't?"

"It will."

"But what if it doesn't, Hale? What if she keeps trying to get more from you until you have nothing left to give?"

His lashes lowered. "I appreciate that the least attractive thing I can offer you is my fortune, Rayne, but it's a substantial one. You're the only woman who's never taken the time to measure it. Jasmine's not going to drain me dry. Trust me on that."

"But when is enough, enough? How much more will you offer her? How much more is she going to take?" How many more trips up the coast to meet with her snake lawyer and rip off another layer of flesh?

"You know I can't go back now. I've already established she's in the power seat. There's nothing I can do but finish what I've started."

"This is so unfair."

"People are generally unfair. We aren't in this situation because of Jasmine's sense of honor."

Wasn't that the truth. Leaning into his shoulder, I laced my fingers with his. "I'm sorry this happened to you. You were the victim in all of this and you've done so much to make things right and take care of Elara. I hate that they betrayed you at all." And every day they took more and more advantage of his kindness.

"I have no regrets. Erasing their betrayal removes Elara from my life. I couldn't imagine not having my daughter."

And that was why he was so amazing. He'd found a silver lining in the shittiest storm cloud. "I love you."

His hand tightened around mine. "You know, if I actually get my way, this house will be ours. Do you like it?"

"*Yours*. And yes, it's very *Beauty and the Beast*. I want to eat baguettes in the kitchen and dance around with teacups and books."

He laughed. "Did they do that in *Beauty and the Beast?*"

"You really need to expand your horizons. Your music is all from last century and you never get my movie references."

"That's not true. I get some of them."

I sighed, my belly hungry and my eyes tired. "Do you think we'll get married, Hale?"

He shifted and turned to fully face me. "Where did that come from?"

I shrugged. "Just wondering."

"I'd marry you tomorrow if that was what you wanted. Is it?"

"I don't know. I love you, but..."

"We're still new."

"It's not just that. It's me. This is *all* new to me. You've had tons of relationships. But for me … you're it."

"Well, I'm not letting you see other people, so if that's what you're getting at—"

"No. I just mean I have no point of reference with this stuff. I don't know if what I'm feeling is normal at this stage or super advanced or what."

"Are you happy?"

"Yes."

"Then that's all that matters. Whatever came before means nothing. All those relationships… Not a single one measured up to what we have. You're it for me, Rayne. I don't want to go backward when I'm convinced I've found the absolute best person to share my future with."

I smiled and gave him a shoulder bump. "Charmer."

"Should I be shopping for rings?"

"I'm not answering that. I think—whenever you pop the question—*if* you do—you'll be as surprised as me by the answer. I won't know until we get there."

"For the record, I'm perfectly fine with waiting until you're ready. Unlike the Davenports before me, I intend to marry once and make my marriage a happy one."

And *that* was why I loved him.

Complications and Calamities

22

We were greeted by silence when we returned to the house, all traces of Odette gone. As we approached the stairs, I saw the light on in the parlor and let go of Hale's hand. He paused and looked over his shoulder.

"Do you care if I..."

"Go ahead. I'll see you upstairs." He pressed a kiss to my temple and left me to talk to Remington.

I walked slowly toward the parlor, unsure what I wanted to say when I got there. As I stood at the entrance of the room, he lifted his eyes from a stack of papers. "Long day?"

I shuffled across the carpet and took a seat across from him. "The longest."

He held up his glass, offering me some of whatever he was having.

"No thanks." My mouth sort of tasted like the 1700's and my head felt like an apple that wanted to be a watermelon.

Remington continued to watch me with those assessing silver eyes that never missed much. "Did you talk to Hale?"

I nodded, not that he had any idea how an honest relationship worked. "Yes, but not about our fight."

"Keeping that one to yourself?"

I gave him a measured look. "Remington ... why don't you fix this for him? You said you could." Part of me believed Remington could fix anything.

"Hale would never allow that."

"Like you're one to wait around for permission."

He tilted his head, his gaze calculating. "I could make it go away, but not the way he'd want. He wants to be the shining hero in a terrible situation. If I interfered he'd be just as angry with me as he was in the beginning."

I wasn't sure if that was possible. "Do you think your way is better than what he's doing?"

"Of course. It's *my* way."

"I'm serious."

He sighed and took a long sip of his cocktail. As he placed it on the table there was nothing left but ice. "When you have children,

Meyers, you always want to protect them, even if it means endangering yourself. My way would protect Hale."

Then why was it even a question? "Then do it."

He raised a brow. "You're asking a lot. There's always a cost. Burdens don't just disappear. They're passed off to others."

"I'm tired, Remington. I'm tired of the games, the maneuvers, and the drama. Hale just wants a peaceful life and I want that with him, but on *our* terms. He's not a puppet and he doesn't do well with strings. If you honestly believe your way is best, then do it—for your son."

"He'll never see it as a favor."

Showing how much this mattered to me, I folded my hands and rested my arms on my knees, leaning in to look him right in the eye. "*I'll* see it as a favor—to *me*."

He drew in a long breath and let it out slowly. With a nod, the conversation was over. I wasn't great at reading people, but something told me this was one of those conversations that *never happened* and would never be mentioned again—like in the movies.

I returned his nod and stood. "Thank you."

Once upstairs, I stopped at Elara's room.

Pressing open the door, I stilled at the sight of Marta giving her a bottle. "Is she up?"

"Just a little hungry, Nena."

I crept softly into the room and leaned over the rocker to see Elara's silver eyes twinkle behind the nipple of the bottle. She opened her mouth and smiled widely when she saw me.

"She loves you. Look at that smile," Marta commented.

That smile was worth so much. "I can take her. You can go back to bed."

"Are you sure?"

I nodded. "Thanks for taking care of her today."

"She is a pleasure, Nena." Passing the little bundle to me, I settled into the upholstered rocker and lifted Elara on my lap.

"I missed you today, pudgy butt."

She cooed and grinned, mouth full of milky gums. I nuzzled my nose to hers, breathing in her innocent freshness, and lowered her into my arm, cradling her as I reached for the bottle.

"Let's get you back to sleep."

Elara drank and fell asleep shortly after she finished the bottle. The rocker was a newer model with wide upholstered arms and a cushioned back, the sort that sucked you in with the contours of a beanbag chair. I stared at her until my eyes grew heavy and then I fell asleep holding her in my arms.

I woke up the next morning, startled from sleep by some sort of commotion coming from downstairs. Elara must have heard it too because her eyes opened and she let out a long babble of syllables.

"You have no fucking right to get involved!" Hale's voice roared from below.

"Uh-oh." I glanced at Elara, who held a fistful of my hair. "Let's get you a fresh diaper and find Marta."

I quickly changed the baby, as the shouting grew louder on the first floor. Something slammed and shattered and then more yelling followed. Taking the stairs quickly, I raced to find Marta in the kitchen. She was mumbling in Spanish and rolling out dough.

"What's going on?"

"Mr. Davenport and Mr. Hale are having another argument. Last time they fight like this they break half the house."

My eyes widened. "Can you take Elara?" Not giving her a chance to object, I shoved Elara into her flour-covered arms and went to find the two idiots tearing the house apart.

Hale towered over the dining room table, knuckles pressed firmly into the surface as he shouted at his father. "Stay the fuck out of it! You've done enough!"

"Stubborn!" Remington yelled. "You're wasting time *and money* dicking around with this lawyer. As much as it hurts your pride to admit it, you know I can get through to her better than you can. I know what she's after."

I stepped to the edge of the table since no one noticed when I entered the room. "I think you both need to calm down."

"Not now, Meyers!"

"Rayne, *please,* go in the other room!"

I jerked back. "Um, no, that's not happening. You two are family. Enough with the fighting."

"Meyers! Not now!"

"Rayne, other room!"

"*No!*" I shouted back. "I love you both and I don't want to see you fighting. All of this has to end. Hale, your dad has a solution. At least hear him out."

I'd never seen a person actually turn red before, but Hale was doing just that—more of a burgundy or burnt sienna. Either way, not good.

"I don't fucking believe this." He staggered back from the table. "You know what? Do whatever the hell you want. I'm out of it." He tossed his hands in the air and stormed from the room.

Remington sighed.

I'd never seen Hale so angry and I wasn't sure interfering had helped defuse the situation or made things worse. Biting my lip I turned to Remington and pointed a sharp finger. "Your plan better work."

With that, I went after Hale.

When I entered our guestroom he was throwing clothes into a suitcase. Without looking at me he said, "Is Elara's stuff together? We're leaving in a few minutes."

"We're leaving *now*?"

"What did you think, Rayne, that you'd go to him for help and he'd turn you down?"

So much for my theories on *this conversation never happened.* "He's trying to help you, Hale."

"He's trying to make a point."

"And what point is that?"

He shook his head. "We'll need bottles made for the flight home."

There was no way we could just show up at the airport and hop on a flight. He obviously wasn't thinking clearly.

"Hale, stop packing. Our flight isn't until tonight."

Flustered, he crammed the last of his

clothes in the suitcase and shoved it across the bed. "I'll do it myself."

As he stormed toward the door I shouted, *"Hey!"*

His head snapped back and he scowled at me with an expression so cold I hardly recognized him. "*What*?"

"Why are you taking this out on me?"

He shook his head and laughed coldly. "You went to him. I told you I had it handled, and you went to him anyway."

"I was trying to help you! I know you were taking care of things in your own way, but this has been so stressful on you and with your constant traveling back and forth and missing your family... You said you just wanted it to end. You wouldn't be in this predicament if I hadn't pushed you to change your original agreement."

"Is that what you think, that you did this?" He ran a hand through his hair, leaving it standing on end. "Rayne ... adopting Elara was *my* choice. Trying to hold onto my portion of the estate was also *my* choice. Walking out of here right now before I say something I'll regret... *My choice!*"

I flinched as the door slammed.

Afraid to follow him, I packed my belongings and closed his suitcase then went to the other room to gather Elara's things. The house was silent, but I felt the energy pumping through the floorboards. Blinking back tears, I carefully folded Elara's clothes and placed them in her bag.

This was supposed to be a chance for us to be together. It was supposed to be relaxing, once all the Jasmine crap was handled.

I should have never asked Remington to get involved. He was probably dying for someone to tell him he could handle this better than Hale. How foolish of me to be that idiot. And stupid Hale. Was this all about pride? About who could fix it first? Who cared! Just make it go away.

I carried the luggage to the front door and found Hale buckling Elara in her car seat. He didn't address me or even look at me. Once she was snug, he stood.

"We'll be in the car." He picked up the car seat, the diaper bag, Elara's bag, and his suitcase, leaving only mine by the door.

I went to the kitchen and found Marta. "We're leaving now."

She sighed and came to give me a hug. "You don't let those boys worry you, Nena. They fight. They make up. It is how this family works."

I was no longer worried about Hale and

Remington. I was more concerned with my relationship with Hale. "Okay."

"Have a safe trip home. We will see you again soon."

"Do you know where Remington is?"

"He went out."

I frowned. "Where did he go?"

She shrugged. "He only said to take care of something. But he drove himself."

I'd forgotten Remington could drive. He always had a chauffeur take him wherever he needed to go. "Will you tell him I said goodbye?"

"Of course. You better run. Mr. Hale is not so patient when he is upset. Be safe."

As it turned out, Hale also wasn't very chatty when he was upset either. He said not a single word to me the entire journey home. And when we got to the house, he carried Elara to bed and went to our room alone.

Ashes ... ashes

23

Finding myself standing outside of our closed bedroom door, I hesitated. Hale and I had never fought like this. When I first met him, he said he could be an asshole, but in this situation, I wasn't even sure if the asshole was him or me.

My eyes closed as uncertainty took hold. All the words between us fell clumsily through my mind, landing wherever. I had no idea if his feelings from yesterday still applied or if my asking Remington for help had done too much damage to repair.

I stepped away from the door, too terrified to see what awaited on the other side. Walking past Elara's room I knocked softly at Elle's door. A light flipped on and there was a soft shuffle of movement before the door opened.

"You're back," she said, hair messy and eyes looking half asleep.

I had so much to say, but not a single word came out. My lips pressed tight as I drew in a jagged breath and started to cry.

"Oh, honey." She pulled me into her room and walked me to the bed. I sat and wiped at my eyes but the tears kept coming.

"What happened?" she asked, brushing the fallen hair away from my face.

"I don't know. I don't know anything. I'm so stupid."

"No. Did you and Hale have a fight?"

"I guess. He won't talk to me. I've never seen him this angry and I don't know how to take it back."

"Shh..." She handed me a box of tissues and I blew my nose.

My chest hurt terribly. No matter how hard I cried, the pain only multiplied. I couldn't catch my breath.

"Rayne, calm down, honey. Tell me what happened."

I stared at my best friend, searching her eyes and finding the girl who had stood by my side since the day she shared her brownie with me at lunch in kindergarten when I'd accidentally dropped my entire tray on the floor. Twenty-five years of friendship and this was the first time I ever had a problem I couldn't share with her.

"I can't talk about it."

"Sure you can. You can tell me anything."

She sounded so much like old Elle, the friend I'd feared losing forever and had been desperate to find again. I'd thought she was just a familiar girl with misplaced memories, but my best friend was still in there. I saw it in the way she looked at me with such concern, the way she took up the position that anything was possible and no problem was too big for the two of us to figure out.

But I couldn't get her help with this one because it was tied up in too many secrets and lies, secrets that weren't mine to share. I sniffled and blew my nose again.

"Everything's a mess. I screwed up and I don't know if I can undo it."

She pressed her head to mine and smiled. "No calamity's that bad, babe. We can figure it out. I'm sure of it."

We. I wished there was a "we", but this time it all came back to me.

"I'm not allowed to tell you. I gave the Davenports my word and I can't betray them like that."

I saw a flash of hurt in her eyes before she covered it. "Oh." She sat back. "Is that because of me, or is this a secret you can't tell anyone?"

"No one can know. It's a private situation and it's not my place to talk about it."

Her lips twisted. "Well... I'm sure we can figure something out without you breaking their trust. What started the fight? Keep it general."

"I went to Hale's dad about a problem thinking he could help."

"Whose problem?"

"Hale's. But it didn't help. He flipped out when he found out I went to Remington."

"*Can* Remington help?"

"He says he can. He said he could make the whole issue go away."

"So why is Hale mad? You were clearly looking out for him."

This was why secrets sucked. "You don't understand. Hale doesn't have a great history with his dad. He loves him, but he hates him, too. There's a lot of bad blood between them and this all has to do with that. He thinks I betrayed him by going to his father." Was that it? "Or he thinks I don't have faith in him or something. I'm not sure. I just know he's furious with both of us."

"You and Remington?"

I nodded. "Elle ... what if I can't fix this? What if we break up?"

"Ray... Sometimes things like loyalty and betrayal leave deep scars. If Hale has some baggage with those things, you have to honor his limits. He trusts you and somehow you shook his trust today. The only thing you can do is apologize and prove to him you're on his side. I honestly don't think that man would break up with you over something small."

"But this is big."

Elle sight and squeezed my hand. "I see how he is with you. Barrett says he's never been like that with *anyone*. Ever. Hale loves you. Trust that. Trust what you two have and try to work this out."

"You know I'm not good with that sort of thing."

"Because of your dad?"

A shiver tiptoed up my spine as I looked at her. "You remember?"

She nodded. "Things haven't been as jumbled lately. I don't know if it's the meds or all the fresh air or what, but things are a little clearer now. The weeks before the accident are still fuzzy, like, I can't remember you leaving or anything, but stuff before that is pretty clear."

I started to cry again, only now they were

tears of relief. I hugged her. "You have no idea how much I missed you."

She laughed and wrapped her arms around me. "I missed you, too."

Easing back, I let out a shaky sigh. "What should I do, Elle?"

"What do you want? Do you want to run home and hide or do you want to fix this?"

"I want to fix this."

She chuckled. "That's a first."

I smirked, a little amazed myself. "I love him. I don't know how to not love him. I love Elara, too. And Remington. They're my Davenports. I can't lose them."

"Then clean yourself up and march down the hall and tell him that. Don't pick a fight, just say what you just said and tell him when he's ready to talk you'll be ready to listen. That's the most you can do right now."

It would be great if that could play out as simply as she just made it sound, but chances were it would be much more complicated and messy. But I had to at least try. "Okay. I can do that."

She smiled and nodded. "Go. Go now."

"Now?"

"Yes, right now, Ray. Why wait?"

"Oh. Okay." I stood, clutching a crumpled tissue. "I'll go."

She walked me to the door. "You got this. I believe in you."

I nodded, borrowing a good heap of her confidence. "I got this."

"I'll see you in the morning."

"Okay, good night."

I stood in the hall as Elle closed the door. The entrance to our bedroom loomed at the end of the carpet, big and closed and frightening. I should probably have a plan B. Maybe tell Elle I'd be back if things didn't go peacefully.

Thinking a plan B was always a good idea, I opened her door and—"*Naked!*"

"Fuck!"

"Oh, Jesus!" I slapped a hand over my eyes. "Barrett?"

"Hey, Meyers."

"What the hell are you doing here?"

"Umm..."

"Oh my god! I knew it! Goddamn it!"

"Ray, it just sort of happened when we were away."

Dear God, had he been in there the whole time listening to me fall apart? I needed to get out of there, but first... I pointed a finger out, unsure where he stood. "You hurt her, Davenport, and I'll find a rusty blade and cut off that thing you love so much. Get me?"

"Loud and clear, Meyers."

I groaned. "I can't believe you were in here. Gah! This family sucks! Goodnight."

I reached blindly for the door and when I found it I pulled it open and left. Apparently, Elle remembered how to screw. Maybe that was why her mind seemed so much sharper all of the sudden. Maybe her vagina was a magic gateway to Memory Lane. *I can't believe she's sleeping with Barrett.*

Lowering my hand I huffed out a breath. Now I really had to work things out with Hale, because if there was going to be a Davenport wedding it had better be mine!

Oooh! Double wedding! No. Way too fast.

Shaking my head, I walked to our door and sucked in a deep breath and turned the knob. The frosty tension of the room smacked me in the face like a brick.

There seemed certain things one should never do. Name your child Adolf after 1945, eat gum off of furniture, or walk unarmed into a room that felt as hostile as this one. But I was never that smart to begin with. "You awake?"

He sighed. I supposed that was as good as a yes.

I moved to the bed and sat on the foot, trying to recall what I'd said in Elle's room.

"Hale, I'm sorry about what happened. I didn't do it to upset you. I only wanted to help and your father seemed to think he could do just that. I swear my heart was in the right place."

Silence.

The tightness in my chest returned, pinching sharply. "Please talk to me." When he still didn't answer, I lowered my head and battled back my tears. "I'm sorry," I rasped, unsure what else there was to say. "If you want me to leave I will."

"Damn it, Rayne. Just stop."

"I don't know what I'm doing," I pleaded. "You won't talk to me. I don't know if you hate me or if you just need some time to yourself or if you want me to get the hell out of your life."

Tears rushed down my cheeks and he was suddenly holding my face between his hands, but his eyes were still angry. "You're supposed to trust me, Rayne. When I say I have something under control, you don't go to my dad for a fucking safety net. I'm pissed, but I don't want you to leave."

"How long do you plan to be pissed?"

He released my face. "I don't know."

"Hale—"

"I'm tired. Can we just leave it for now and talk tomorrow when we're both thinking a little clearer?"

I nodded, but deep down I didn't want to

table it. I wanted to lay everything out and hack it to bits until we knew what was what. Dear God, I wanted to *communicate*.

But Hale didn't and, as an ex-non communicator, I had to respect that. I remembered what Elle said.

"I just want you to know, whenever you're ready to talk, I'll be ready to listen. I love you and I don't want to lose you."

He sighed and looked away. "I ... love you too."

Was that a pause? I heard a pause.

My lip trembled as he rolled to his side, facing away from me, and pulled the covers over him. Conversation over.

Hale: score unknown. Calamity Rayne: negative infinity.

I had to leave the room so he didn't hear me cry.

24

Apparently, some sort of fucked up karma was after me. I'd told Hale I was ready to talk, but several days of silence passed and he still wasn't ready open the gates of communication. There had been no word from Remington or Jasmine's lawyer. Clayton was at a loss and Barrett hadn't been able to say two words to me since I accidentally saw his junk.

Hale's penis was nicer. Not that it mattered, but it was good information to have.

While Hale continued to ignore me and avoid eye contact, I passed my days playing with Elara by the ocean and talking to Elle, who seemed like her old self again. She still had a lot of questions, but they were fun questions, sort of like binge-watching a favorite sitcom we'd seen a thousand times before.

"And Travis Jones?"

"Mmm…" I swallowed a sip of water. "You dumped him because he had an obsession with twisting your nipples."

"Oh, yeah!" Elle laughed. "He was awful! It was like he was trying to crack a safe every time he got my bra off. What about Lee McGuire?"

I thought back for a moment. "I think you broke up with him because he was too into manscaping."

She scrunched her nose. "His face?"

"No, down there."

She made an expression that told me that wasn't high on her violation list these days. "Barrett manscapes."

"Ew. And I know. Let's not discuss Barrett's penis."

"It's a nice one."

Not as nice as his brother's… "Anyway…" When we got back to the house, Hale was on the phone. Elle sent me a look and bailed, leaving me alone so she could take a shower. I carried Elara to the sink and rinsed the sand off her body then took her upstairs to change into something cozy. The beach had a way of tuckering her out, so once she was changed she was ready for a nap.

After laying her in the crib, I went to find something to eat. Walking down the steps, I spotted Hale sitting on a chair in the den, sipping from an almost empty glass. "Hey."

"Hey."

Be still my heart. Words! "You okay?"

"I guess I am. That was Clayton. Jasmine dropped the charges and she's giving me the house in New England."

I gasped. "*What?* That's great!"

Remington had done it! I wasn't sure how, but he did and now everything could go back to normal.

"She's also not taking my last offer—the additional money and the place in New York."

Even better! Or was I missing something? "So why don't you look happy?"

His phone buzzed and he briefly glanced at the screen, swiping his finger over the bottom. "This is why."

Uh-oh. I slowly walked toward him and looked at his phone. It was a picture of a newspaper clipping. "What is it?"

"Look."

I took his phone and stretched the screen so I could read the words.

Remington Davenport announced his fifth marriage today during a private interview held at his New England estate. The reception was held at a secluded location in Costa Rica, imme-

diately following the ceremony with only one wit-ness and the couple on the beach.

My heart pounded. "Your father got married?"

Wouldn't he have invited us? I would have loved to have gone to Costa Rica with him and Odette.

"Notice they didn't print the bride's name."

"Maybe he and Odette want to be discreet. She is his *fifth* wife. I knew there was a spark there."

He laughed coldly, hoisting himself out of his seat and walking to the bar, refilling his glass with a generous hand. "He didn't marry Odette, Rayne."

"Who..." My words fell away as a cool sweat broke over my skin like a fever, my stomach instantly nauseous. Chills raced up my spine.

"No," I breathed.

Hale sipped his drink then lifted his glass as if on second thought. "Cheers. May Rachel not roll over too hard in her grave."

This couldn't be happening. "He *married* her?" *Jasmine?*

"Technically," Hale said, thick with sarcasm. "He made my problem go away."

"I don't understand any of this!" My legs

gave out and I dropped into a chair. "They couldn't have a baby together but they can get *married*?"

"She didn't want a baby. She wanted money. Father had more than son, so she fucked him. Dad's counter offer was more enticing as well. You see the trend. Now she'll have plenty for the rest of her life."

"Who does this?"

"Remington. Davenport." His glass was again empty so he refilled it.

"Hale..." He didn't look good. His tie was undone and his shirt was only half tucked in and his eyes were the most haunting shade of silver I'd ever seen. "Have you spoken to him?"

"Nope, and I don't plan to."

"Will you stop acting so blasé? I can't take you like this! Why can't you people be a normal family for once?" I sounded hysterical, but what the fuck!

"How do you expect me to be, Rayne? I wanted that woman as far away from me and my daughter—*and you*—as possible. Now, she's a part of the family. All. To save. A buck."

I couldn't catch my breath. There had to be a way to undo this. Remington's words played back in my mind.

Burdens don't just disappear. They're transferred to someone else.

He took Hale's burden and made it his own—which was exactly what he should have done in the first place, being that it was never Hale's problem to begin with, but that was beside the point. "What the fucking fuck?"

"Exactly. Be sure to send my congratulations when you call him. I'm sure you'll do that tonight, being as he's your go-to guy. Is it proper to congratulate the bride? Or is it best wishes and congratulations to the groom? I can never remember."

His callous comment struck me where all my tender emotions hid and I flinched. This wasn't a side of Hale I liked.

How dare he act like this would make me happy? This was not what I wanted! I had to get out of there. I couldn't take anymore. They were all insane. "You need to stop drinking before Elara wakes up."

He ignored me and sipped from his watered down ice.

"Hale."

"Rayne, I love you, but there isn't a force in the world strong enough to pry this bottle out of my hand tonight. I intend to finish it and then finish its friends over there. If you don't like it, you can get the hell out of my house."

I took a staggering step back. "Did you just tell me to get the hell out of your house?"

Something snapped inside of me. Maybe it was that crazed, psycho rage some women got when their boyfriends offend them. I always thought that was hormones and too much crazy, but now I knew. It was an intricate part of female genetics, a force of power that stemmed from all the crap tied into our uterus and the miraculous strength possessed by the female soul. It was the innate wrath and métier that allowed women to flip over cars and rescue babies. And now it was pumping through my veins, full speed ahead, ready to spew all over Hale.

"Oh, I'll get out." I spoke in a frighteningly quiet tone.

His head jerked and I saw the flash of fear in his bloodshot eyes. Wise boy.

"And I won't come back until you're ready to talk to me like a man and a partner. I've had about enough Davenport bullshit for one lifetime—"

"You're a part of this bullshit—"

"Your father did this! Not me. God, you can be just like him sometimes! I'll be damned if I let one more asshole pin his problems on my back. Do *not* try to follow me!"

I marched up the stairs and packed a bag. Then I packed a bag of Elara's clothes because she wasn't staying here either. It briefly crossed my mind that I was kidnapping Hale's daughter, but that was a risk I was willing to take because I was fucking fuming and he was drunk!

Once I had everything, and my precious cargo, I pounded on Elle's door. "Elle! Come on, we're leaving!"

Her door flew open. "What?"

"Get your stuff. We aren't staying here."

"Where are we going?"

"Just get some stuff! I'll meet you in the car."

I carried Elara down the steps and stopped into the kitchen to grab some bottles and snacks for her.

"You're not taking her," Hale said from the den.

"Try to stop me, Hale. You're drunk, angry, and in no condition to take care of her right. You told me to get *the hell* out. I'm taking her with me. You can pick her up in the morning when you're sober."

"Where are you going?"

"I'll let you know when I get there. Elle!"

"I'm coming!" Elle came down the steps with a bag slung over her shoulder. "Hey, Hale."

"Hey."

I rolled my eyes. "I'll meet you in the car."

Once I had Elara buckled in the back of

Hale's Rolls and Elle was ready to go, I shifted into reverse and backed out of the driveway.

"Where are we going?"

"I'm not sure." I ground my teeth and gripped the wheel. If not for the little bundle of snuggles in the back I'd have peeled out.

It was Key West so we didn't have to go far to find a place to stay. I parked valet style at the first sizable hotel I passed. "Give me some money."

"I don't have any cash," Elle said.

"Great." The attendant opened the door and I reached under the seat, fishing around until my hand landed on a thin strip of plastic. "Ah-ha!" I withdrew a shiny black card with HALE DAVENPORT embossed on the front.

We climbed out and instructed the valet to charge it to our room. We then entered a lavish lobby and Elle held Elara as I made my way to the front desk.

"I'd like the nicest suite you have available."

The clerk typed some words into the computer and said, "I have a King available with an ensuite lounge and Jacuzzi tub."

"Perfect." I slid him the card.

He swiped and we were passed a key. I was breaking so many laws I was a little dizzy and high with authority, but nothing could stop me now.

The room was fucking bananas. Champagne chilling on ice, pillows and gossamer drapes cloaking the bed like something from Cinderella's palace, and a view to die for.

"Wow," Elle said, stepping up to the glass and taking in the sight of the sun setting over the ocean. Even Elara seemed impressed.

I plopped on the bed and dialed room service. "Hello, I'd like to order two ice cream sundaes, two steak dinners—medium rare—some applesauce, a fruit tray, and what do you have that's chocolate?" The receptionist listed several things that sounded amazing. "Yes, one of each. Thank you."

"What the hell did you just order?" Elle asked, balancing Elara on her knees as she sat in one of the club chairs by the window.

"Don't judge me."

I popped the cork on the champagne and took a long sip from the bottle. I didn't offer Elle any because someone had to keep a sober eye on Elara. Falling back on the pillows, I held the cool bottle between my thighs and sighed.

"Men. Suck."

Elle groaned. "Here we go again."

This is Armageddon!

25

"Rayne! Enough!" Elle snapped. "I don't know what's gotten into you, but I miss my things and I want to go back to the house."

I stood on the bed, bouncing Elara on my hip. My hair was a disaster, my legs hairy, and my last clean shirt was freckled with spit up. But I was not giving up!

"We can't quit now. We're winning!"

"Do you hear yourself? You sound crazy. We've been cooped up in this hotel room for two days. We don't have a charger and you have someone else's kid! Barrett's probably trying to text me."

I blew raspberries into the air. "Screw Barrett. This is about us women! Don't you get it, Elle? They have to learn. They say we're the

363

ones with PMS and all that crap, but it's really them. They're the crazy ones!"

She plopped onto the chair. "I wouldn't be too sure."

There was a knock at the door and we both stilled. I sniffed. Elara needed a diaper change, but we were running low on supplies. The knock came again.

"Do you want me to get that?"

"No! It could be a trap!"

Elle rolled her eyes and went to the door. I lowered myself to the mattress and cradled Elara on my lap. "Shh ... be very quiet."

"Thank you," Elle said and shut the door.

"Who was it?"

She came around the corner holding a vase of vibrant lilies. "It was a delivery for you."

I eyed the flowers like a bomb. "Who are they from?"

"Get a grip, Rayne. They're from Hale."

She put them on the dresser and plucked out the card. "*Rayne, please forgive me for being a first class jerk. Come home. I miss my family. I miss you. Love, Hale.*" She tossed the card next to the flowers. "Can we please leave, now?"

"How did he know where we were?"

"*You have his credit card!* Oh, my God, I can't take you like this!" She went to the closet and grabbed her bag.

"What are you doing?"

"I'm leaving. Barrett and I were supposed to go out sailing this weekend and he's going to think I'm blowing him off."

"You can't leave! We're in this together."

"No, Rayne. This is all you. I told you to talk to him and be an adult. This..." she waved her hand around the messy room. "This is like a luxury undercover op gone wrong. And the room stinks like sour milk and baby shit."

"Don't be a turd in a sandbox, Elle. Stay!"

"No, my Thelma and Louise days are over. Now, are you coming with me or do I have to call a cab?"

My shoulders slumped. I was no match for Elle when she got her mind set on something. It was like the old days again and I told myself to be happy my friend was well on her way back to her former self, but part of me wished she'd stay my reckless sidekick—as irrational as I was being.

"Fine. I'll go with you. But for the record, I feel like a prisoner of war and this is not how I wanted to go down."

She looked at me and sighed. "Why are you doing this? I mean, how long do you want to drag this out?"

My head lowered. I'd done a fair job at keeping my hurt feelings at bay, focusing on the rage, but the truth was I was more hurt than angry. "You weren't there. He told me to get the hell out of his house."

"Ray." She came to sit next to me on the bed. "Couples fight and say stupid shit. He didn't mean to throw you out *permanently*. He's obviously tense about whatever happened with his dad, but he'll get over it. By the flowers and card, I'd say he already has."

But those words... *Get the hell out.* "I don't want to love someone who can just throw me away."

Her lips pressed in a sad smile. "He's not throwing you away, babe. He's lashing out. All of this is because *he* wants to be the man you turn to when you're in trouble. I know you love Remington and count on him, but you have to stop looking for a father figure that isn't there and start looking at what's real. Hale loves you. He told Barrett he plans on marrying you. No one needs to walk you down the aisle for you to have that happy ending. You just have to be brave enough to trust that Hale will be waiting for you at the other end."

"You think I should marry him?" Why didn't anyone else care that we'd only met this summer? Wasn't that supposed to be a thing?

"I think you love him. Never in a million years did I expect you to actually find a real relationship like this and be brave enough to commit to it. Think about who you are. Calamity Rayne doesn't do commitment. But here you are, raising his daughter, making him lunches, taking care of his house, and worrying about the future." She grinned. "I think you're finally growing up."

Come to think of it, I was doing an awful lot of adult things—before I kidnapped Elara and hid out in a hotel. But that skittish little girl was still lurking inside of me. "I'm scared."

"Love's scary. But so is being alone. Only you can decide what you want."

The mere thought of a life without Hale made my stomach hurt. I didn't know how to go back to being the girl I'd left in Oregon.

"What about you? Will you stay here?"

"For a while. I'm having fun right now, but eventually, I need to get a job. Barrett told me about an opening at the marina. I might check that out, but ... you can't base your life on me. It's time to start deciding for *you*."

A world without Elle seemed a dark and lonely place. "We'll need a good phone plan if you move home again."

"I think I outgrew Oregon a long time ago. I'm going to find a lawyer to help me sell the house and split whatever's left with Chris. Right now, I have no roots and I sort of like it.

It's like I'm a brand new person and I want to find out how far she can fly before I clip her wings."

"Aren't you scared?" She always seemed so confident, so fearless. I wasn't any of those things.

"Yes, but it's an exciting fear. I'd rather jump than spend my life staring at the view and wondering what if."

I'd taken a jump when I flew to Jersey for an interview last summer. Things hadn't gone too badly. I mean, I had Hale, got to know a fascinating man like Remington, figured out babies weren't so scary, and it actually turned out sort of nice.

The other day when Remington joked about Elara eventually calling me Mother... I'd be lying if I said the idea didn't fill me with joy.

I looked down at her as she sucked on my knuckle. Would she eventually want a little brother or sister? I wanted to give her everything she wanted and I wanted to give her those things with Hale.

I looked around the hotel room. The place was in shambles. Hale would never tolerate such a mess. I laughed to myself.

"We're really opposite, me and Hale."

"Sometimes opposites attract in the best possible way."

I sighed, my heart missing home, missing him. God, I missed his face, the scent of his clothing, the way he hung my towel when I left it in a sopping heap on the counter. All of those little quirks added up to the man I loved. And no matter how many times I arranged the pillows wrong or put the milk away empty, he never got frustrated with me.

"How can I be so in love with him and so mad at him?"

"He's a boy, Ray. They're totally annoying. But I'm convinced he's one of the good ones. We'll go home, I'll give you guys some privacy, and you'll talk it out. Then you can have make up sex."

I twisted my lips and eyed my legs. "I'd need to shower first."

"Let's go home, Calamity. Your man's waiting for you."

Within an hour we were packed up, checked out, and on our way home. Elle had me drop her off at Remington's where Barrett was staying. As she got out of the car I felt like a kid being sent off for college for the first time.

I looked back at Elara, my little partner in crime. "It's just you and me, kid. Should we head for the border or go home?"

The binkie in her mouth bobbed.

"Yeah, I miss him too." Exhaling, I backed out and turned the car toward Hale's.

Hale appeared on the front step before I had the trunk open. He looked much better than when I'd left him. I on the other hand... Well, it wasn't great.

He approached slowly and took Elara, giving her a kiss. So much for war. The turncoat practically squealed with glee the moment she recognized him.

His gaze met mine. "Hey."

"Hey."

"Can I get your bags?"

"I got them." Of course, I *had* them. But once I tried to juggle my bag, the leftover room service, and the flowers, I nearly dropped everything.

With a sigh, Hale took the flowers and walked us inside.

Situating Elara in her swing, he watched me as I tossed my bag on the steps and took my leftovers to the kitchen. I planned on eating them later, but he was watching me and that made me nervous, so I peeled back the top of the brownie tray and popped a piece in my mouth.

"Did you have fun?"

"Not particularly."

"Did you visit the pool?"

"No, we just stayed in the hotel room."

"You could have used the card to visit the spa if you wanted."

"We had Elara."

"Right."

"Right."

How were we supposed to shatter this wall of awkwardness between us? I closed the brownies and tucked them in the fridge. "I'm going to take a shower." Which was really code for *nap*. Playing nanny twenty-four-seven was a lot harder than taking turns with Hale.

"Should I order dinner?"

"Do whatever you want." Gah! I didn't mean to come off as such a bitch, but some womanly part of me demanded he didn't get a pass simply because he sent flowers and a sweet card. I needed to actually hear him say the words *I'm sorry*. And maybe a few others... *I was an asshole. My love for you is undying and will never fade. You were right to go to my dad...* Something like that.

I carried my bag up the steps and didn't exhale until I was safely inside the bedroom. As I showered, I thought about my life, not just the *me and Hale* stuff, but all the crap that came before.

I never tried to be much of anything, and not trying too hard had a way of making me feel fine with who I was. It wasn't until my thirtieth birthday that I wasn't fine anymore.

Then I found the Davenports and realized there was *my sort of weird* and a whole other level I never considered. The sort of weird where fathers steal their children's lovers and babies are seen as leverage, and scandal is a real word with serious consequences.

I thought about Remington, no longer as furious as I'd been when I first discovered what he'd done. It still didn't make sense though.

How did bringing Jasmine into the family make Hale's problems go away? I kept having strange visions of Thanksgiving dinner with the Davenports and Jasmine sitting to Remington's left while her daughter sat between Hale and I. *Mega weird.*

And I needed to stop thinking of Elara as being anything to her. Elara was ours—well, Hale's.

When I got out of the shower my phone had a charge and several missed calls and texts from Hale, but none from the last hour. I sat on the bed and considered if calling Remington was a wise choice or a very bad one.

Undecided, I hit send.

"I was wondering when I'd hear from you," Remington answered.

I sighed. "Remington ... what have you done?"

"Exactly what you asked me to do. I made a problem go away for my son."

Was she there right, listening to him talk? "By *marrying* her?"

"Meyers, my heart died with Rachel. What difference does another wife make?"

I scoffed. "It's *marriage*, Remington."

"And we've discussed our different positions on the subject ad nauseam. This doesn't change much for me, but it changes everything for Hale."

"She's your wife now, Remington. She'll be around forever."

"She'll be gone when I die."

"Don't say that."

"It's the truth. Besides, holding the title of spouse doesn't affect much more than a bank account. She'll have her money and then some. For now, she's on an allowance, meeting with realtors who can find her a home in Europe or any American city she wants. I get her attention whenever it suits me, and she's legally bound to never cross my children or my grandchildren again. Hale's safe. My granddaughter is safe."

"But what about Odette?" They were so

cute together, singing dated jazz tunes and sipping old fashioneds.

"Odette's fine. She understands this is more of a business arrangement than anything else. She's upstairs in my bed as we speak."

"Odette? She's there?"

"Of course."

"Where's Jasmine?"

"She went back to Europe yesterday. I imagine she'll be there most of the time. Given the nature of how we met and my circumstances back then, she's aware she didn't marry a saint."

"And what about *her* loyalties?"

He chuckled. "This ain't my first rodeo, Meyers. Her prenup's ironclad. Any signs of infidelity and it all goes away, the allowance, the houses, the widow perks. I might not be an angel, but I learned how to write a contract from the devil himself. Trust me when I say the situation's handled."

He was so calm about everything, so accepting. "I just ... don't understand why you would do this. You changed so much so fast."

"I thought my motive was clear. I did it for Hale."

My lips pressed tight as I understood none of this was what he really wanted. It was an arranged inconvenience he'd tolerate for the rest of his life. But he'd suffer that if it made his son's life a little easier. He was trying to make amends. Maybe trying to thank his son for bringing Elara into this world, even when she'd never know how she got there.

"Oh, Remington."

"Now, don't get all emotional. Christ. You asked me to help him and I did. That's ... what a father's supposed to do."

Hale might not see it now, but what Remington did was significant. He'd never wanted a part of any of this, but he caved on account of his love for his son. "You're a good dad, Remington." Finally.

"I've seen better. There are a lot of things I'm great at, but fatherhood isn't one of them. I'm not too arrogant to admit Hale helped me. That child, my ... granddaughter ... she's a Davenport. I think it will be interesting watching her grow up under a good father, which Hale is. I would never let one of my children play the pawn to someone else's greed."

Only if his was the hand in control, I thought, but maybe he was turning over a new leaf. Remington said he'd never love anyone after he lost his first wife, Rachel, but maybe he was discovering a new love, the sort fussy old men discovered when their grandbabies were born.

I didn't know what to say. "Why didn't you do this from the start?"

"I didn't want to."

I laughed. "Are you saying you wanted to now?"

Remington was strangely silent. "Jasmine was a mistake I should never have made. I knew it the minute I left her bed and I knew it in the weeks that followed. I didn't want my wife to know what I'd done. Rachel was different. I … loved her in a different way than all the others. But mostly, I didn't want Hale to know. For a brief moment there, I thought they never would."

"Then you found out she was pregnant."

He sighed. "Rachel was devastated and my hands were tied. I'd do anything to prove she was it for me. I'd never been good with regret, but there was no escaping the mistake I'd made with Jasmine. I was trying to make it right, but…"

Rachel had passed away suddenly.

"Hale was a separate issue. The way he looked at me… I hope you never have a child look at you with such hate. I just wanted the entire mess to go away. I'd lost my wife. I couldn't lose my son."

"But Hale wouldn't let it go away."

"No. He's always had a better moral compass when it came to doing the ethical thing. But he didn't know what he was getting in to. I've met a thousand Jasmines in my lifetime and they're vicious. She knew exactly what she was doing, betraying Hale to jump into my bed. She saw a bigger opportunity and went after it. I was just the dumb fish that took the bait.

"When Hale told me what he intended to do, I panicked. Losing Rachel, the constant battling with my son, the heart attack... It wasn't an easy defeat, but I'd lost. And then you came along."

"Me?" What did I have to do with any of this?

"Yes, Meyers, you. Marta, the staff... They all adore Hale. The walls are only so thin and you've heard how loud we can shout at each other. They knew what I'd done and it didn't make my days easy. But you... You came in, with your cheap clothes and clumsy chaos, and you looked at me like I might actually be able to help you in some way. It was the first time in months that I felt needed."

A soft smile curved my mouth. "No wonder you hired me. You were desperate."

He grumbled. "You were a delightful distraction. I probably would have tried to—"

"Don't."

"It doesn't matter. The minute Hale got involved I knew I'd never cross him like I had in the past. You were his the moment he set eyes on you."

"But what about all that warning me away stuff?"

"I couldn't bear to see him hurt again. He was all in. I needed to make sure you were just as deep."

I shut my eyes. "I'm all in."

"I know, sweetheart."

"So as you see, the time hadn't been right to marry her before. But there was nothing holding me back now. I stole something from Hale that I can never give back. But he loves you. You're a part of us, Meyers. You asked me to help him and I did. For Hale. For you."

"Thank you."

"Now, I'm going to say goodnight. I've had a long week and Marta brought me a slice of cake that's sitting here begging to be eaten and I have a company waiting upstairs. You take care."

"You, too. And Remington?"

"Yeah?"

"I..." It was probably a mistake, but I said it anyway. "I love you."

"Don't start, Meyers. You'll spoil my dessert."

I smiled. "Goodnight."

"Goodnight, sweetheart." The line went dead.

That wasn't so bad. I actually had a better understanding of things now that I spoke to him. But my problems were far from over. Time to go after the man who owned the rest of my heart. I texted Hale.

Can you come up here?

26

There was a scratch at the door a minute later. "Come in."

"Hey," Hale said, as I slipped my phone into the pocket of my robe.

"I spoke to your father."

"I figured you would." His hands were deep in his pockets and he looked like a censored young version of himself as he shuffled closer to the bed.

"Do you know what it was like for me growing up without a dad, Hale?"

He shook his head. "I imagine it was difficult. A daughter needs a father in her life."

"The funny thing is, she sort of doesn't. But it's always nice to have someone you can depend on, someone to go to when life gets tough and you feel like no one's on your side. I've never had anybody like that in my life, but dads seem like they'd be handy in those situations."

"Not always," he commented, coming to sit next to me.

"No, not always." I kept my gaze on the floor. "I have a dad, but he's terrible. There have been moments in my life when I would have given anything to see him take an interest in me, even if it was to just pop in and tell me I was doing something wrong. I didn't care what he might say. I just wanted to know he cared about me on some level."

His hand slid into mine and squeezed. "I'm sure he cared, Rayne. He just didn't know how to show it."

"A trademark of fathers everywhere," I commented, deliriously happy that Hale was actually touching me.

Keeping hold of his hand, I turned and faced him. "Your dad loves you, Hale. What he did, it helped you. It helped *us*. There was no getting out of that mess without you suffering in some way or another. That lawyer would have pushed until there was nothing left. And when you couldn't have squeezed out another dime, he would have threatened you with Elara's custody. You would never have had a moment's peace the way things were moving. Now, you can focus on what's important. Leave the past behind."

He tried to remove his fingers from my grip, but I held tight. Looking away, he said, "I didn't want him to interfere."

"I know you didn't, but he did because I asked him to. I couldn't bear seeing you so beaten down by this. You're a good guy and you're the hero in all of this, no matter who wrote the last chapter. What they were doing was wrong and I wanted it to stop. I want to protect you the same way you want to protect me."

Time stretched as he stared away from me. I knew his pride and experience with betrayal only made my actions more hurtful, but he had to understand my heart had been in the right place.

He sighed. "I shouldn't need my father's shitty track record to prove I'm a good guy."

"No one said you do. He just makes all of us look a little better." I gave him a shoulder bump. "But Hale, you are a good guy. She's yours. No one will ever try to threaten your situation with her again. And I know you might have eventually hit Jasmine's price, but you've already given so much. Let Jasmine be your father's worry. Let Elara be yours."

"Maybe you're right. I'm glad she's off my back, but I hate that *he* ended it when he fought me so hard in the beginning. I told him I didn't need him and I meant it."

"There's no shame in counting on the ones we love to be there for us, especially when they're willing to help. It's over. That's what's important."

"It doesn't feel over."

I gave him another shoulder bump. "Give it time to sink in."

He fell back onto the bed and pulled me with him. Our hands held, entwined, as we lay with our feet dangling off the edge. "I used to look at him the way you do, like a god or something all-powerful. Everything he touched turned to gold."

I waited, not wanting to interrupt his thoughts.

"Then he put his grubby hands on my life and everything turned to shit. I never held deep feelings for Jasmine, but I loved him. It wasn't what he did, but the fact that he tried to hide it when I continued on the same ignorant path. If not for the baby, I never would have known. I hated feeling so deceived by the one person I've always trusted."

"I can't imagine how much that hurt."

"My hurt was one thing, but Rachel's was another. She was so good to him, so loyal. When she died I remember feeling envious. I was *that* miserable. Everything I was and owned was tied to the person who betrayed me. I wanted to hate him. It should have been easy, but then he had a heart attack and ... I just couldn't."

My cheek pressed to his shoulder. "That's because you have a good heart."

"It's not right for me to ask you not to love him when I can't command the same of myself. I get it. He has this energy about him that's always been able to suck people in. I don't have that."

"But you have other qualities he doesn't. You're honest and loyal and honorable. You do the right thing even when it's the most difficult thing in the world. That's what really matters, Hale. That's what makes you the better man."

"I should have never talked to you like that the other day. I was angry."

"I know. But it wasn't like I acted my age this week either. I mean... I kidnapped your kid."

He chuckled then sobered. "I couldn't see anything past my rage. But when I woke up the next morning, hungover, and you and Elara were gone... It was too familiar. That miserable empty feeling... That's how I felt every day before I met you. I can accept that you love me and love him in different ways, but you'll always be my favorite, Rayne. I've never loved anyone the way I love you."

My heart seemed to dance in my chest at his words. "He's probably the closest thing I'll ever have to a father, Hale. It's nothing like what I feel for you. You're ... my world. I don't need a father. I *need* you."

"I need you, too."

I glanced at our hands, seeing the diamond anchor ring. "I love you."

"I love you more. Do you forgive me for the last few days?"

"I think it's safe to say neither of us was at our best this week. But if you can forgive me for kidnapping your kid and acting like a crazy person, I think I can overlook your drunken comments."

He laughed softly. "I forgive you."

"I forgive you, too."

I was so tired of bickering and strategizing. Now that everything with Jasmine was finally over, I could see the future. It was fuzzy, but alluring at the same time. I wanted to move forward. "Hale?"

"Yeah?"

"Ask me."

He turned his head to face me. "Ask you what?"

"*Ask* me…"

"What do you want me to ask?"

"For the love of Pete. Forget it." I let go of his hand and sat up, fixing my robe and sliding off the bed. Men were so blind.

"No, what are you talking about?" He sat up and frowned at me.

"Moment's over. Never mind. I thought we had this whole Felix and Oscar thing happening and were oddly in sync for a change, but I guess I was wrong."

I moved to the dresser to find a pajama shirt. Hale went to his. I changed out of my robe as drawers opened and closed behind me. Moving on, I decided we should order Chinese for dinner. I removed my robe and turned. "I'm in the mood for kung pao—"

"Is this what you were hoping for?"

My eyes went wide as I stared down at him, on bended knee, holding a small velvet box.

"Where did you get that?" I wheezed.

He shrugged. "I had it for a while … Oscar."

I was *so* the Oscar. "Are you going to ask?"

He cracked open the box. "Rayne, I love

you. Are you crazy enough to become a Davenport and marry me?"

I laughed as chills raced down my shoulders making my fingers twitchy and then numb. I would forever be the Oscar to his tight-assed Felix. "Lucky for you, I'm just that exact amount of crazy, so *yes*!"

He laughed and stood, pulling the ring out and tossing the box on the bed. "Come here, Calamity." He jerked me into his arms and kissed me soundly. "I love you."

"I love you more. But I have to warn you, the sheets are about to get very, very messy."

He slipped the ring on my finger and nibbled my ear. "I'm not worried."

I looked down at my hand and gasped at the iceberg weighing down my ring finger. "I'm becoming very sparkly. This is lovely. *Cracker Jack* box?"

"Nah, found it at the bottom of some *Lucky Charms*."

It was really rather incredible, and surprisingly heavy. As was my chest, my full heart now pounding rapidly with uncontrollable joy. "I love it, Hale. Honestly. It's the prettiest thing I've ever worn."

"Good, because you're wearing it for the rest of your life."

I grinned up at him. "There was a time a

comment like that would have terrified me."

"And now?"

"It's the best promise I've ever heard."

He kissed me deeply, corralling me to the bed until we fell into the pillows, laughing and touching. "My future wife," he purred, spreading my body out beneath him.

"I like the sound of that." I arched against him, so glad to be back home where I belonged.

We made love until Elara awoke from her nap and then we ordered Chinese and had a picnic in bed. Hale was against crumbs mixing with sheets, but I persuaded him.

"You should text Elle," he said as we split an egg roll.

"I'll tell her in person. She's on a date right now anyway."

"Barrett?"

"Yup."

"You okay with that?"

"We'll see. I threatened to cut off his penis if he hurts her."

"Do me a favor and keep away from my brother's dick. If he hurts her, I'll take care of it."

I shrugged and bit into my half of the egg roll. "Wha-evah. Yours ish 'icer anyway," I mumbled over a mouthful.

Hale stilled. "What was that?"

I swallowed. "Nothing, dear. Eat your egg roll."

The End

**Want more billionaire romance from Lydia Michaels?
Read Sacrifice of the Pawn next!**

Claim your FREE book when you subscribe to Lydia's newsletter!
<u>Click here to sign up for Lydia Michaels' Newsletter.</u>

Are you follow Lydia Michaels?
Stalk her on <u>TikTok</u>, <u>Instagram</u>, <u>Facebook</u>, <u>Goodreads</u>, and <u>BookBub</u>!
<u>TikTok @LydiaMichaels</u>
<u>Instagram @lydia_michaels_books</u>
<u>Facebook @LydiaMichaels</u>
<u>Goodreads</u>
<u>BookBub</u>

Show Your LOVE
If you enjoyed this book, please don't forget to <u>leave a review</u>.

LYDIA MICHAELS' READING ORDER

MCCULLOUGH MOUNTAIN
Almost Priest
Beautiful Distraction
Irish Rogue
British Professor
Broken Man
Controlled Chaos
Hard Fix
Intentional Risk

JASPER FALLS
Wake My Heart
The Best Man
Love Me Nots
Pining For You
My Funny Valentine
Side Squeeze

CALAMITY RAYNE
Calamity Rayne Gets a Life
Calamity Rayne Back Again

THE SURRENDER TRILOGY
Falling In
Breaking Out
Coming Home

SURRENDER GAMES
Sacrifice of the Pawn

About Lydia Michaels

Lydia Michaels is the award winning and bestselling author of more than forty titles, a certified life coach, and transformational speaker. She is the consecutive winner of the 2018 & 2019 *Author of the Year Award* from *Happenings Media,* as well as the recipient of the 2014 *Best Author Award* from the *Courier Times.* She has been featured in *USA Today, Romantic Times Magazine, Love & Lace,* and more. As the host and founder of the *East Coast Author Convention,* the *Behind the Keys Author Retreat,* and *Read Between the Wines,* she continues to celebrate her growing love for readers and romance novels around the world.

In 2021, Michaels released the groundbreaking, non-fiction series, ***Write 10K in a Day,*** to commemorate her career in the publishing industry. She looks forward to many more years of exploring both fiction and non-fiction writing, teaching about the craft, and learning from the others in the author community.

Lydia is happily married to her childhood sweetheart. Some of her favorite things include the scent of paperback books, listening to her husband play piano, escaping to her coastal home at the Jersey Shore, cheap wine, *Game of Thrones*, coffee, and kilts. She hopes to meet you soon at one of her many upcoming events.

You can follow Lydia at <u>www.Facebook.com/LydiaMichaels</u> or on Instagram <u>@lydia_michaels_books</u>

<u>Read By Mood</u>
Billionaire Romance
<u>Falling In</u> | <u>Sacrifice Of The Pawn</u> | <u>Calamity Rayne</u> | <u>Blind</u>

Contemporary Romance
<u>Wake My Heart</u> | <u>The Best Man</u> | <u>Love Me Nots</u> | <u>Pining For You</u> |<u>Almost Priest</u>| <u>My Funny Valentine</u> | <u>Side Squeeze</u> | <u>Almost Priest</u> | <u>Beautiful Distraction</u> | <u>Irish Rogue</u> | <u>British Professor</u> | <u>Broken Man</u> (LGBTQ) | <u>Controlled Chaos</u> | <u>Hard Fix</u>|<u>Intentional Risk</u>

Emotional Favorites
<u>La Vie en Rose</u> | <u>Simple Man</u> | <u>Wake My Heart</u> | <u>Sacrifice of the Pawn</u> | <u>Crush</u>
Romantic Comedy
<u>Calamity Rayne</u>

Erotic Romance
<u>Breaking Perfect</u> | <u>Protégé</u> | <u>Falling In</u> | <u>Sugar</u>

First in Series
<u>Almost Priest</u> | <u>Falling In</u> |<u>First Comes Love</u> | <u>Wake My Heart</u> | <u>Crush </u> | <u>Original Sin</u>

Paranormal Vampire Romance
<u>Original Sin</u> | <u>Dark Exodus</u> | <u>Prodigal Son</u>

LGBTQ+ & Menage Romance
<u>Broken Man</u> (MM) | <u>Breaking Perfect</u> (MMF) | <u>Crush</u> (MMF) | <u>Hurt</u> (Non-Consensual) | <u>Protege</u>

Sexy Nerds & Second Chances
Blind | <u>Untied</u>
Teacher Student, Workplace, and Age-Gap Love Affairs... Oh my!
<u>British Professor</u> | <u>Pining For You</u> | <u>Breaking Perfect</u> | <u>Falling In</u> | <u>Sacrifice of the Pawn</u>

Single Dads & Single Moms
<u>Simple Man</u> | <u>Pining For You</u> | <u>First Comes Love</u> | <u>Controlled Chaos</u> | <u>Intentional Risk</u>

Dark Tortured Hero Romance
<u>Hurt</u>

Non-Fiction Books for Writers
<u>Write 10K in a Day</u>: Avoid Burnout